TO
HELL
WITH
CRONJÉ

ALSO BY INGRID WINTERBACH

The Elusive Moth
The Book of Happenstance

IN AFRIKAANS

Klaaglied vir Koos
Erf
Belemmering
Karolina Ferreira
Landskap met vroue en slang
Buller se plan

TO HELL WITH CRONJÉ

INGRID WINTERBACH

TRANSLATED FROM THE AFRIKAANS BY ELSA SILKE
IN COLLABORATION WITH THE AUTHOR

OPEN LETTER
LITERARY TRANSLATIONS FROM THE UNIVERSITY OF ROCHESTER

First Open Letter edition, 2010

Library of Congress Cataloging-in-Publication Data:

Winterbach, Ingrid.
    [Niggie. English.]
    To hell with Cronjé / Ingrid Winterbach ; translated from the Afrikaans by
Elsa Silke. — 1st Open Letter ed.
        p. cm.
    ISBN-13: 978-1-934824-30-6 (pbk. : alk. paper)
    ISBN-10: 1-934824-30-5 (pbk. : alk. paper)
    1. South African War, 1899-1902—Fiction. I. Silke, Elsa. II. Title.
    PT6592.32.I44N5413 2010
    839.3'635—dc22
                            2010018522

Printed on acid-free paper in the United States of America.

Text set in Bembo, an old-style serif typeface based upon face cuts by
Francesco Griffo that were first printed in 1496.

Design by N. J. Furl

Open Letter is the University of Rochester's nonprofit, literary translation press:
Lattimore Hall 411, Box 270082, Rochester, NY 14627

www.openletterbooks.org

For Villiers and Doret Terblanche

TO
HELL
WITH
CRONJÉ

CHAPTER 1

When they arrive at the farm the sun is setting.

At first glance the place seems deserted but the dogs are barking and presently the farmer comes out to greet them. He invites them into the house, once they have seen to their horses.

He insists that they share his meal. They ask if they might wash before supper. In their present condition they are unfit to sit at a decent table.

In the kitchen the farmer blows on the fire vigorously, fanning the flames with care.

His wife died three months ago, he tells them. He'll show them the grave the next morning—if they care to see it.

They eat meat and coarse white bread with jam. They eat hungrily, hardly able to get enough of the food. After supper the farmer carefully measures out some brandy with their coffee. A sense of well-being spreads through their veins.

The house is not big but the precise way in which each object is arranged suggests the hand of a woman.

Reitz notices how meticulously the farmer wipes all objects and surfaces after use. With a kind of lingering yearning, as if the replacing of each object summons a particular memory.

"My wife was a fastidious person," he remarks later that evening. It is not clear whether this is intended as an apology or an explanation.

He pours more coffee, more careful measures of brandy.

Later still he asks if he might tell them of a dream he had the night before. Willem nods on behalf of the rest of them.

He dreamed, the farmer says, of the trickster woman—he's always thought of the trickster as a man, but in his dream it was a woman. A small crowd had gathered at the town church. He recognised no one. Then he saw a woman he knew. She had red hair, her face was powdered white and she wore a little feathered hat.

He can't even begin, the farmer says, to describe how becoming that little hat was. Soft as the wings of a bateleur, with a flash of blue-green light.

In due course he and the woman moved away from the others, to a room where there was a bed. When the time came to lie together and he held out his arms to her, a strange man was suddenly in her place and he heard *her* laughing on the stoep outside. It was then that he realised she was the trickster.

Ben nods attentively.

Reitz glances over his shoulder at the shadows beyond.

"Have any of you ever met the old prankster?" the farmer asks. "In any of his or her guises?"

No one answers at first. Ben seems to be giving the question the most serious consideration.

Young Abraham has been remarkably calm all evening. He sits motionless and silent, not uttering any of his usual incoherent phrases.

When they are ready to turn in—they plan to set off early the next morning—the farmer offers to give up his bed, but Willem won't hear of it. It has been so long since they slept in a bed anyway, he says.

They sleep in the spare room, on feather mattresses, under clean blankets and jackal skin karosses.

Unable to sleep, Reitz gets up during the night and steps outside. The house lies in a hollow between the mountains. In the moonlight the silent farmyard seems utterly desolate. Reitz feels a chill, and a premonition of woe such as he has seldom felt of late. It may be because of the silence. Or perhaps the orderliness of the yard, or the symmetry of the flowerbeds in front of the house.

The next morning Reitz notices anew how carefully the farmer performs each little task; with small, tidy, controlled movements. The neatness of the house also strikes Reitz again. As if a woman has very recently taken pity on it—before she left. A woman whose half-faded fragrance still clings to each object.

When they take their leave, the farmer remarks that he truly hopes to see that little feathered hat again in his lifetime. "It was indeed remarkable," he says.

CHAPTER 2

They leave the farmer's land early in the morning, travelling up the steep mountainside, leaving behind them the hollow where the farmhouse lies among the foothills. After a while they reach a narrow pass where they are able to cross the mountain. The narrow track is flanked on either side by a sheer cliff. Thick sedimentary layers of mudstone and sandstone are clearly visible, Reitz notices, with dolerite sills. A mountain range of the Karoo system, with the rock formations strikingly different from the dramatic undulations of the Cape fold mountains. The horses' hooves echo noisily on the loose stones and from the narrow ledges birds fly up in alarm. In the caves there will be wild honey, baboons, leopards crouching and hiding. A chill runs down their spines even though it is broad daylight. Above them the sky is a thin strip of resonating blue.

Once they have passed through the mountain, a wide expanse opens at their feet. They follow a northeasterly course along the dry bed of a river. Whenever they stop to dismount and rest, Reitz's practised eye scans the riverbank for evidence of fossils. They continue in this way for at least half a day.

At noon, their shadows hard upon their heels, they come across three black men on horseback. The men are wearing hats and blankets. One is clad in the threadbare tunic of a Khaki uniform. Another wears a feather in his hat.

"A motley crew," Ben mutters.

The two groups come to a halt, facing each other.

"What do you want?" Willem demands. "I trust you're not helping the Khakis."

The men confer in Xhosa. The leader raises his hand in what appears to be a peace sign.

He and Willem bow to each other formally.

The group passes them without further greeting.

"Tonight they'll be joining General Pettingale," Ben says.

"At least they're unarmed," Willem says, "and rightly so."

They meet no one else for the rest of the day. They travel through a landscape of low hills, tall grass and thorn trees. The flat, unbroken landscape gradually opens up even more. After a while they leave the Koueberg behind.

In the late afternoon they cross a fairly broad stream—possibly a tributary of the Seekoei River, they surmise, though they cannot be sure. They keep going in a northeasterly direction, heading towards the Orange River.

"O bring me back to the old Transvaal," Ben sings softly.

"We're still some distance away, Ben," says Reitz, "thanks to Senekal's tactical skills."

"The hero of Skeurbuikhoogte," Ben says.

"Of Allesverloren and Droogleegte," Reitz says.

They find shelter on the slope of a rocky ridge strewn with large, loose boulders, where there is a shallow cave. They light a fire. They eat the food the farmer packed for them.

Young Abraham is incoherent again.

"Bandy botherings," he says.

"What's the matter, Abraham?" Willem inquires, distractedly.

"Crimmenings! Futterings! Foots!" says Abraham, his eyes rolling slightly.

"Bad night ahead," Ben says to Reitz. "Abraham is distraught."

It is mid-February, the worst heat of summer starting to subside.

"It gets very cold in these parts at night," Ben says.

"There are kimberlite pipes under the soil," Reitz says, "but whether they contain diamonds, I can't be sure."

"Whatever you do, don't mention it out loud."

They hollow out shallow sleeping places around the fire.

Willem tends to young Abraham.

"Uneasy tonight, Reitz?" Ben asks.

"Ah," and "Oh Lord," sighs Reitz, running his hand over his face.

For a long time he stares into the flames, for behind his back and in the shadows there is the intimation of a presence. A nagging something he has left behind, that will in time catch up with him.

·

The sun rises. They left the farm the day before, and it has been two days since they departed from Commandant Senekal's wagon laager. Senekal's commando has been based in the Beaufort West district for the past two or three weeks, having tried in vain since last October to join up with General Smuts during one of his incursions into the Cape Colony. In December, having missed him once again in the Vanrhynsdorp district, and soon after the skirmish with the English at Allesverloren, Senekal appeared to lose hope, and abandoned his search for Smuts.

Ben and Reitz could not decide which was worse: the fruitless roaming in search of Smuts, or the ensuing tedium of remaining in one place.

Now the four of them are taking young Abraham to a more beneficial environment—to his mother at Ladybrand—if she is still there.

Commandant Senekal (his eyes narrowed suspiciously, head wreathed in tobacco smoke) gave them leave, provided that on their way they deliver a letter to General Bergh. The general is hiding somewhere in the Cape Colony, near the Orange River, in the area west of the Skeurberg.

Upon leaving, Senekal handed them a sealed letter addressed to the general and a map with directions to his camp.

Willem Boshoff is in his fifties—the oldest of the four. He is tall of stature. Solemn, slow, dignified: a man of few words. His eyes are clear as water. Before the war he was postmaster in his home town. He took Abraham under his wing the day after Abraham's older brother had fallen by his side during the battle of Droogleegte. Ever since that day young Abraham has been incapable of uttering an intelligible sentence.

Though Abraham Fouché cannot be much older than twenty, his youth is spent. Who knows what his life might have been in more favourable circumstances?

Reitz Steyn is tall, with a certain languor and hesitancy in his movements. His complexion is ruddy and freckled. His eyelids are heavy, his mouth sensual, somewhat petulant, suggestive of someone excessively attuned to the pleasures of the senses. But what then of the underlying nervousness, the reticence in his interaction with others?

Ben Maritz is shorter than Reitz, of medium build, his curly hair dark and thinning. He has a broad, high forehead (remarkably deeply lined for a man his age). His ironic smile belies the expression in his eyes, which is surprisingly mild and sympathetic. His reaction to a situation is sometimes apparent from his unusually expressive nostrils. Not one for drawing attention to himself, but rather someone whose energy flows spontaneously to the world around him.

Ben is about forty-five, Reitz perhaps three years younger.

They share a passion for the natural world. This mutual passion formed the basis for their friendship—when they found themselves in the Lichtenburg commando under Commandant Celliers, each having joined a different commando at the outset of the war.

Both have been occupied since their youth with observing and recording nature. For as long as he can remember, Ben has been engaged in studying and collecting plants and insects, always searching for new species. He studied natural history at the South African College in Cape Town. Reitz studied geology in England and worked in Johannesburg as a mine geologist before settling in Pretoria, where he had been in the process of documenting the geological features of the Middelveld when war broke out.

•

In the early morning they shiver and pull their jackets closer around their shoulders as the chilly air settles on their necks, cheeks and ears. It is the second morning of their journey.

Initially they are talkative. They admire the seemingly endless land-scape stretched out before them. The tall, waving grass, the few rocky outcrops ahead and the low mountains rising in the distance like mole-hills.

Ben points out a shrub here, a bird there.

It is still hot during the day.

At noon they rest in the shade of a tree.

Reitz looks closely at the ground, always on the lookout for a rare stone or fossil.

Ben makes a small sketch of a pod. Inspects another plant. "Carrion flower," he says.

Young Abraham sits with his back against a tree. He sits woodenly, like a doll. Willem speaks to him in soothing but firm tones, trying to coax him into taking some food and water. The youngster seems to have lost his will to eat.

They consult the map. There are still no recognisable landmarks in the vicinity, though Willem's compass shows that they are travelling in the right direction. Due northeast.

In the afternoon they are more subdued. Large clouds scud across the land.

In the distance they see a herd of buck. They notice dassies on the scattered boulders, and a few springhare.

At least they are certain of meat when they reach the end of the biltong and flour the farmer packed for them.

At dusk they dismount at the base of a small koppie. Like the night before they seek shelter under an overhanging rock. Again they hollow out sleeping places alongside the fire.

They cook some porridge. Eat in silence.

After supper Willem reads from the Bible. He reads from Proverbs, chapter three, and offers a prayer.

As on every other evening, Reitz makes a few notes in his journal. As opposed to the Cape system that came into being during the vacant, twilit prehistoric world of the Devonian, the Karoo system is younger, with an unimaginable abundance of water during the Permian and Triassic periods that supported a profusion of plants and animals, he writes. It was formed after a time of widespread glaciation, followed by a lengthy period of lakes, deltas and swamps, and ending in desert-like, volcanic conditions during the Triassic. It remains cause for wonderment, he writes, the many relics of our earliest and most primitive mammalian ancestors preserved in the soil beneath our feet—in the rock strata of the Beaufort, Ecca and Stormberg Series. So many secrets the earth has yet to surrender. So much still to learn about her unfathomable mysteries.

Because the overhanging rock and the koppie provide scant shelter, they do not sleep well. Until recently they enjoyed the safety of the numbers provided by the commando. Now they are on their own. By day in this unbroken landscape they are fair game for whoever may lie in wait to launch a stealthy attack on them.

Reitz is still mulling over the farmer's tale of his deceased wife and his dream of the trickster woman. He does not know why these tales have struck a chord with him. He only knows they have left him unsettled.

•

The morning of the third day breaks gloriously on the horizon, its beauty constricting the throat.

There is a bite in the air. They consult the map. According to their calculations they should have come across at least one of the landmarks by now. There is the possibility that they are lost. Or that Senekal has played a trick on them.

As they travel on, they observe their surroundings even more keenly than the day before.

The landscape is still changing. Thorn trees and shrubs are diminishing; the waving grass making way for low bushes and smaller scrub.

They hear the call of a bird: weeet-weeet-weeet. A black-shouldered kite, Ben observes.

Another bird cries out: gug-gug-gug. Sand grouse, says Ben.

Now and then Ben questions Reitz about some aspect of the land; about the geological features of the area.

They dismount at regular intervals to give young Abraham a rest.

They sit him down in the meagre shade.

Willem speaks to him encouragingly. Take heart, Abraham, it won't be long now. We're on our way.

Then Willem looks up at the sky, his pale blue eyes clear as the surface of water ready to receive the reflection of clouds.

Abraham stares straight ahead, his dark eyes intense in his thin, pale face.

Ben scrutinises the activity of some ants at his feet.

"Are you any the wiser from their movements, Ben?" Reitz inquires.

"Not only am I wiser," Ben replies, "but I've just had the most interesting insight regarding their endeavours."

While they are resting, Ben points out the tiger beetle and the sand beetle, the bombardier and the tapping beetle.

·

According to Willem's compass they are still travelling in a northeasterly direction.

They talk—about one thing and another—but not about what they recently left behind.

Namely the commando under leadership of Commandant Servaas Senekal.

The hero of Skeurbuikhoogte, Ben would sometimes call him—in muted tones, of course.

Hero's backside, Reitz would say.

By day the commandant could mostly be found in front of his tent, smoking. Making his fruitless plans. Unless the commando happened to be on the run, of course.

He wore a black tailcoat and tophat (like General Maroela Erasmus, the men joked). His mood was seldom good. His eyes were unfocused from smoking and narrowed with suspicion. His talent for making the wrong tactical decisions seemed boundless.

Old flathead on the loose, Reitz would mutter.

Reitz, Ben would say, the man has a responsibility to the people to make his plans.

Like hell, Reitz would reply. Or: Oh heavens. Or sometimes in an unguarded moment: The downfall of the people has already been secured.

Careful, Ben would admonish, some things are better left unsaid.

When the commando moved from one encampment to another, Ben and Reitz used the opportunity to do field work in the area. They documented their findings in their journals. These journals they took with them everywhere they went—in the event of anything unforseen.

The other burghers spent their days sleeping in the shade, or playing cards, or gambling. Few of them still read, or wrote regular letters home to fill the dragging hours.

The past weeks have seen Ben and Reitz become increasingly disillusioned with the course of the war. (Neither had ever been a passionate believer in the cause—Ben even less so than Reitz.)

Is there still a leader worth his salt, Ben? Reitz asked. And Ben replied: You're asking the wrong man. Or the wrong question.

Over which hill or low ridge, from which direction, Reitz wondered, would the harbinger of good news appear—to present them with an order, or the possibility of a way out?

Commandant Senekal's judgment had not improved since they were obliged to join his commando in the early autumn of the previous year. In fact, it seemed clear he was losing what remained of it. Moreover, he had a weakness for female flesh and any accompanying form of intoxication: whether obtained from the bottle, from tobacco, or some other substance.

Accordingly the movements of the commando were determined by the availability of the above, rather than the whereabouts of the enemy.

At Norraspoort, with the commandant in hot pursuit of a certain widow, they narrowly escaped being lured into a fatal ambush. Fine examples of sills formed by intrusive rock, Reitz just had time to notice in passing.

At Skeurbuikhoogte and at Allesverloren shortly afterwards they had a quick brush with the enemy and did not come out of it well, but at Droogleegte—about three weeks ago—after two days of bloody battle they buried fifteen men in the late afternoon, including the able scout Faan Oosthuizen, and young Abraham's older brother. The confrontation at Droogleegte could have been avoided—Faan himself had strongly advised Senekal against engaging with the Khakis in that specific spot.

That evening Reitz's gaze swept across the graves, across the sandstone plains, and he thought: I've had my fill of bloodshed.

We've lost a good man here, Reitz, Ben spoke quietly beside him. One of the last good ones.

Willem stood facing them, his pale blue eyes grimly searching the sky. As if in anticipation of a vision or a sign.

At Droogleegte young Abraham's brother fell by his side. His head and chest blown away. For hours Abraham sat with his dead brother in his arms—until Willem led him away, subsequently taking him under his wing. The fallen brother had been his friend.

After this, young Abraham's condition deteriorated. He lay curled up in the tent next to Reitz and Ben's. He never spoke coherently again—he uttered gibberish, unrelated phrases, confused cries; at night he suffered nightmares and delusions. He did not eat, he did not move. His body was rigid, like a corpse.

It was there—at Droogleegte, in the evenings beside the cooking fires—that Reitz and Ben began to confer with Willem in monosyllables and undertones.

A word here, a remark there. At first Willem said: The brother's blood is calling for revenge. Forget revenge, Ben replied, this is neither the time nor the place for revenge.

Finally they decided: There was no other way. Willem had to get young Abraham away from Senekal's laager and take him to his mother, where he could be cared for, and Reitz and Ben would accompany them, for Willem would not cope on his own with the debilitated, bewildered young man.

In the meantime Ben—more so than Reitz—had begun to consider laying down arms, signing the oath, going back to his wife and children. Reitz said: You know what the Boers do with traitors.

The plan was to take young Abraham back to his mother in Ladybrand. From there Ben would visit his wife and children in his home town Burgershoop, southwest of Ladybrand. (It has been more than a year since he last saw his family.) Then he and Reitz would perforce join another commando. They would not, however, be returning to Commandant Senekal's laager. Time would tell, but they certainly weren't going back to Senekal.

Reluctantly Senekal gave them leave to take Abraham home, and one morning seven days ago the four departed, carrying with them the letter and the map.

•

In the late afternoon they meet up with three men and a dog. They have been watching the group's approach from a distance.

The men are clad in indigenous dress—mostly dressed skins: karosses worn like cloaks, the fur on the inside. Around their necks, hips, ankles and wrists are beads made of wood, seeds, shells and buttons, and necklaces made of teeth. They wear feathers, and thongs round their ankles, leather sandals, and earrings. They wear strange little hats made of skin. The hat of one has the ears of the dead animal pricked up on either side of his head so that they appear to be listening. Another carries something resembling a flyswatter—a wooden stick with a tuft of horsehair on the end. They have no rifles—their long spears are handcrafted. The leader has a broad, open face. They do not appear unfriendly or unreasonable.

Reitz thinks: We trust in God that these people are well disposed towards us, for on this wide open plain there is neither shelter nor escape.

The leader turns to Willem, whose large frame is imposing, exuding authority.

The man gesticulates with great emphasis. His right hand performs a sweeping gesture in the air in front of him. His arm describes a circle past his ear and comes to a halt at eye level—four fingers held up together—before dropping to his side. This movement is repeated another four or five times.

Willem is clearly doing his best to understand what the man is trying to put across.

"I wouldn't be surprised," Ben remarks quietly, excitedly, "if these people were descendants of the !Kora. They might even be Gonna Hottentots. Who could have known there were still some of them around here? I'd have thought they'd have been extinct for many years."

Willem's eyes keep shifting between the direction in which the man is pointing and the man himself.

A ringing silence surrounds them.

Slowly Willem shakes his head from side to side.

The leader gesticulates again. Then he draws his index finger across his throat in a cutting motion, and gestures again with his hand.

"Good grief," Reitz exclaims. "Slit throats, Willem. Either ours or theirs."

"Someone else's," Willem declares with conviction.

"These people don't speak any language at all," Reitz remarks. "Just a collection of gurgles and rattles."

"Their language is a form of !Kora-Hottentot," Ben explains, "all but extinct, I believe. No wonder we don't understand a word of it."

Ben is delighted, Willem deeply worried.

The men smell of meat. Their skins glisten as if they have rubbed themselves with animal fat. Reitz catches himself inhaling deeply, and realises how hungry he is.

From the layered depths of his clothing the leader produces a leather pouch.

He takes out a scrap of paper.

Squatting on his haunches, he slowly unfolds the paper: a map.

With an eloquent wave of the hand he summons Willem to approach.

Willem squats by his side.

The dog stands with ears pricked.

The others keep a respectful distance.

"Our fate is being sealed here, my friend," Reitz speaks quietly, "and we aren't even aware of it."

"Astounding," Ben remarks in awe. "Astounding that these people should be here."

A low sound escapes from Reitz's throat: a muffled exclamation or cry, for something has emerged from the folds in the clothing of the smallest and most likely the youngest of the three men—something live. The snout of a smallish animal. A meerkat, possibly. The man allows the small creature to crawl out and perch on his arm. Reitz tries to point it out to Ben surreptitiously.

The dog pricks up its ears more sharply.

Willem unfolds the map. "I can't make much sense of this," he says. He shows it to Ben and Reitz. It is indecipherable at first glance. Willem hands it back to the leader.

Keep the map, the man indicates.

Slowly Willem folds the map. Puts it into his jacket pocket.

The young man with the tame meerkat, who has kept his face averted the entire time, suddenly looks up archly. On the side of his face, halfway across the smooth cheek, Reitz sees for a moment the glint of a tuft of feathers. Deep purple and reddish green in the late afternoon glow.

They bid their farewells. Mount their horses. The men turn and trot off, fading swiftly into the distance.

"It can mean one of two things," Willem says. "An ambush by the English or a deputation sent by General Bergh."

"Willem," Ben observes laconically, "for the sake of our peace of mind I propose we believe the latter. What interests me more is where these people have come from. I swear—I'd lay my head on a block. The clothes. The language. Everything points to it."

In the late afternoon they once more seek shelter at the base of a low ridge, one of a few in the area. Though it can hardly be called a ridge— rather a cluster of loose boulders.

They make a fire. They study the map they have been given. It is thin and worn from repeated folding and unfolding. Some information has been pencilled in and is all but illegible. There is a word that appears to be Skeurberg and they distinguish a few other almost indiscernible landmarks: crosses, circles, arrows. They decide the map may mean anything, that they might as well accept it in good faith and see whether it becomes any clearer in time. But in truth they still have only Senekal's map and Willem's compass to rely on.

They realise that they have been moving too sharply northeast during the past two days.

"Inexplicable," Willem muses. "Inexplicable where these people could have found this map."

When they have crawled into their hollowed-out sleeping places, Reitz asks whether Ben also noticed the meerkat on the man's arm.

That wasn't a meerkat, Ben replies, it was a mongoose—a banded mongoose, to be precise.

They take it in turns to stay awake—someone has to be on guard at all times.

When it is Reitz's turn, the moon is high and bright in the clear night sky. A jackal howls. The night veld seems limitless. The firmament is so lush and glorious, so boundless from one end to the other, that it appears as if the dome of the heavens has lifted. He sits beside the fire, trying to warm himself, his jacket and blanket wrapped around his shoulders.

Reitz knows she is there. A presence: behind the rocks, behind the daily bustle, and at night behind the dreams and the night smells and the soft calls and scurrying of small animals. He thinks: They are separated by a membrane and she is pushing against it, pushing, trying to penetrate to where he is.

•

In the early morning they are stiff from the night's sleep.

They huddle around the fire to dispel the morning chill. They cook some porridge, drink a mug of coffee. The farmer's rations are being depleted.

"Consider this," Ben says suddenly, staring into the fire. "Two and a half years ago we were called up in the name of the president. We joined our commandos because it was our patriotic duty."

He remains silent for a while. Willem and Reitz look at him expectantly.

"At Boskop Frederik Botha was shot in the head," Ben says. "Our fathers knew each other well. At Elandslaagte my cousin Johannes was struck in the side by shrapnel; he died three days later. At Nicholson's Nek Frans Bothma and Kleinjan Beukes fell side by side. Wounded in the liver and the stomach respectively. I knew them both well. At Leerlaagte, Vleesfontein and Skulpkraal we lost two hundred men altogether—my brother-in-law Jurie Botes was one of them. In January this year Sakkie Ehlers and six others signed the oath. All seven were executed. Sakkie and I played together as children. At Paardeberg four thousand men surrendered and were captured. Prisoners of war. Sent away. At least three of those men were known to me. At Skeurbuikhoogte some of our best men were taken prisoner, and at Droogleegte," he looks at where young Abraham is sitting. "What can one say?"

He is quiet for a while.

"I have no idea how matters stand with my two brothers. I haven't heard from them in a long time." Ben stares into the flames. "Yes," he says softly, "so it goes." He blinks without taking his eyes off the flames. "I knew right from the start," he says, "that no good would come of this war."

They are all quiet. What's most important has remained unsaid, Reitz thinks. Ben makes no mention of the welfare of his wife and children; he does not know for certain where they are. Neither does Willem know whether his wife is still in town with her two married daughters and their children.

Willem's hands dangle helplessly between his knees. His eyes are pale as pebbles in a stream.

"I still believe in the honour of our cause," he says. He rises and walks over to where young Abraham sits bundled up against a rock. Scrawny and undernourished.

Reitz turns away from the fire. "Ben," he says after a while, "one of those men yesterday. One of the men we met. The one with the tame mongoose. Could it perhaps have been a woman?"

•

As they ride deeper into the country, armed with Senekal's map as well as the indecipherable map given to them by the three men dressed in skins, with the days almost imperceptibly becoming shorter and the nights longer, proceeding more directly northwest according to the compass, they behold sunrises of exceptional beauty and sunsets of exceptional glory in purple, rose and gold—more impressive, more majestic, more dramatic than any they have encountered during all of their meanderings of the past months.

In the mornings they speak little. They are stiff after sleeping uncomfortably in the cold. Uncertain of what the day may have in store—friend or foe coming to meet them from wherever. They are uncertain whether they are on the right track, nervously on the lookout for an ambush or obstacle, for a suspicious cloud of dust on the vast, ringing horizon encircling them.

During the day they are also becoming less inclined to talk. Willem keeps a constant eye on young Abraham. At night he watches over him carefully. The young man seldom spends a peaceful night. He mutters and groans and calls out unintelligible phrases. Then Willem's voice is comforting, and it breaks through their restless dreams. In this way they allow themselves to be comforted as well—Reitz and Ben. They sleep with ears pricked up like dogs, turned in any direction whence comes the slightest hint of a sound—other than the usual nocturnal sounds, the scurrying of small animals, the distant call of a jackal and sometimes an owl, the swishing of bats, the low, restless snorting of the horses.

She is there by day for Reitz, transparent as the moon's disc, and at night, becoming steadily more urgent, the hint of her presence behind dreams, in sounds, and in the glittering paths of shooting stars.

On the fourth morning they come across a wagon with the skeletal remains of three people underneath. Two adults and a child. Among the ant hills in the barren veld scattered with sparse tufts of grass. Oxen and horses missing, and no sign of their remains. Someone must have got away with them. Only the bare wagon, apparently plundered, for nothing has remained, even the wheels have been removed.

"These must have been the people whose . . ." Ben makes certain Abraham is out of earshot, "throats were slit according to those men."

Abraham gazes at them with wide, stricken eyes. He gives no indication that he has heard what is being said.

"Everything looted," Willem says.

"And the vultures and scavengers cleaning up afterwards," says Reitz.

"Vulture eats the flesh, jackal eats the flesh and bones, crow waits for vulture to open up the carcass, bearded vulture eats the marrow in the bones, bluebottle lays her eggs in the flesh, and ant eats the scraps that have remained," says Ben, pensively.

They dismount.

Willem leads Abraham away to rest in the meagre shade of a few stunted trees.

"This is where their fire was extinguished," Ben says, kicking at a big blackened stone.

"Uncanny," says Reitz, and feels a shiver run down his spine.

Young Abraham looks as if he is about to have a fit. As a precaution Willem gives him a small sip of brandy—still part of the farmer's contribution. During the past few days Reitz has increasingly avoided looking at Abraham. Their water is running low—they are constantly on the lookout for a stream. Their flour is all but depleted. Fortunately Ben has knowledge of edible bulbs in these parts.

•

They feel as though they are no longer making progress. They are moving through a barren region dotted with small shrubs, with low hills in the distance. No trees or streams. Only ant hills and an occasional rock lizard.

As they move further north, deeper into the unknown, they speak even less, or they speak in a different manner. Immediately after leaving the commando it was different, but after their visit to the farmer they seem gradually to have quietened down. And so every day, as they move deeper into the land, they become less inclined to share their thoughts. Perhaps their thoughts, like the vegetation, have become sparser too.

The landscape gradually opens up and becomes flatter. The distance from horizon to horizon appears greater. Their thoughts simply waft away, become wispy and as light as tumbleweed. They see the horizon. They see the changing cloud formations. They see the shadows of clouds moving across the landscape. They see bushes, rocks and ant hills. What is there to add to this?

Taaibos, Ben sometimes remarks. Hard pear and kriedoring, he says pensively, preoccupied. Aloe and bitter aloe. Bitter buchu. Cancer bush. Bitter root and cancer leaf. They no longer know whether he is pointing out anything specific or merely reminding himself of the names.

By day they allow themselves no more than a mouthful of water, and in the evening they moisten their lips with brandy. They chew on leaves. Veld bulbs and tubers. By day it is hot. The nights are cold. Where possible they take shelter against a rock, or a slope, anything in the flat expanse providing the least bit of cover so that they may light a fire without being seen.

They have left the farmer behind, with his veiled sorrow, as though he never told them about his dream. Earlier they left the commando behind, as if they had never during all those months been subjected to its dragging daily routine. They are becoming disconnected, detaching from where they came, and from where they are heading. Their earlier lives are dissolving. How soon it has happened, Reitz thinks. How soon they have left everything behind. They no longer have any discernible roots.

Willem's solicitude towards young Abraham forms a solid web, a firm but invisible net in which they are caught when they threaten to disappear, to disintegrate like little swirlings of dust.

Their language was more robust before, their reactions sharper; they were more attuned to one another. Now Willem is their keeper, their mother, no less than he is young Abraham's. It is Willem who speaks encouragingly by day: Well done, Abraham, take courage. There now, Abraham, be strong. Calm down, Abraham, calm down. We're on our way.

To freedom, Ben once says, laughing softly.

The sun hangs low towards sunset. Soulful, says Reitz. Soul's affliction, says Ben, and: Not a soul in sight.

Abraham's silence deepens by day; towards evening they sometimes find him shivering; at night his feverish mutterings become increasingly urgent. Presently, Willem murmurs in his sleep. There now, he murmurs. It will soon be over, Abraham, he murmurs, his tongue thick with dazed but wakeful sleep. When Willem comforts Abraham, they find comfort too: a rampart against the weight of evil dreams and suppressed longings, and the painful memories of a fragile order.

One morning Willem's eyes are clear as pebbles in a stream and his cheeks are awash with tears. Reitz looks away startled and sees that Ben's face, when he notices it, turns a deep crimson.

•

22

When the plain lies outstretched in every direction, providing no more than the scantest cover and shelter, the silence between them is deepest. Then the land takes over, removing all thoughts from their minds and all words from their mouths. They note the sun's trajectory; they see the place where the earth meets the sky; they hear the sound of the horses' hooves.

While their days go by in wordless silence, their nights are haunted by chaotic dreams and terrifying visions. They hollow out their sleeping places deeper each night to protect them from the vicious early morning cold. Like Hottentots, Reitz remarks. He has become more and more afraid of sleep, no matter how badly he needs it. For in the hour before dawn, during the phase of deepest sleep, he is often jolted awake by repugnant dreams. Dead eyes. Dead teeth. Bloodied hair. These leave him half dazed, but too petrified to sleep again.

The earth around here was once an enormous swamp, he says one morning, his voice filled with awe.

When they reach a place a few days later where it is so barren and desolate around them, so devoid of God and man and history, so quiet that the silence by day is an onslaught on the inner ear, they see in the distance the scant curve of a low mountain range.

"That must be the Skeurberg," Ben says.

"Boon," Abraham interjects without warning. Everyone laughs, surprised at the recognisable word. Even Abraham gives a brief, lopsided grin. They take it as a sign, if ever there has been one, that they have survived so far.

•

The landscape that has constantly been changing is taking on more solid contours. There are small shrubs, some undergrowth, a few rocky ridges in the distance, more birds, more insects, even buck far off, and dassies on a rock.

On the fifth morning after they have left the farm, there are vultures in the sky. There must be a cliff nearby, Ben remarks, watching the birds.

"Buzzard," Reitz says, "predatory bird."

"Bird of prey, that hunts animals for food," says Ben.

"Bone," says Reitz, "the remains after death."

"Botfly," says Ben, "dipterous fly with stout body."

"Carrion," says Reitz, "dead, putrefying flesh."

"Carrion crow," says Ben, "bird feeding mainly on carrion."

"Devonian," says Reitz, "geological period."

"Devil," says Willem, "lord of the kingdom of evil."

"Devil's coach horse," says Ben, "large rove beetle."

"Eland piss," says Reitz, "the piss of an eland."

"Everlasting," says Ben, "plant used as remedy for a cold."

"Goldfield," says Reitz, "district where gold is found."

"Gold," says Willem, "streets of jasper and gold."

"Good heavens, Willem!" Ben exclaims. "Goldcrest, with its heavenly warbling."

"Heavenly body," says Reitz, "celestial object."

"Hay," says Willem, "to feed the horses."

"Helpful," says Ben, "more helpful than Peternella one could not hope for."

Even Willem smiles.

They carry on in that vein, but keep their eyes on the distant low mountain range, steadily acquiring more substance. Taking courage?

They are forced to dismount when a violent dust storm overtakes them. They failed to notice its approach in the distance. They sit huddled against the horses' flanks, moisten their lips with the last of the tepid water, and chew on some leaves that Ben carries with him.

Once they have saddled the horses and resumed their journey, Willem declares: "Kaffir-melon preserve—mouth-watering, to say the least."

"Kaffir thorn," Ben says, "a kind of tree."

"Kaffir cow," Willem says, "cow belonging to a Kaffir."

"Kaffir sheeting," says Reitz, "a thick, soft cotton."

"Kaffir cherry," says Ben, "a raisin bush."

"Kaffir beer," says Reitz, "beverage drunk by Kaffirs."

"Kaffir work," says Willem, "work not fit for white people."

"Kaffir copper," says Ben, "a large russet butterfly."

"Kaffir hangman," says Reitz, "an executor or oppressor of Kaffirs."

"Kaffir chief," says Ben, "bird with extremely long tail."

"Kaffir captain," says Willem, "chief of a Kaffir tribe."

"Kaffir pebble," says Reitz, "pebble found in gravel to indicate the presence of diamonds."

"Kaffirboom leaf miner," says Ben, "insect found on the kaffirboom."

"Kaffir grave," says Reitz, "hump across a road to prevent water erosion."

"Kaffir kraal," says Willem, "dwelling place of Kaffirs."

"Kaffir swallow," says Ben, "a kind of swift."

"Kaffir pound," says Reitz, "nickname for a penny."

"Kaffir war," says Willem, "war between white people and Kaffirs."

"Kaffir-corn midge," says Ben, "small gallfly with bright wings."

"Kaffir corn," says Reitz, "fine, diamond-bearing gravel."

"Kaffir missionary," says Willem, "missionary that works among Kaffirs."

"Kaffir crane," says Ben, "large bird with long legs and neck."

"Kaffir half-crown," says Reitz, "another name for a penny."

"Kaffir nation," says Willem, "nation consisting of Kaffirs."

And so they amuse themselves until by late afternoon they reach a greenish area with plenty of thorn trees and aloes and—to their great relief—a small, sandy stream. (A tributary of the Orange?) They drink. They fill all receptacles. The horses drink. At dusk they come across a rocky outcrop with a convenient overhanging ledge. They will be able to make a proper fire, without fear of being seen. They cook a little porridge. Brew some weak coffee. As on every other evening, Willem says grace before they partake of the frugal meal. After he has read from the Bible, he offers up a deep, grateful prayer, thanking the Lord for His mercy, and for today's water to quench their thirst.

They lie in their hollowed-out sleeping places, close to the fire. (Willem and Abraham some distance away, up against the rock face.) As usual, Ben and Reitz lie with their heads on their journals for support as well as safekeeping, should something happen to the horses.

They speak in undertones, as is their habit, so as not to disturb Willem and Abraham.

"Have you ever wondered, Reitz," Ben asks, "what it would be like if some or other heavenly body collided with the earth?"

25

Reitz gives it some thought. Wipes his hand across his face.

"I imagine," he says, "that at first an enormous glow would appear on the horizon, like a fire—an inconceivably large fire. Then the shock of the impact, followed by a colossal reverberation, and then the heat—wave upon wave, scorching and shrivelling everything in its path. Heat waves that would lay waste to the earth."

"Ah," says Ben, "goodness."

"Leaving it much more desolate," says Reitz, "than anything we can imagine."

"Worse than the devastation of war," says Ben with a smile.

"Much, much worse," says Reitz. "Much worse than any devastation we have beheld."

"Ah," says Ben. "Inconceivable."

"Yes," Reitz agrees, "inconceivable."

·

In the late afternoon of the sixth day since their departure from the farm they reach a rise—a slight plateau—from where they can make out a farmhouse in the distance.

They study the map. There is a faint marking that might indicate a homestead. They approach cautiously, but the closer they come, the more apparent it is that the place is deserted. There are no barking dogs to herald their approach, no smoke, no movement in the yard.

At sunset they dismount near the homestead. They investigate cautiously. The house is large and sturdy, built of stone, with wide, flagged verandas at the front and at the back. The windows and doors are boarded up. A gigantic vine clings to the back wall, trailing over a trellis. Ben thinks it could easily be more than a hundred years old. The front garden is overgrown with weeds, but the rose bushes are still visible. The windows of the outbuildings have likewise been boarded up. The chicken coop is empty. The dam nearby is half full, with a green film on top, and there is the rank smell of decay. The orchard is choked with weeds, the late summer harvest rotting under the trees. They search desperately for something to eat. To their delight they find the occasional overripe or half-shrivelled fruit, which they devour, worms and all.

They inhale deeply the putrid smell of the orchard. Everything is suddenly so cool and aromatic, so fruitfully rotten, so shady, so sweet, so inexpressible, after the harsh, barren, unbounded landscape which they have traversed during the past days.

The kraal at a distance from the house is also deserted.

There is no sound in the yard. A sombre mood engulfs them—a desolation that grips and holds on to the heart.

"Where could the inhabitants have gone?" asks Reitz.

"Who knows," says Ben, "who knows what calamity befell them here?"

"Khakis in pursuit of rebels," Willem declares with conviction.

"It's entirely possible," says Reitz, "that the occupants have gone into hiding somewhere in the ridges."

Entirely possible indeed, for the rocky ridges would afford excellent shelter. In the half-light they stand surveying the surrounding landscape, but not much is visible in the gloom.

They sit on the stoep at the south side of the house, at a loss as to what to do, overcome by fatigue and dejection, thoroughly disheartened.

"I have a feeling," says Willem, and he holds up his hand, as if listening for voices, "that there are people close by."

Reitz groans under his breath.

"Goodness, Willem," Ben inquires, "friend or foe?"

"Friend," Willem counters without hesitation.

The moon rises, almost in her first quarter. The cold sets in, and reluctantly they build their fire beside the orchard, away from the house.

"Patience," says Willem. "We must keep good faith."

"What faith is he talking about, Reitz?" Ben asks softly.

They sit close to the fire, warming their hands.

"Now that we're in the vicinity of people," Reitz says, "I'm suddenly nervous."

"The true believer has nothing to fear," Ben teases.

Willem gives him a reproachful look.

They cook a meagre pot of porridge. Though the heat gives some comfort, the quantity is hopelessly inadequate. Willem reads from the Bible. He reads from the book of Daniel, chapters three and four:

Daniel's friends in the fiery furnace; Nebuchadnezzar's madness. In his prayer he thanks God for keeping them under His protection, so that they have nothing to fear. (Reitz shoots a sidelong glance at Ben.)

During the prayer they become aware of movement near the kraal. Ben and Reitz instantly reach for their rifles. Careful, Willem warns, as two persons step out of the darkness into the glow of the fire. A white man and a black man. Both have their rifles trained on them.

"What are you men doing here?" the white man demands brusquely. He looks at them mistrustfully. He is short. Sturdy. A broad face, wide across the cheekbones. Curly hair. The face of a thug: head thrust forward challengingly—belligerent, brutal. His frayed jacket is fastened at the front with spike-thorns.

Willem explains why they are there.

"Aha!" says the man. He is swaying slightly and his speech is somewhat slurred. "On some or other mission. You want to see the general. You look like deserters to me."

"A touch inebriated?" Reitz murmurs to Ben.

The black man hovers in the shadows behind the white man. He is tall, strongly built, with a well-shaped head, broad cheekbones and a dark, prominently arched mouth.

Kaffir hangman, Reitz thinks involuntarily.

The man turns suddenly to the black man behind him.

"Ezekiel," he says, with a sweeping gesture, "is a Kaffir to be reckoned with. You can ask him anything. Ask him something!"

They stare, dumbfounded.

"Go on!" the man urges impatiently. "Ask him something from the Bible!" With the butt of his rifle he strikes the ground impatiently. "Or don't you deserters have any questions?"

Ben and Reitz glance at Willem, the only one with a sound knowledge of the Bible. Willem is offended, does not like the insinuation, colours slightly.

"Who," Willem asks solemnly, after a moment's thought, "who were the twin sons of Tamar, the daughter-in-law of Judah?"

The black man raises his head. He takes a step forward. The whites of his eyes gleam for a few moments in the glow of the flames.

"The sons of Tamar," says Ezekiel, "were Pharez and Zarah."

"Right?" the white man cries.

"Right," Willem declares solemnly.

"What did I tell you!" the man cries and stamps triumphantly on the ground with his rifle butt.

"Something else," he says. "Ask him something else. Ask something from history. Our own history. Not Kaffir history or Khaki history."

"Who was the commander of the Boers," Ben asks, "at the battle of Nooitgedacht in the Transvaal?"

Willem looks at him reproachfully, as if he has gone too far.

Is Ben being wilful? Reitz wonders.

Again the man steps forward, rolls his eyes so that the whites gleam in the firelight, and thinks for a moment.

"The Boers," he says, "were under the command of General De la Rey, General Smuts and General Beyers."

"Right?" the white man insists.

"Right," says Ben.

"What the hell did I tell you!" cries the man.

The minute Ezekiel has given his answer, he steps back into the shadows and his face becomes expressionless again.

"Come," says the man suddenly. "My name is Gert Smal. I've no time to waste. Get your things. Bring the horses. Come along."

They walk along a footpath that leads past the kraal, through a hollow and up a fair-sized koppie, following in the footsteps of Gert Smal, with Ezekiel, the clever Kaffir, bringing up the rear.

CHAPTER 3

Gert Smal leads them to a camp behind a large koppie strewn with loose boulders. Near the crest there is a cave with a deep overhang, flanked by a solid rock wall. In front of the cave is a large, open space with a fireplace. Among the large boulders are a number of shelters. The loose rocks and dense shrubbery appear to afford ample shelter. (Better than they have seen in a long time.) The farmhouse is clearly visible in the slight hollow below.

By the time they arrive, it is dark. The men sitting around the fire are eating. There is the intoxicating smell of meat and porridge.

Gert Smal shows them where they can make their beds. They can use grasses and dried shrubs as mattresses. Ezekiel will build them shelters tomorrow, he says; no one can build a shelter like that Kaffir.

Ezekiel is ordered to tend to their horses, which have been left with the others lower down the slope.

Gratefully they join the company around the fire. Apart from thug-faced Gert Smal there is also Japie Stilgemoed—a thin, wiry man with a sharp, intense face and wild hair that springs energetically from his high forehead. He is clean-shaven, except for a moustache. There is Kosie Rijpma—a small, delicately-built man, with a fine head of dark, curly hair, a short, neatly-trimmed dark beard and dark, soulful eyes—who sits hunched up, avoiding all eye contact. There is Reuben Wessels—a big man with a lively but weathered face, a bushy beard and hair, large hands and one leg ending at the knee. There is Seun—a scrawny youth, younger than Abraham—not much more than fourteen or fifteen years of age—with a shaven head and a harelip. There is Gert Smal's dog, a slender beast with yellow eyes that growls warily and keeps her distance mistrustfully. And finally there is Ezekiel, squatting just outside the immediate glow of the fire.

"Heavens, Ben," Reitz says softly, "what have we got here?"

Ben makes no reply but his nostrils flare nervously, a sign that he is ill at ease.

At first they are hardly able to focus on anything but the food. Even Abraham has to be cautioned by Willem to eat more slowly.

"Slow down," says Gert Smal, "or the lot of you will be throwing up all night." Every now and then he fills his tin mug from a bottle.

"Been hungry lately?" Reuben asks. And he throws a bone at the dog that slinks from the shadows to pick it up before returning to her place at Gert Smal's feet. "Yes," he says, "hunger can certainly gnaw at a man's guts. You can't tell me anything about hunger!"

When they have finished eating, Japie Stilgemoed moves closer to the fire and reads from the Bible. He reads from Job, chapter twenty-seven, verses one to twenty-three: Job maintaining his innocence before God; Job pointing out to his friends how little resemblance there is between him and a wicked man; Job acknowledging that the righteousness of God is often revealed in the downfall of the wicked, although this does not pertain to him, for he is not wicked.

After the Scripture reading he prays—a bashful but sincere prayer. He thanks God that the newcomers have reached them safely, and he prays that God will soon reunite them all with their loved ones. They sing a hymn. Willem especially is in full voice tonight—his singing is filled with gratitude and praise.

Then Gert Smal brings out another bottle, and pours them each a generous measure of brandy. (They dare not refuse this token of hospitality. And Reitz, for one, feels no inclination to do so.)

Young Abraham has a coughing fit and Willem pats his back and wipes his mouth carefully. Before long a feeling of well-being spreads through their bodies, and Reitz does not decline when the bottle makes the rounds again and again.

"The general," says Gert Smal, "never has a shortage of firewater. Spoils of war," he adds with a sanctimonious sneer. "The general has no qualms about taking what's his due."

Whereupon he inquires how they ended up in Senekal's wagon laager, all the while looking at them askance, as if he has no great interest in their reply, the prominent, heavy fold between his eyebrows drawn together in a scowl. He takes frequent swigs from his mug.

At the beginning of the war Reitz joined the Johannesburg commando under Commandant Ben Viljoen, but after the battle of Donkerhoek he ended up with the Lichtenburg Commando led by Commandant Celliers, where he met his friend Ben. They were in the Northern Free State with the men of the Kroonstad Commando for a while. Under the leadership of Commandant Nel they moved as far as Kimberley, but the battle of Slangfontein resulted in their joining up with Commandant Senekal.

Ben initially joined the Winburg Commando under Commandant Vilonel, before he ended up in the Lichtenburg Commando with Reitz.

Willem fought in the Middelburg Commando under the leadership of Commandant Fourie before joining Commandant Senekal's laager. Then his good friend Frederik Fouché was killed in the battle of Droogleegte, and since then Willem has taken his friend's younger brother under his wing. He points at young Abraham, who is staring fixedly into the flames.

"Scutties," Abraham says tonelessly.

"Celliers, Vilonel and Fourie can all go to *hell*," says Gert Smal.

"And may we ask," Willem inquires politely, "what byways brought you men here to the general's camp?"

Gert Smal spits out the piece of twig on which he has been chewing. He takes a swig from the bottle. Laughs curtly.

"Old Japie over there," he says, pointing at Japie Stilgemoed, "is a bit hard of hearing—a shell exploded right next to him. He had the runs for a long time. He was so emaciated and weak, he wasn't fit for anything."

Japie Stilgemoed listens attentively; nods in agreement.

And is he quite recovered now? Willem asks solicitously.

Yes, oh yes, he's much better, says Japie Stilgemoed, and looks the other way.

"Old Kosie," and Gert Smal points summarily at Kosie Rijpma, "used to be a predikant in the women's camp not far from here before he went off his head. We found him wandering in the veld—batty. No one could make head or tail of his blathering. He's still not all there half the time."

Kosie Rijpma stares impassively; does not refute the information.

"Poor man," Willem remarks sympathetically.

"Spibush," young Abraham says tonelessly.

"Reuben lost his leg at Dwarslêersbos," Gert Smal continues. "Now he's no use whatsoever in the field."

Reuben nods.

"Bends," says young Abraham. He appears pale and restless. Willem looks worried.

"There now, boy," he says, trying to persuade him to take a sip of water.

Not a word from Gert Smal about his own movements, Reitz notices.

Gert Smal is gradually warming up, helped along by his inebriation. If he happens to forget a name or a place, he snaps his fingers at where Ezekiel keeps to the shadows, and the missing fact is immediately forthcoming.

"To *hell* with Piet Joubert," Gert Smal says. "He should have chased the English into the sea, right at the beginning, when we still had the advantage of mobility. The siege of Ladysmith was a farce! Our men could have been put to better use. Joubert should have given chase at Nicholson's Nek. The Free Staters were the best snipers—the Heilbron commando alone could have whipped the Khakis' arses at Nicholson's Nek! By the end of April the men had lost heart. They were starting to go home. They had no more drive. They'd been lying around for far too long, waiting for action. Joubert made them lie around, bored stiff, when they were still full of dash—when he should have let them loose to chase the enemy into the sea!"

Thus and in that vein Gert Smal holds forth, with Reuben now and again adding something. Japie Stilgemoed has little to say and Kosie

Rijpma does not utter a word, and the two of them are the first to get up and go to their shelters.

Not only is Seun's speech impaired by his cleft palate, Reitz notices, but he also seems rather slow on the uptake. He communicates—only with Ezekiel and Gert Smal—by means of signs and unintelligible sounds.

Drowsy from the heat of the fire, the food and the drink, Reitz finds it difficult to focus on the conversation; he barely makes an effort to follow what Gert Smal is saying.

Later, when Gert Smal's eyes are fixed and glassy, when his language has steadily become more uncouth, Willem—ever tactful, as they have come to know him—speaks on behalf of them all: "And may we ask where the general is at the moment?"

"You may ask, Neef," Gert Smal replies, "but I can't tell you, because the general's movements are secret. All I can say is that he's out on a little punitive expedition with a group of men. They've gone to give those damned fat-arsed Khakis a bloody good thrashing."

Much later, in the small hours, when the night air is cool and fragrant, the chirping of crickets deafening, the cool rustling of poplar trees down at the river barely audible and the stars are shooting furiously across the dark sky, when Willem and Abraham have already turned in and Reitz and Ben are decidedly the worse for drink (though not unpleasantly so), Gert Smal suddenly declares: "Tomorrow we're going up the kloof to fetch honey. You two are coming along," and he points at Reitz and Ben.

They reach their beds just in time, grateful for the grass bedding on the ground. They are scarcely aware of the night chill and the early morning dew, they sleep as never before, sleep like logs, under the swirling and pitching of the stars.

•

The next morning both Reitz and Ben wake with pounding headaches. They groan when Gert Smal wakes them. They are to get up. He can't wait all day.

Willem and Abraham stay in camp. Reitz and Ben accompany Gert

Smal, who leads the way energetically. He appears to be much more resistant to the excessive intake of intoxicating fluid than the two of them.

Heading away from camp, they follow a narrow footpath, picking their way among loose boulders until they emerge near the river. There is no bank on the opposite side—a cliff face reaches up to the sky. With the river on their left, they proceed downhill for a while, past the poplar grove, to a place where the opposite bank plunges sharply downward. At a shallow drift they cross the river, leaping from stone to stone. At the base of a narrow kloof they swing left.

Reitz and Ben battle to keep up with Gert Smal, muttering from time to time under their breath. Gert Smal is out to kill us, Ben, Reitz says. He'll think of crueller ways if that's what he's really up to, Ben replies.

After a while the rocky, uneven terrain gradually gives way to grassland dotted with aloe and thorn tree. The sudden transition in the landscape is beautiful—the unexpected greenness in this predominantly arid, stony environment. Up ahead they hear the rushing of water. Must be a waterfall further up the kloof, Ben remarks.

He points out a variety of things. A grasshopper with long, slender body and folded wings, uniformly green and motionless on a blade of grass. The quill of a porcupine, the droppings of a red rhebok, the lair of the small-spotted genet and the red mongoose. They hear the cry of a hamerkop and see a tawny eagle circle overhead.

Everything has to be pointed out at the double, for Gert Smal brooks no loitering.

Despite his energy, Gert Smal is sullen this morning. Their cautious inquiry as to where they will find the honey is met with silence. They soon discover Gert Smal dislikes questions—unless he is asking them himself.

When they have covered a considerable distance, Gert Smal says out of the blue: "Oompie knows a lot of tricks. And he can see into the future."

Oompie? Reitz glances at Ben, who shrugs in mid-stride.

"What kind of tricks?" he asks circumspectly.

"You'll see soon enough," is Gert Smal's curt reply.

"And what does he see?" Reitz asks later, also warily.

"Anything," says Gert Smal, "he sees anything."

"Be prepared, Ben," Reitz says softly.

"Is one allowed to ask him things?" Ben inquires.

"There's no need to ask him anything," Gert Smal answers brusquely.

"What do you want to know, Reitz?" Ben asks as they walk along, having made certain they are not being overheard.

"Ah," Reitz wipes his hand across his face, flushed and damp by now. "That is the question—what do I want to know!"

Some distance into the kloof they are suddenly pelted with stones from higher up. They fall to the ground.

Gert Smal, flat on his stomach, cups his hands to his mouth and shouts up the mountain: "Dammit, Oompie, stop your nonsense! We come in bloody peace!"

Bloody peace, it echoes through the kloof.

Dead quiet from above. But there are no more stones.

"Goodness, Reitz," Ben says softly, "what are we to expect now?"

Shortly afterwards, about midway up the kloof, a hut becomes visible on a level grassy plain.

"This is where the old bugger lives," says Gert Smal.

An old man comes to meet them. He approaches with arms outstretched, wearing a crumpled raincoat—like the one (Reitz imagines) the defeated Piet Cronjé wore when he emerged from the bunker after twelve days, having just about lost his bearings after the English had subjected them to twenty-four hours of non-stop shelling.

On Oompie's feet are home-made sandals, artfully woven of grass and leather, with thick leather soles.

When he reaches them, he greets them warmly. He gazes into their eyes long and searchingly, as if he recognises something in their unfamiliar faces. His pupils are small and black, Reitz notices, scarcely visible specks.

"My friends," he says, "I've been expecting you!"

First pelted with stones, now heartily welcomed.

Oompie is of indeterminate age with a short, stocky frame. His eyes are small and pale. His skin is oily and his complexion somewhat swarthy. His beard is sparse; the hair long, sleek and greasy. There is something Oriental about him, Reitz thinks. He emits a smell like rancid butter.

Oompie escorts them to his hut and bids them sit on a bench in the sun.

He himself takes a seat on a large loose boulder.

Today is a special day, he says. It's the birthday of his old father, who departed this life some years ago.

Reitz notices the small fleshy hands: hairless, with sharply pointed fingers and a bluish tinge under the nails. Oompie is like someone from a different era; from another, an older realm.

While at first he peered eagerly into their eyes, he now stares steadfastly over their shoulders and seems to be directing his words at a spot somewhere behind them—so that neither Reitz nor Ben can resist the temptation to steal a backward glance once or twice at what Oompie observes in the distance while he is talking.

He speaks of his late father. He speaks of the bounty of creation and the mysteries of nature. He speaks musingly and at times he seems deeply moved. For long moments he is silent.

Reitz is struck by the fervour in Oompie's expression—while holding forth, his face draws Reitz like a magnet.

Gert Smal, chewing on a piece of wood all the while, abruptly interrupts. "What can you tell us, Oompie?" he asks. "Seen anything lately?" His voice holds a mixture of deference and scorn. Reitz takes note of this near-respectful tone, which, as far as he can tell, is unusual for Gert Smal.

"Do you have any tobacco?" the old man asks suddenly—his emotional reverie suddenly at an end. "Did you bring the old man something nice?" he asks plaintively, insidiously.

Gert Smal reaches into his jacket pocket and hands something over. Oompie unwraps it: a roll of chewing tobacco. He chews, his eyes shut in pleasure.

Reitz wonders whether Oompie remembers Gert Smal's question or has in fact even heard it.

Gert Smal restlessly picks his teeth with the piece of wood.

Oompie scratches his head. He spits out a piece of tobacco and looks at the ground in front of him.

"These are dry times, brother," he says. "Even the bees know it." He makes a dramatic gesture with his right hand, without looking up. Reitz had not noticed the beehives on the right earlier; beyond them two cows are grazing and higher up a few sheep.

The meat and milk supply of the camp, Reitz realises.

Oompie gets up. Suddenly old and haggard—an old man in a shabby, greasy raincoat. He beckons them into the hut.

After the brightness outside it takes Reitz's eyes a while to adjust to the gloom. It is the smell that he notices first, a mixture of animal pelts, rancid butter and something else, something he cannot place immediately. A cool smell, of fungi, or silt: something medicinal. He notices that Ben is also sniffing, unobtrusively trying to identify the smell.

The hut is warm inside. There is a bed on one side, a rough wooden table and chairs, and a stove on the other side—facing the door. On a wooden shelf against the back wall are a variety of glass jars and milk cans. On the stone floor buck and jackal skins lie scattered, also karosses of dassie skin. A snakeskin is stretched on one wall. A door leads to what is apparently a second room.

Oompie motions for them to sit at the table.

"Formalin," Ben whispers suddenly, and Reitz instantly recognises the cold, medicinal smell.

From a clay pot on the table Oompie pours sour milk into tin mugs. His movements are slow and deliberate. In the dim light his coat takes on a greenish tinge—as if it has been exposed at length to dripping water, as if it is covered with moss; as if he has been swimming in it underwater.

Though Reitz is thirsty, the sour milk sticks in his throat.

They sit at the big, coarse wooden table, facing the door, but Oompie does not join them. He busies himself at the stove. "You have books," he says. "You have big books in which you write. You are educated men. You have knowledge of hills and vales. Of the forces that create mountains. Of the birds of the sky and the flowers of the veld. Of the small animals and insects. You know each one by type and by name. But you have not reached the end of your long journey."

"Show them a few tricks, Oompie," Gert Smal interrupts.

The old man does not seem to hear. "You've been wandering for a long time," he continues, his back still turned to them. "You're weary of travelling. You left a leader who was ill-disposed towards you. Keep your eyes open. God's ways are mysterious, but the ways of man are treacherous. God makes Himself known through His creation—but man's motives are always inscrutable. One of you has a problem. It is linked with feelings of guilt."

Reitz feels the hairs on his arm stand on end.

Gert Smal is becoming more restless; he is still cleaning his teeth with the piece of wood.

"Show them a few tricks, Oompie," he insists.

But Oompie ignores him as one ignores a troublesome child.

At this point Gert Smal decides he has had enough. He gets up. They have to go, he says. They can't sit around here all day.

Instantly Oompie's expression changes.

"You wouldn't happen to have something—pleasurable—for an old man to look forward to?" His demeanour is sly again, almost lewd.

"We'll see what we can do, Oompie," Gert Smal says brusquely. "We can't promise anything."

Before they leave Oompie gives Gert Smal a jar of honey and three cans of milk.

When they take their leave, he embraces them again. He bids them a warm and fond farewell and extends his arms over them in blessing as they depart.

·

Going back down the mountain is much quicker than going up. Gert Smal leads the way, leaping from rock to rock like a klipspringer. He certainly has energy to spare after their visit, and after his sullen silence of the morning, he is now positively garrulous.

"The old scoundrel is as randy as a billy goat! Every so often he takes himself a new wife."

Gert Smal leaps from rock to rock with great flourish. "There was a time when he had a great many wives around here. We couldn't keep up with his demands," he declares.

"Goodness," Ben remarks. "How long has he been here then?"

Gert Smal chooses not to reply.

Reitz casts a quick, furtive glance in Ben's direction.

"Once he and his new bride have worked each other over good and proper," Gert Smal continues, "the old bugger's words take wing. In times of plenty his prophecies make the hills resound."

"And how often does that happen?" Ben inquires cautiously.

"By God and the devil," Gert Smal replies. "Not often these days. Not easy to keep up the supply nowadays. Not many young Kaffir girls left in these parts. All dead or carried off to camps, or so starved they've lost their appeal."

"Really?" Ben inquires, pausing for a few moments to study an interesting-looking insect at his feet. Reitz can see Ben would dearly love to linger and inspect the beetle, but it is obvious Gert Smal will not put up with dawdlers.

"The general keeps the old fellow up here," Gert Smal remarks over his shoulder as they struggle to catch up with him, "because he's a bad influence on the men. He unsettles them."

"How?" Ben inquires from his position a few paces behind Gert Smal—still cautious, for he knows the man does not welcome questions.

"The men see things. They imagine they hear voices. They have dreams."

For a while they continue in silence.

"And besides," Gert Smal continues, "he's our bee man. He has a way with bees. He talks to them. He never gets stung."

"Is that so?" Ben remarks, trying not to sound too interested.

Later still, when they have almost reached the camp, Gert Smal declares: "Actually, the old man is a great sorcerer. He was just out of sorts today."

•

That night around the fire Gert Smal is surly at first, his high spirits of the afternoon apparently flown.

Before long, however—after their devotions, and once the evening hymn has been sung—he brings out the bottle again, and once more launches into a tirade. This time Ben and Reitz are more careful when it is their turn to drink.

"To *hell* with Piet Cronjé," Gert Smal proclaims. "In 1899 he intercepted Jameson at Doornkop, and that was the only thing he ever did worth mentioning. By 1888 Paul Kruger was buying up arms for all he was worth. Wily old sod. Alfred Milner was steering the negotiations towards a declaration of war. To *hell* with Alfred Milner too. Twenty-two thousand Uitlanders signed a petition. Oom Paul should have shown them who was in charge right from the beginning, even before he and Milner met in Bloemfontein."

Gert Smal spits out a piece of wood. "Milner outwitted Oom Paul right from the start—pretending to negotiate a period for giving the Uitlanders the vote. That was just his way of putting the pressure on until Oom Paul was forced to give in. No, Oom Paul said at first, there's no way. Later he couldn't take it any more. You want my country, he said, and bawled like a bloody woman." Gert Smal's voice is bitter. He takes a swig from the bottle. He continues.

"While Oom Paul was drying his tears, Milner was laughing up his sleeve. Bloody hell! To *hell* with Milner. No, Oom Paul said after each new concession, no, no further. Send the troops, Alfred Milner said. He knew—the bastard knew. On September the twenty-second the ultimatum came: the Uitlanders are to be given full equality, and the franchise after a year. That's what happens when you don't show them who's in charge right from the start. Some people thought Oom Paul was bluffing. He had Jan Smuts draft his own ultimatum. They asked for arbitration. He should have known, Oom Paul should have known there'd be no arbitration. And Alfred Milner got what he wanted—he got his war."

Gert Smal takes a huge swig from the bottle. He gazes into the fire grimly, as if all these events have only just taken place instead of three years ago. As if things could have gone differently.

"Alfred Milner be damned, his complete bloody English arse be damned," he declares in measured tones, taking another swig from the bottle. (Tonight Gert Smal is too far gone to be bothered with a mug.)

"We raised our army," he goes on. "Three generations taking up arms together. But we weren't prepared for war. Neither was the god-damn British army."

Shortly afterwards Japie Stilgemoed and Kosie Rijpma go to bed. But Ezekiel remains in the shadows a short distance away, just outside the light of the fire. And the dog with the yellow eyes keeps watch at Gert Smal's feet.

"Ezekiel was reared by hand," Gert Smal declares suddenly. "He never knew his own people."

"Poor Kaffir," Willem comments.

"Ezekiel knows our history," Gert Smal says. "There's nothing you can't ask him about history and the Bible."

"Poor Kaffir," Ben confirms softly.

"The only thing you can't teach him," Gert Smal continues, "is to catch a joke. There's just no way he can make head or tail of what we find funny. What do you say, my old Kaffir?" Gert Smal asks as he turns to Ezekiel, passing him a chunk of meat skewered on his pocketknife.

"You can ask him anything," Gert Smal repeats, pausing expectantly.

"Ask him if he has a soul," Ben remarks softly, out of earshot.

Willem, overhearing, eyes Ben reprovingly. "He's accepted the Lord as his Redeemer, Ben. He's a Christian, like the rest of us."

"Well?" Gert Smal urges impatiently.

"Can he describe the descent of President Steyn?"

Crouched in the shadows, Ezekiel throws back his head, his eyeballs gleaming in the dark. For a few moments his lips move in a wordless litany before he proceeds to recite.

When he is done, there is a deathly silence.

"Right?" Gert Smal inquires triumphantly.

"Sounds right enough to me," replies Reitz, whose father was the old president's second cousin.

"What did I tell you?" Gert Smal cries exultantly. "In the entire land there's no Kaffir that's his equal!"

Shortly afterwards Willem and young Abraham turn in as well. Later, when Reitz and Ben rise, Gert Smal is still holding forth, with no one but the silent Reuben and the sleeping Seun in attendance.

That night Reitz dreams of towering cliffs and of fire upon water.

•

The next day Gert Smal orders Ezekiel to help them build shelters—like those the rest of them have. He has instructions from the general, he says, that they are to stay here for the time being.

"Goodness," says Ben softly, "when did he get those?"

"Oh Lord," Reitz remarks quietly to Ben, "we may be here for a long time. This calls for deliberation. Long and serious deliberation."

"It looks that way," says Ben.

First Ezekiel builds a strong frame of lattice and matting. He cuts the switches from the stand of poplars. Then the structure is lightly covered with thatch-grass. Ezekiel works slowly, methodically and with precision. He loops and interlaces the young green switches. He thatches and rethatches. He knots and weaves. The framework stands firm, the covering is dense. Finally the inside is lined with dried shrubs, and other aromatic grasses are laid on the ground.

While he is working, Ezekiel sings hymns in a deep, pleasant voice.

Japie Stilgemoed approaches timidly and suggests that the opening of the shelter should face north, as the cold winds blow from the south.

The shelter is sturdy and virtually waterproof; together with the soft grass mattress on which they can spread their meagre blankets, it differs considerably from the wet blankets and leaking tents that have been their home during the past months, and which they left behind when they departed from Commandant Senekal's laager. An admirable shelter in any kind of weather; the best protection they have ever had in all their months on commando.

"Do you have peace of mind, Ben?" says Reitz. "Or does this bed come with a price?"

"Peace?" asks Ben. "Who said anything about peace?"

Later that morning they ask Gert Smal's permission to wash their clothes down at the river. He agrees, but not without an assortment of threats. After their visit to Oompie the day before, they have a great deal to discuss. They prefer to do it out of earshot of the others.

Although they are permitted to go unaccompanied, they remain conscious of the constant presence of Seun behind some boulders further up the slope.

From the camp they follow the same path to the river as the one used the previous day when they accompanied Gert Smal to visit Oompie.

They wash themselves, they wash their clothing. In spite of the fresh morning breeze they cavort in the water like otters—for when last did they have the opportunity to do just this? Afterwards they sit on a rocky ledge to dry off in the sun.

Their necks, faces and forearms have been darkened by the sun, but Reitz notices how delicately pale the rest of Ben's body is. He is so thin that his ribs show, and his skin has a bluish pallor that contrasts sharply with his dark hair. Reitz's own body, though ruddier, is also much gaunter than before.

A large variety of birds are nesting on the sheer cliff face that reaches up to the sky on the opposite side of the river. Ben immediately identifies the sandmartin, the speckled pigeon. The red kaffir finch and the kingfisher. From lower down the river the fizzing zt-zt-zt of the yellow weaver, the cry of the red bishop bird on the wing and the loud whistles of the sparrow weaver are clearly audible. In the distance they hear baboons barking. Down here it is paradisiacally lush.

There are definitely otters in the area, Ben declares, he has noticed the small piles of crushed snow-white crab and other shells that they excrete. The water mongoose will also be found around here, he thinks. There are insects in abundance: dragonflies, Ben says, moths and butterflies, beetles and bugs, wasps and caddis flies—a large variety of species. He is excited. This place is so different from the barren regions through which they have been travelling for the past months.

In the afternoon the cliff will cast a deep shadow over the river, but at the moment it is sunny, the only shade provided by the shadows of overhanging branches.

Reitz shows Ben the horizontal and vertical dolerite sills clearly visible between the successive sedimentary layers of khaki-coloured shales, clay-pellet conglomerates and siltstone. These dykes and sills intersect the sedimentary layers like plumbers' pipes, he says, and through which the red-hot lava escaped upwards. He shows Ben how the lava bed scorched the surrounding sandstone in some places, indicating how hot it must have been.

And the bank of the river opposite the cliff face, rising higher further downriver, will also be an ideal place to look for fossils, Reitz imagines.

But it is not only the geological features of the area that he finds interesting—he senses that his attention is also engaged in a different, less definable manner.

"Ben," Reitz inquires cautiously after a while, "who and what have we got here, do you think? Where have we landed?"

"Consider it a transit camp," Ben says, "for those temporarily and permanently unfit for battle."

"What are we?" Reitz asks, "temporarily unfit?"

"We are still of uncertain status," Ben says. "Something between deserters and traitors. Spies, even."

"Yes, well," says Reitz, "there you have it. Senekal's doing."

"It will all become clearer in due course," says Ben, "I've heard good reports of General Bergh. Apparently he's an intelligent, reasonable man."

"Unlike Senekal," says Reitz.

"Unlike Senekal. In the meantime each of us will be assigned a task," says Ben, "until our fate has been determined."

"Darning socks," says Reitz. "I couldn't take it."

"Weigh it up against Senekal's lunacy," Ben counsels.

"Each of our camp-fellows seems more frightened and bewildered than the next," says Reitz. "Gert Smal can hardly be called a rational interlocutor. Kosie Rijpma has yet to say a single word. Poor Seun barely manages to utter a few incoherent sounds. Reuben appears to be a somewhat rough diamond and Japie scurries off if one even happens to look in his direction."

"As timid as an aardvark," Ben says.

"And Ezekiel doesn't count," says Reitz.

"No," says Ben, and smiles, "he doesn't count."

Ben lifts a small plant from the water by its roots. "Let's count our blessings for now, Reitz," he says, "until in due course our fate is determined. Young Abraham seems calmer. Apparently we aren't expected to take up arms for the moment. Our surroundings are interesting. Our movements aren't unduly restricted. We have a dry sleeping place."

"It's interesting around here, I agree," says Reitz, "but I feel uneasy. There's something in the air that makes my hair stand on end."

Ben looks at him with interest.

"It's not after our visit to Oompie, is it?" he asks.

"I can't put my finger on it," Reitz says evasively. He runs his hand across his face.

"Does it have anything to do with what Oompie said?" Ben persists cautiously.

"With that too, yes," Reitz replies "but it's also this *place*. Down here as well as back at camp."

Ben still observes him keenly. "It's bound to become clearer later," he says after a while.

It is noon. The sun is directly overhead. The heat makes them drowsy. Their clothes are draped over rocks to dry. Lizards bask on the rocky ledges. Under the flat rocks are large river crabs. Damselflies hover motionlessly above the surface of the water.

After a while Reitz wonders aloud why Gert Smal took them along to visit Oompie. He thinks there has to be a reason. Could it have been to intimidate them, Reitz speculates. Could he have hoped the old man would say something to make them watch their step?

"Quite possible," Ben says, "with a man like Gert Smal."

"The old fellow made a few accurate observations," Reitz says carefully.

Ben nods. He thinks Gert Smal might also have taken them along to learn something about *them* from Oompie's observations—something about their plans and intentions. "But," says Ben, "it's important, Reitz, not to start imagining things at a time like this."

He speaks while scrutinising an interesting sheathlike cocoon on a twig. "Gert Smal is obviously a restless and disagreeable soul, and for all we know Oompie really does have exceptional powers. Each of our camp-fellows has clearly been injured in his own particular way and is no longer suitable for active combat—but let's keep the issues separate and hope that the general is a reasonable man."

Reitz cannot but agree. He resolves to keep the issues separate and not to become unnecessarily agitated.

Ben explains that the little cocoon in his hand is the permanently inhabited grass house of a caterpillar. "The wingless, worm-shaped female moth lives inside," he says. "It's also called the bagworm or caseworm."

For a while they lie on the rocks in the shade of the overhanging branches without speaking.

"Those guilt feelings, Reitz," Ben inquires carefully after a while, "that Oompie referred to yesterday—are they for your account?"

Reitz hesitates for a while before nodding affirmatively.

During the time they spent together on commando neither of them ever spoke at length about the life they had left behind.

When their clothes are dry, they put them on and return to camp, where a surly Gert Smal awaits them. Why did they take so long? he asks. Cooking up some or other defection, he says. But don't try anything, he warns, the general isn't someone you'd want as an opponent.

•

On the third evening after their arrival at the camp, the day after their trip up the kloof with Gert Smal, Japie Stilgemoed suddenly breaks his silence after the evening devotions. At twilight Ezekiel turned up at camp with some potatoes. Potatoes he seems to have grown himself. They must have been here for a long time then, Ben remarks to Reitz.

Japie Stilgemoed speaks of the time at the camp where he was before when they went to fetch sweet potatoes. Everything around them had been burned down by the Khakis—except for the sweet potatoes. They dug them up and stacked them in piles. Then they put them into bags and loaded them onto a wagon. The moon was full. He will never forget it—they passed the place where General De la Rey had destroyed one hundred and sixty British wagons the year before. The wreckage still lay scattered in the moonlight.

Japie Stilgemoed stares into the fire for a long time.

"It was July of 1901 if my memory serves me right," he says. "The sweet potatoes were a welcome respite from our daily fare of porridge without meat."

"Cronjé had De la Rey to thank for his victory at Magersfontein," Gert Smal says. "Without his advice the old sod would've been buggered."

"That was when I began to realise that times of tribulation teach us about our own strengths and weaknesses," says Japie Stilgemoed. He throws another log onto the fire. His gaze is intent, his hair stands on end, his domed forehead is smooth in the firelight.

Gert Smal is silent; Ben nods slowly, absorbed. They wait for Japie to continue.

Kosie Rijpma sits hunched forward with his blanket around his shoulders. He stares into the fire with close attention. His face is austere, his eyes deep in their sockets.

"So," Japie Stilgemoed continues, "from February to May 1901 we trekked with General Kemp's wagon laagers from Roodewal, across the Skeerpoort River, past Hekpoort on the Witwatersberg, through Hartley's Poort, past Grobler's Nek on the Magaliesberg, past Vlakfontein and Dwarsfontein and Leliefontein, across Vlakvarkpan, Tafelkop and Rietpan in the Lichtenburg district. Through Kwaggashoek, Syferfontein and Bokkraal. At Grootfontein we swung sharp north in the direction of Groot Marico and Koedoesfontein, then southeast again, back to Kwaggashoek, and through Swartruggens until we reached Waterval."

Gert Smal chews on a twig, his attention elsewhere.

"I thank the Lord," says Japie Stilgemoed, "that there were times when I could remove myself from the day's tribulations by reading. To this day books have been my salvation. What I would have done without them, I don't know. Whenever we came upon books left behind by the English, or in deserted houses and shops along the way, I found something to provide solace, to support me further along the way."

Reitz thinks of their journals. Without them these past months would also have been much harder to bear.

"Fortunately we had fruit in abundance at the time," Japie Stilgemoed continues. "Our clothes were in rags by then—the men were beginning to make clothes out of blankets. In February we celebrated the victory at Majuba. But at the same time there was Cronjé's defeat at Paardeberg to commemorate."

"My *arse!*" Gert Smal shouts. "Commemorate, my *arse!* Cronjé can go to *hell!* The hero of Paardeberg!" he says scornfully, and spits out the twig he has been chewing so forcefully that the sleeping dog wakes and leaps to its feet.

"Fooking! Fooking!" young Abraham cries, alarmed, and Willem has trouble calming him down.

"Not to mention the hero of Droogleegte," Reitz says to Ben in an undertone.

Japie Stilgemoed, hard of hearing, appears to pay little heed to these interruptions. He seems completely absorbed in his reminiscence.

"Yes," he says, "there was fruit in abundance in those days. We picked a bag of oranges every day. We bathed in the Crocodile River. But even more important than the fruit were the books we found along the way. It was like coming upon a treasure! More precious to me than food—more precious than gold!"

After a while Willem rises to put young Abraham to bed in his shelter. The dog with the yellow eyes has dozed off peacefully again at Gert Smal's feet. Beyond the circle of the firelight night sounds are audible. The noiseless zigzag flitting of bats, the call of the owl and sometimes the cry of a bird somewhere near the river. Overhead the dense teeming of stars. The nights are getting colder. The cold laps at their backs and kidneys.

Reitz and Ben have noticed that nobody is expected to stand guard. Unless it is another of Ezekiel's numerous tasks—assisted during the night by the dog. (It would be futile to ask Gert Smal, for he makes a point of not answering questions.) Would Gert Smal and the others be under the impression that they can depend on the general's protection at all times; that despite martial law they can afford to be less vigilant?

"Even *then* the burghers had had enough," Japie Stilgemoed continues. "Our predikant believed that Mauser and canon would not help us regain our independence; he believed instead in the weapons of faith, love, hope and prayer. Unfortunately some men saw in this an opportunity to make a run for it."

"Probably thought they might as well pray at home," Ben says.

Gert Smal snorts. "Deserters," he says, looking at Ben and Reitz, who make a point of not reacting to his taunt.

"No war can be won with deserters," Gert Smal declares bitterly, and Ben and Reitz glance at each other surreptitiously.

The owl hoots again. "Spotted eagle-owl," says Ben.

Japie Stilgemoed presses on, now that he has begun.

"During one trip we lost a great many horses, some to horse-sickness. On another occasion three horses were struck by lightning. The number of dismounted men was growing all the time—there was too little room on the wagons for everyone."

"Never seen a dead horse myself," Reitz tells Ben softly. "Never seen a horse or a mule that has died of horse-sickness being dragged away."

Ben shows no reaction, continues to listen politely to Japie Stilgemoed.

"And everywhere," Japie Stilgemoed continues, "the dismal sight of burned and ruined farmhouses—the work of the Khakis."

"Oh no," Reitz whispers to Ben, "I don't have the strength to listen to this."

Ben's nostrils flare almost imperceptibly, the only evidence of his slight irritation. "Give him a chance," he whispers. "He needs to tell his story."

"One day," Japie Stilgemoed says, "we came across a swarm of flying ants. We'd never seen anything like it before. They crawled into everything."

"Oh no," Reitz repeats in a whisper. He can neither ignore nor explain his growing exasperation with Japie Stilgemoed.

"Sometimes it rained all night and the men would sleep in ant hills," Japie continues, unperturbed. "I kept urging myself to endure the ordeal with patience. Of the future I asked nothing more—as I still do today—than to be reunited with my loved ones."

At the mention of loved ones a great silence falls upon everyone, interrupted suddenly by the yellow dog, which utters a low growl, and raises the hackles on her back. An inspection of their immediate surroundings reveals nothing. The dog calms down and shortly afterwards everyone crawls into his shelter. Everyone except Ben and Reitz, who enjoy the warmth of the flames a little longer while each makes a final entry in his journal.

CHAPTER 4

Ezekiel is responsible for fetching water, chopping wood, cooking porridge, tending to the horses. And roasting meat, when the men don't do it themselves around the fire in the evenings.

The somewhat deaf Japie Stilgemoed and the reclusive Kosie Rijpma apply themselves to a small stack of blankets and items of clothing, mending and darning. When they are not thus occupied during the course of the day, they keep to themselves. Japie Stilgemoed reads or writes in a book, and Kosie Rijpma reads or sits hunched in the sun in front of his shelter.

Reuben makes repairs to saddles and stirrups. Otherwise he calmly smokes his pipe or whittles at a wooden object.

Seun makes traps, with which he catches mongooses and dassies and field mice near the camp. These he skins and hangs from spike-thorns to dry—like the butcherbird—much to Ben's horror. He is also supposed to keep an eye on the horses, but it is doubtful whether anything comes of that.

For most of the day Gert Smal sits in front of his shelter, cleaning his nails with his pocketknife, chewing on a twig or a piece of wood. He is the one who supervises events. He gives the orders, he apportions their duties, the dog with the yellow eyes never far away. Reitz and Ben soon realise a close watch is being kept on the four of them.

Gert Smal cautions them not even to think of leaving before the general has seen them.

Willem solemnly declares that they have never planned to do so, as they have a message from Commandant Senekal to deliver to the general.

The purpose of their journey, he explains once again, is to get young Abraham to a more settled place as quickly as possible. Gert Smal seems unconvinced. They have no hope in any case that he might further their cause. They put their faith in the reasonable disposition of the absent general—the length of whose punitive expedition no one seems to know, nor when he may show up again.

At night everything that has kept them occupied by day is stowed in the rock shelter under the deep overhang. A deep, cool cave that serves as storage room and cold store, where flour, wood, meat, milk, biltong, broken saddles and stirrups, and probably also rifles and ammunition are kept. Not everyone is allowed inside—at any rate not Ben, Reitz and Willem.

It is no use sounding out Gert Smal about the movements of the general. This they discovered on their very first day. It is no use asking the others either. Kosie Rijpma does not speak. Japie Stilgemoed claims to have very little knowledge of the general's manoeuvres—Gert Smal doesn't divulge any information, he says. Reuben says he has no idea what the general is up to, though he knows him as a fellow who takes no nonsense from a Khaki. And if it wasn't for his leg, he would certainly be in the field with the general today. Ezekiel goes about his numerous daily chores impassively—they do not expect him to supply them with information.

They soon learn to wait for Gert Smal to drop some scrap of information, as happens from time to time. The general takes no prisoners, he declares. When he captures the Khakis, he finishes them off straightaway. First he makes them dig their own graves, before he pots them there and then. He recently gave Colonel Fairisle and his men a devilishly good thrashing just the other side of the Skeurberg. Lured them into an ambush, lay in wait for them, and *mowed* them down. When the general has finished with the English, they regret ever having boarded the ship that brought them here.

"That is to say, if anyone survives to regret it," Ben mutters under his breath. Though he wouldn't be surprised if considerable embellishment was taking place here, he adds.

When Gert Smal is in a good mood he sings:

Jan tick, Jan tack, Jan haversack
Jan up-the-pole
Jan finger-in-the-hole

Then Reuben chuckles heartily to himself while carving his objects from wood. Japie Stilgemoed and Kosie Rijpma show no reaction; either they do not hear or they are simply too disengaged from their surroundings to take note of whatever ribaldry may reach their ears. At times Willem blushes slightly and looks as if he wants to protect young Abraham from whatever crudeness he may be exposed to, though Abraham never shows any reaction at all.

When Gert Smal is in a bad mood, he snarls at everyone and sits in front of his shelter, chewing grimly on a piece of wood.

After going down to the river for the first time, Reitz and Ben asked Gert Smal's permission to do field work there by day. He wanted to study the cliff face and the rocks, Reitz explained, and Ben was interested in the plants and insects of the area. Initially Gert Smal seemed sceptical and disinclined to allow it, but after a day or two they could leave in the mornings without having to ask permission—provided they did not go anywhere near the horses, and given the understanding that they would be hunted like rabbits if they tried to escape.

"The rocks have eyes," he warned.

Thus they fall into the habit of going down to the river with their journals and small tin trunks in the early morning and staying there until late afternoon.

Though he keeps a close watch on them, Gert Smal never shows the slightest interest in what they are doing.

Meanwhile Reitz fears the day they too will be assigned mending and darning duties. Ben teases him about it: "Watch your step, Reitz," he says, "it's just a matter of time before Gert Smal puts us to work here."

Over and above their daily excursions to the river Gert Smal seems to have no objection when they go for walks in the immediate vicinity. As long as they remain on foot.

He warns them anew. If you men give me any shit, he says, you'll be sorry. Just try leaving here without permission. You won't even reach the farm gate. You'll be shot like rabbits. The general wishes to meet you in person.

"And we look forward to making his acquaintance," Ben replies, with only the slightest movement of his nostrils.

"Reitz," Ben remarks later when they are alone in the veld, "I suspect Gert Smal is not a dependable source of information. It won't come as a surprise to me at all if the general turns out to be a very reasonable man."

•

In the evenings around the fire they listen chiefly to Gert Smal's ranting or Japie Stilgemoed's tales. No one else contributes much apart from a few desultory remarks.

Gert Smal gives a sneering exposition of the battlefield and everything pertaining to it. He lays it out like a corpse.

When something slips his mind, the date a battle took place or the name of a commanding officer, he snaps his fingers over his shoulder, and Ezekiel fills in the missing information. When was Graspan, my old Kaffir? Graspan was in November of 1899, Baas Gertjie. When was the damned Union Jack raised over Pretoria again? On the fifth of June 1900, Baas Gertjie. When was it that Eloff was forced to surrender? Commandant Eloff surrendered at Mafeking in May of 1900, Baas Gertjie. Where did De la Rey and Smuts whip Clement's arse? At Nooitgedacht, Baas Gertjie. And so forth, and not once does Ezekiel leave Gert Smal in the lurch.

Japie Stilgemoed speaks musingly, his eyes mostly fixed on the flames. He takes them with him, step by relentless step, in his recall of his sojourn with General Kemp's laager.

Yet, despite Japie Stilgemoed's merciless solemnity, Reitz wonders who, apart from Ben and himself and perhaps Willem, actually pays him any heed.

Kosie Rijpma seldom shows any sign of listening, Gert Smal seems to hear only those parts of the conversation that he can comment on derisively, and Reuben is permanently engaged with either the weed or his pipe.

"Once we had a debate," Japie Stilgemoed says one evening, "about the desirability of intervention for the sake of peace. The result was: no intervention—we would fight to the very end. Though I had my doubts whether all the burghers understood the exact meaning of the word intervention—despite voting against it.

"We had another debate. This time about the Native question. I was asked to defend the position of the Native." Whereupon Japie Stilgemoed gives a detailed account of his own as well as the counterarguments.

"Needless to say," he says—with just a trace of a smile—"my viewpoint was voted out with a resounding and incontestible majority."

Ben smiles.

"Why don't we ask Ezekiel what *he* thinks of the Native question?" Reitz asks under his breath.

"Because Ezekiel doesn't know that he's a Native," Ben replies surreptitiously.

"A year ago," says Japie Stilgemoed, sighing deeply, "the prospect of peace talks already existed. At Tafelkop the burghers celebrated for fourteen days in anticipation of peace. They played sports—took part in races, long jump, tug-of-war, fencing, boxing. The men were in high spirits. Little did we know. Yes, little did we know then what still lay ahead."

He stares into the fire, on his face an expression of bitter defeat.

"In my memory Tafelkop will always remain a place of dull grey light and howling wind, with ceaseless rain," he says. "I wouldn't know how long it rained there continuously."

Japie Stilgemoed pulls his blanket closer around his shoulders.

"We, on the other hand," Reitz says to Ben in an undertone, "always slept dry. Our tents never leaked." He runs his hand across his face. He does not expect Ben to react. Which indeed he does not, but Reitz feels the need to voice his exasperation with Japie's sombre tale.

"In March General Kemp went out with a group of men on horseback to help De la Rey in an attack on General Babington at Geduld."

"Kemp and De la Rey can go to *hell*!" Gert Smal says. "Kemp moved too slowly and De la Rey was too cautious. They should have *known* they were outnumbered! They should have come up with a different strategy."

"I sat reading in my tent all the while with a blanket around my shoulders to cut myself off from the present, from its unrelenting affliction," Japie Stilgemoed continues, ignoring Gert Smal's interruption.

Reitz sighs deeply, and again runs his hand across his face wearily. Is there no end to the man, he wonders.

"An icy northerly wind blew for days on end," Japie Stilgemoed continues, undaunted. "The sky was dull and overcast. The wind whistled and gusted. It was March—almost exactly a year ago. Winter was on its way. The tent was so low that one could sit up straight only in the middle. The grass was nearly flattened by the wind. In the distance the veld was greyish yellow and a muted blue where it met the heavy clouds on the horizon. If our circumstances had been different, one might have called it a scene of picturesque beauty. But I was too down-hearted, and the rain too unceasing—a fine, misty, mournful rain. Every day I yearned intensely for the end of the day, for at least night brought oblivion."

At Gert Smal's feet the yellow dog sleeps fitfully, making soft yelping noises as she dreams.

"Glums," says young Abraham tonelessly, and: "Glooming glums."

Willem starts at the first sign of incoherent speech in the young man.

"Take it easy, boy," he says.

Japie Stilgemoed, staring into the flames unwaveringly, seems to have been transported completely to the past.

"I realised it was no use longing for the end of the war if I still had so much to learn—and if I was so reluctant to do so! Would I be a better person when it was all over, I kept wondering. Was it not deplorably clear, day after day, that privation had little to teach me?" Japie Stilgemoed asks, with increasing fervour.

"That time is much more real to him than the present," Reitz remarks softly to Ben, who nods in agreement.

"How could I pray for salvation for myself if I'd done so little to bring salvation or blessing to others? Those were the questions I battled with," says Japie Stilgemoed, "on that comfortless plain, amid that endless drizzle. I had no idea it could rain for so many days on end. Kemp's offensive failed. They were forced to retreat. The Khakis seized four cannons and a number of machine guns. Some of the fleeing men were overtaken from the rear and," he adds quietly, "shot with revolvers."

"Like dogs!" cries Gert Smal. "Shot dead like dogs! A hell of a lot were captured and sent to Madras! The Khakis are going to pay for that! As true as hell!"

"The blast, the blast," young Abraham says, shifting uneasily in his seat.

"The rain that never stops reminds me of the time my late father, my brothers and I went hunting for hippopotamus along the Olifants," says Reuben. "That was also a damn muddy affair."

Willem tries to placate Abraham before putting him to bed in his shelter.

"What did you expect?" Gert Smal exclaims, scornfully spitting something into the fire. "What did you expect of those two old fools? That they would get it right?"

Japie Stilgemoed's eyes remain fixed on the flames. He hears nothing, he sees nothing, he is reliving the past, a time of drawn-out misery.

"Must have been unpleasant," Ben remarks, "the continuous rain."

Japie Stilgemoed gives no sign that he heard.

Reitz nudges Ben to repeat his words.

Ben repeats his observation, but with less conviction.

Japie nods, absently. He draws his blanket closer around his shoulders.

"We were a miserable lot," he continues. "Sometimes we didn't even take the trouble to pitch our tents. Merely drew the canvas over ourselves to keep dry. Two days later a report from General Botha about the peace proposals was read to us. He refused to accept Kitchener's proposals. We returned to our tents. No matter how I counselled my heart to be patient, I was overwhelmed by bitter despondency. I could hardly endure the knowledge that there was no happy future within reach, and I realised how much I had pinned my hopes on the peace talks."

He remains silent for a long time. "And during the entire month of March," he continues, "not once was it dry underfoot."

"Hell," says Reuben, "wet ground like that can be a goddamn nuisance! I remember it well—that time on the banks of the Olifants."

(Despite Reuben's large, battered, coarse-grained face, Reitz is struck by his childlike manner.)

There is no stopping Japie Stilgemoed now—he is not to be diverted by chance remarks, for he is reliving the past with such unrelenting passion that the present hardly makes any impression on him.

Growing increasingly irritable as he listens to Japie Stilgemoed's narrative, Reitz after a while feels compelled to get up. He is no longer able to listen to Japie's story. He does not know why it unsettles him so. It rouses distressing emotions in him—feelings he may have ignored for too long, he thinks. More than once in the course of Japie's tale the thought has come to mind: Enough of this. Enough of everything.

It is no use turning in early, before the others. To be alone in his shelter with only his thoughts—that is not to be endured. And moreover, his chances of falling asleep are slim. But to remain sitting around the fire, listening to Japie Stilgemoed—that is no longer possible tonight either.

He rises, walks away a short distance on his own, and sits down on a loose boulder. He has been so intent upon the small circle of light cast by the fire that the sudden vastness of the night sky makes him reel slightly.

Around him the night comes to life. The silent bat goes its apparently aimless way. He hears the scrabbling of small warm-blooded creatures close by. Further off in the veld a bird flies up in alarm and cries shrilly. From the river comes the silvery sound of frogs. The soft, muffled call of an owl, hu-hooo, hu-hooo, sounds from the direction of the cliff face. In the distance something howls like a jackal. The stars are nearly audible in their teeming presence.

Reitz forces himself to calm down. His exasperation with Japie Stilgemoed nearly got the better of him tonight.

Never amid the privation and constant vigilance of the past months did he feel himself as rankled as during these past few days here in camp. In all those days and months he succeeded in warding off the feelings of futility, loathing and boredom he is experiencing now. In Senekal's laager he allowed himself to be swept along thoughtlessly by the daily routine of commando life and at times by the terrifying diversion of battle. What kept him going was their field work—the notes Ben and he made in their journals whenever possible. But lately he fears that even his journal, a fixed point from the start, can no longer protect him against the troubled feelings that have surfaced in him. And that is not all.

She has caught up with him. She is here. She is in the whispering of the trees by day and in the shooting paths of the stars by night. It began with the farmer's dream of the woman with the feathered hat, but it did not end there.

·

General Bergh surprises them early one morning—he arrives at camp before break of day with two of his officers. Where did they leave their horses? Why did no one hear them approach? Bewildered, Reitz and Ben crawl from the shelters, put on their jackets, wipe their faces with their hands, smooth their hair and beards. They want to look present-able for their meeting with the general. Reitz swears softly, *hell*, the man might have warned us. He is still dazed after being awakened from a deep sleep in which a woman smiled at him wonderfully sweetly, and was going to lie down with him, after making her carnal intent appealingly clear.

Who among them was expecting the general at this hour? Not even Gert Smal. No one but Ezekiel, apparently, because he is calmly fanning the fire. The general blows in his hands and stamps his feet while he waits for his coffee. Gert Smal comes crawling out of his shelter, head over heels and on all fours from his shelter of branches, his face distorted with sleep and his eyes glazed after the previous night's vigorous sam-pling of the spoils of war. Or it may have been the heady weed, Reuben and Seun having joined in with gusto.

Reitz and Ben, rumpled and unwashed, greet the general.

He is shortish, but sturdy. His eyes are permanently narrowed, like someone used to sizing up the situation at hand while keeping his eye firmly fixed on the horizon. In his face the horizontal lines dominate over the vertical ones: the narrowed eyes; the wide, slightly squashed nostrils; the thin, wide mouth; the broadness across the cheekbones where the upper jawbone hinges with the lower jaw. Broad across the jaw and broad across the cheek, broad of shoulder and broad of hand; a broad, flat man, with eyes perpetually fixed on a point in the distance. A man of minimal eye contact and, moreover, a man of few words. The general is clad in military uniform and riding boots and he cuts a fine figure—making them even more mindful of their own frayed and ragged state.

The two officers with him are one Blackpiet Petoors and one Sagrys Skeel. Neither makes a favourable impression on Reitz. Not men he would like to cross swords with. Especially Blackpiet Petoors, sallow of skin, with a short dark beard and dark hair, seems like a fellow to look out for. Whenever he comes near Gert Smal's dog with the yellow eyes her hackles rise and she gives a menacing growl.

Hell and damnation, Reitz swears softly. The man might at least have warned us. Look at us, he says to Ben under his breath, no one can take us seriously in this condition. We look like bloody . . . he searches for a suitable word. Bushmen, whispers Ben.

Gert Smal has clearly been frightened out of his wits, for he scurries around like a maniac, trying to get everyone up and about and standing to attention with their best foot forward. The coffee is being brewed and a large pot of porridge is on the fire and meat is being cooked and Seun is dispatched to fetch eggs from somewhere and it is yes, General, and no, General. (At every opportunity, however, he glowers at Reitz and Ben and addresses the others in hissing undertones.)

The general sits on a camp stool (that has been brought out especially for him) and drinks his coffee. He pays little heed to Gert Smal's frantic scrambling.

In the meantime Willem has made his appearance—grave and un-ruffled. His hair neatly smoothed, as dignified in his shabby attire as if he were clad in his Sunday best.

When they have finished their coffee, the general calls them aside. The hour of reckoning has arrived, Reitz thinks. Willem explains their situation. They are taking the raving young Abraham to his mother in Ladybrand so that she can look after him. The commando is no longer a suitable place for him. Commandant Senekal gave them permission to go, Willem says, on condition that they deliver a letter to the general. Which Willem then solemnly proceeds to do on behalf of them all.

The general reads the letter. He says nothing. He hands it back to them. Read it yourselves, he says. Willem reads first. Then Reitz and Ben.

In Commandant Senekal's decrepit hand with elaborate flourishes that threaten to plunge off the page, the missive states clearly that they are deserters and chancers, every single one of them, and that the general should teach them a lesson before sending them back to Senekal's laager.

Reitz feels his ears burning. His heart is pounding. In his mind he harbours horrendous murderous feelings towards Senekal. May God strike him down. May he come to an unbearable end. Senekal is a turd, it buzzes through his head like the noise of a thousand cicadas. Whether the buzzing reaches the general's well-appointed ears is, however, uncertain.

The relentless shrilling of cicadas is indeed audible and the heat is suddenly palpable—especially in the armpit and groin.

Willem's face is crimson. Ben keeps silent and his eyes are fixed on the ground at his feet.

The general gives a faint smile. He crumples up the letter and throws it into the fire. He turns away from them and orders Ezekiel to pour him another mug of coffee. They remain standing, crestfallen. The general slowly drinks his coffee. He examines the sky. He stares into the distance. At last he turns and fixes his gaze on them once more.

"Where is the boy?" he asks Willem.

Willem points at the shelter.

"He's had a bad night," he says. "He has to sleep for as long as possible."

The general nods. "What is his condition?" he inquires.

"Not good," Willem replies. "Better since we've been here, but not good."

"Are you related to him?" the general asks.

"No," Willem replies. "But I accepted responsibility for him the day his elder brother was shot dead by his side during the battle of Droogleegte, about two months ago. He never spoke coherently again after that. And he is no longer fit for battle."

The general nods again. "I heard of the battle," he says, and turns to Reitz and Ben.

"What is your business," he asks, "apart from escorting your friend?"

"Since we were called up in the name of the president," Ben says, "our business has been the war."

"And before the war?" the general asks, "before you were called up in the name of the president? What was your business then?"

"Before the war," says Ben, taking a deep breath and scratching his left shoulder absent-mindedly with his right hand, "I occupied myself with natural history—with the study of plants and insects—and my friend here," and he motions with his hand, as if presenting Reitz to the general, "my friend worked as a geologist at the Witwatersrand . . ."

The general intervenes and turns to Reitz, who, after a moment's hesitation, continues: "The science of geology has made rapid strides in this country, as you probably know, since the discovery of gold and diamonds—which unfortunately, as we all know . . ." At this point he suddenly falls silent, uncertain how to continue.

"Yes?" the general urges.

"Has led to great conflict and strife in the Transvaal," Reitz completes the sentence in an undertone.

High in the sky a jackal buzzard cries shrilly. They all look up.

"Yes," the general says. "Indeed. Conflict and strife. The rightful ownership of the riches." He looks at the sky again. Gazes over Reitz's shoulder.

"And may I ask," he continues, "whether in the two and a half years since you were called up for duty by our president the two of you have had an opportunity to proceed with your important work?"

A trick question, Reitz thinks. Now we're done for.

"Whenever possible," Ben answers carefully, "where time and conditions have allowed, we have both done field work in the area where we happened to be."

"Which is where?" the general asks without looking at them directly.

Nervously Reitz launches into a description of their movements with the Lichtenburg Commando, but the general interrupts and asks where they have documented their field work.

"In journals," Ben answers, suddenly unwilling to share the information.

"Let me see," says the general.

Ben and Reitz shoot each other a brief glance before turning to fetch their journals from their respective shelters.

They hand over the precious objects to the general for inspection.

The sun is basking on their heads. Reitz feels dizzy. This is the end, he thinks. It is the tragic end. It is the last straw. The man is going to throw the journals into the fire as he did with the letter. He is going to confiscate the journals and send them all back to Senekal's laager. Their fate has been sealed. He dare not look at Ben. There is an uncontrollable crawling sensation in his armpits and groin.

Slowly the general pages through the journals. He takes his time. It is dead quiet in the camp. Reitz has never realised it can be so quiet here. Even the cicadas have momentarily stopped singing.

Turd, he thinks. Senekal is a *turd* and may his end be bitter.

Tick-tick-tick, a bird calls.

At last the general closes the journals. He hands them back to Reitz and Ben without meeting their eyes and says: "On my return I expect from each of you men a brief lecture on your subject."

And with that he turns away. He does not speak another word to them for the remainder of his short visit.

•

General Bergh and his two comrades do not stay long. Reitz watches closely as he speaks a few words to each man in turn. He is polite but curt in his interaction with them all.

When he has asked after everyone's welfare, he takes Blackpiet Petoors and Sagrys Skeel aside and they pore at length over a map spread on a flat rock. From time to time they summon Gert Smal. Between pointing out different places on the map, the general seems to be waving his hand at some location in the distance.

It's not over by far, Reitz tells Ben under his breath. They're still scheming for all they're worth. What made you think it's over? Ben asks. Perhaps I dreamed it, says Reitz, perhaps it's because we're stuck here, with the sick and the lame. We can count ourselves amongst them nowadays, Ben says. It's going to get worse, says Reitz, if we don't get away from here soon.

After the general and his company have left, Reitz and Ben make their way to the river. They want to wash their clothes, they tell Gert Smal. It's too late now! he shouts after them. You should have thought of it earlier.

Of course he's dying to know, Ben says, what the general said to us. It gives us some bargaining power too. We may be able to gather a few scraps of information from him this way.

At the river they proceed to curse Commandant Senekal lustily. May his prospects become less favourable by the day. May he meet his blasted match soon, says Ben. May he die lonely and humiliated, and may his progeny be damned, says Reitz. Ben looks at him as if he is going a mite too far.

At intervals, between bathing and washing their clothes and sunning themselves on the rocks and listening to the baboons high up in the kloof, with Ben inspecting and describing various things as he is accustomed, Reitz exclaims softly: Blast and blasted hell. What now?

But Ben is optimistic. He stands firm. They should be grateful that the general is a reasonable man, for it could have been much worse— had any of the others been in control of their fate.

"Our fate hasn't been conclusively decided," Reitz reminds him.

"As good as," Ben replies.

"He can still decide not to permit us to leave," says Reitz. "In which case we're done for."

"The general is an honourable man," Ben insists, "honourable and reasonable—unlike ninety-nine per cent of the people we've been in contact with during the past few months."

"If we're forced to remain here until the end of the war," says Reitz, "I couldn't endure it." And beseechingly: "I couldn't stand it, Ben. I'm unsettled. I'm not at ease here. I don't trust Gert Smal." And more beseechingly: "I'm enfeebled by that man, Ben—Japie Stilgemoed enfeebles me. If I have to listen to his tales night after night, I'm bound to attack him. I can't vouch for my self-control much longer. It's not good for my state of mind."

Ben chuckles softly.

"You shouldn't take it to heart like that, Reitz," he says. "Things were much worse at Senekal's laager. You forget."

"There's one more thing," Reitz says. More gravely, wiping his hand across his face.

Ben looks at him closely.

Reitz says: "I don't know how to say this."

Ben waits.

"Since we arrived here," he says—hesitantly, shoulders slumped, arms dangling loosely between his knees, "actually since we stopped at the farmer's that night."

Ben listens patiently.

"It's my wife," Reitz says. "My late wife. She wants to make contact with me."

He remains silent for a while.

"Now, after all this time," he adds softly.

The afternoon air is heavy and sweet. The atmosphere is languid and in the crevices the baboons, who have been cavorting and barking exuberantly all morning, suddenly fall silent. Somewhere a dove coos soft and low.

"I can't bear it, Ben," says Reitz, "I don't know if I can bear it much longer."

CHAPTER 5

After the general's visit Ben and Reitz occupy themselves by day with
the preparation of their lectures, over and above their normal field work.
They have no idea when the general might put in an appearance and
they have no desire to be taken by surprise again. In the morning they
take the small trunks containing their journals to the river where they
can work undisturbed.

Gert Smal will not or cannot say when they can expect the general,
and from the general himself there was no hint.

"It's part of our punishment, Reitz," Ben says, "that we're not permitted to know when the general will turn up again. It's expected of us
always to be prepared. Like the wise virgins."

"Oh Lord," says Reitz.

Gert Smal makes devious inquiries into their conversation with the
general, and with equally deft footwork they try to extract from him
what the general's plans are, and so they circle and approach one another
craftily, and each tries to trump and outmanoeuvre the other.

"What happens now?" Reitz asks Ben the morning after the visit.
"What's the general's plan with us? Is he interested in what we have to
say—or is it a test to see whether we have honourable intentions?"

"Do we?" Ben asks teasingly.

"We do want to help Willem get Abraham to Ladybrand," Reitz
says.

"And after that?" Ben asks, still teasing.

Reitz shrugs, avoiding Ben's eyes. "Well, the plan has always been that after you've visited your family . . . we will of necessity join another commando. But it doesn't look as if we'll be able to get away from here soon," he says broodingly.

"This place is good for Abraham at the moment," Ben says. "He won't be better off anywhere else for now. To get him to his mother at Ladybrand safely is going to be more difficult than we surmised."

"We should have thought of that earlier," says Reitz, with a hint of spite in his voice.

"It was important to get Abraham away from Senekal's laager," says Ben. "We couldn't have foreseen it would turn out like this."

So now we're stuck here, Reitz wants to say, but he holds his peace.

Ben looks closely at Reitz. "You've been grumbling and complaining all morning," he says. "What's biting you?"

Reitz shrugs despondently.

"Is it your wife?" Ben asks, more carefully.

Reitz runs his hands across his face. He shrugs again. Ben continues to inspect a small plant he is holding. Reitz, too, tries to apply himself to his work.

"What do you think?" he asks after a while, abashed.

"About what?" Ben asks, not looking up from the sketch he is making in his journal.

"About the general's intention with us?" Reitz says.

"I think," says Ben, "that the general knows very well Senekal is a dead loss. I think he's a shrewd fellow, he sized us up soon enough, he knows where he stands with us." Ben gives a short, furtive laugh. "I think he's interested in what we're doing. I may be wrong." Ben inspects the plant from a different angle. "But I also think he knows very well we can still be useful on the battlefield—and that's probably his chief consideration when determining our fate. In due course the two of us will be assigned some or other mission—you can prepare yourself for that."

"Oh Lord," says Reitz. "I suppose you're right."

Having worked in silence for a while, Reitz asks hesitantly: "And your wife and children, Ben, what about them?"

Ben looks up. He stares into the distance. He seems suddenly older to Reitz, his shoulders slumped.

"It's been too long since I heard from my wife," he says. "I still plan to stop at home. As soon as I'm able to."

They let the matter rest.

Besides flour, biltong and coffee (*where* could they possibly have found it, Reitz wonders), the general and his men have again brought a few saddles, blankets and clothing items in need of repair. No shortage of work for Reuben, Kosie Rijpma and Japie Stilgemoed. But despite the watchful eye of Gert Smal no one seems to work very hard.

Sometimes Kosie Rijpma sits staring into space for hours on end, or he snaps twigs and plays with them, or immerses himself in a slim volume with a tattered brown-paper cover—the pile of clothing and blankets forgotten by his side. Japie Stilgemoed writes in his diary or reads—apparently whenever he feels the urge to do so.

By day young Abraham sits in the sun. He is no longer so painfully thin. It seems his health is indeed improving. He is still not talking—now and again he utters a word or an incoherent phrase that appears to have no connection with anything identifiable, but he sleeps more peacefully at night and he is less prone to fits of agitation.

By day, when he is not carving cutlery out of wood, or quietly smoking his pipe, Willem often reads to Abraham from the Bible.

From time to time Ben tries to initiate a conversation with Japie Stilgemoed, but Japie is so timid and distrustful that he soon gives up trying. It is because Japie is hard of hearing, Reitz and he decide, and they leave it at that.

In the evenings around the fire, however, it is still chiefly Gert Smal and Japie who hold forth. Sometimes Reitz handles it better than other times, depending on his frame of mind.

•

On the evening following the general's unexpected visit, after Willem has read from the Bible and they have sung together, Japie Stilgemoed continues with his fervent account. (These days Willem and Japie Stilgemoed take turns to lead the evening devotions.) As text, Willem chose the parable of the wise and the foolish virgins. Ben and Reitz shoot each other a furtive glance.

"Seems even old Willem took fright this morning," Reitz says softly.

This evening they sing more lustily than usual—each grateful in his own way that the general with his appraising eye is no longer in their midst.

Gert Smal especially has been jittery all day after the surprise visit, and the last notes of the hymn have barely faded before he fetches a bottle of the war booty from the cave, at the same time asking Reuben to start rolling the weed.

Reuben needs no encouragement; his face glows at the prospect of a peaceful stupor. (Reitz wonders whether Ezekiel counts among his numerous duties the cultivation somewhere of dagga—as well as potatoes.)

Meanwhile Japie Stilgemoed has pulled the blanket closer around his shoulders and is staring intently into the fire, Reitz notices with dismay. Onward then, he thinks, onward with the account.

"My main diversion," Japie Stilgemoed begins, "was reading. It was the only way I could tolerably pass the hours and days."

"Couldn't they have found something for him to *do*?" Reitz mutters to Ben.

"I spent too much time reading, actually," Japie Stilgemoed says, "I spent too much time reading, too little time doing anything, and—more's the pity—not enough time thinking either. The more I chided and tried to restrain myself, the more I tried to force myself to become more aware of events, to reach out to people more—at least to those in my tent, the less I could resist the temptation to lose myself in the pages of a book. Time and again I resorted to picking up a book in an attempt to escape from the pain of the moment, from feelings of futility and despair. I simply couldn't exist in the present without being stripped of all sense of fortitude and meaning. I lived in constant fear that, failing to detach myself, I might be deprived of my senses."

"It's only natural," Ben says in the silence that follows, "that a person will try to remove himself from difficult circumstances."

Japie Stilgemoed nods without looking at Ben. Reitz wonders if he heard.

"I fell short," says Japie Stilgemoed. "Over and over it became clear to me that I fell short. That I didn't live up to my own requirements and standards."

"Prepare yourself for another great outpouring tonight," Reitz says to Ben, running a weary hand across his face.

"See it as the testimony of a soul in need," Ben says softly, "see it as someone giving voice to the ordeal of war on behalf of all of us."

Reitz gives a muted exclamation; makes a dismissive gesture, as if he wants to make it clear—not on *his* behalf.

"There were days," Japie Stilgemoed continues, "when the separation from hearth and home and loved ones weighed on me twice as heavily. If only I could know, if only I could be certain they were safe, that we would be reunited, I could persevere in the struggle with greater peace of mind."

Reuben takes the first deep draw at the weed. It is rolled in something that looks suspiciously like a page from the Bible. He holds it in his lungs for so long that Reitz expects the man to fall down in a dead faint right in front of their eyes. Not in the least—Reuben hands Gert Smal the tightly-packed hand-rolled cigarette, swings his powerful torso in a great sweeping arc as the weed kicks in, but remains firmly in the saddle. The firelight accentuates the rough contours of his broad, animated face, which seems to wear a permanent expression of slight surprise. Gert Smal takes an equally deep draw and grimaces from ear to ear. The weed's sweet scent hangs heavily in the air.

"Tonight," Reitz tells Ben softly, "everything will converge in one mighty revelation again—from the whore of Babylon to Cronjé's defeat at Paardeberg."

"In a deserted Khaki camp," Japie Stilgemoed continues, "I came across a copy of Goethe's Faust! I threw myself into it with such abandon that I frightened even myself!"

"Khaki, my *arse*," says Gert Smal.

"The weed has taken hold," Ben remarks softly.

"Do you think the general would approve of this habit, Ben?" Reitz inquires.

Ben smiles.

"Stick up Khaki's arse," says Reuben.

"Stick up his grandmother's arse," says Gert Smal.

"Oh, the depravity of it," says Willem, casting a worried glance in young Abraham's direction.

Seun, who has also partaken of the weed, capers joyously, with much unintelligible moaning and bleating.

"Daily I heard the voice of my conscience saying: Don't try to remove yourself from your own hell," Japie Stilgemoed continues, unperturbed. "Don't pass up an opportunity for the growth of your soul!"

Reitz feels an immense, uncontrollable irritation welling up inside him.

"But what good did the voice of my conscience do me?" Japie Stilgemoed asks. "I was no match for my conflicting impulses—I wanted to seize the opportunity *and* I wanted to escape! And time and again it was the lesser impulse that got the better of me."

Reitz wipes his hand across his face. Sighs.

"That's understandable," says Ben softly. And adds: "Who amongst us has *not* wished to escape from his unpleasant circumstances during the past years?"

He is the only one still listening to Japie with undivided attention.

Reitz is listening with mounting resistance; Kosie Rijpma gives no indication that he is following the conversation. No one expects young Abraham to listen or react. Willem smokes his pipe calmly, sometimes dozing for a few moments, otherwise keeping a watchful and protective eye on young Abraham. Gert Smal, Reuben and Seun follow the path of the befuddling weed, and Ezekiel squats silently in the shadows—unable to retire before Gert Smal gives the word.

Thus Japie Stilgemoed continues, not allowing himself to be interrupted. He describes the desolate plain through which they trekked, bathed by night in unvarying moonlight, giving everything a bleak and godforsaken appearance.

On one occasion they outspanned towards midnight, a small, bitter wind blew from the south, and he was overcome by a feeling of emptiness and unbearable longing. It was then that they looked up at the sky and saw the comet. And everyone read into it his own omens and attached to it his own meaning.

And always the evening was the best time, for it was less harrassing than daytime, and the small fires created a semblance of peaceful familiarity. It was May by then and bitingly cold at night, and during the day they bartered salt for goat skins. One night they camped under some thorn trees, and through the branches he gazed at the stars, and shortly afterwards, at the battle of Vlakfontein, they solemnly buried their nine fallen dead.

And here Japie Stilgemoed grows silent for a while, before he goes on to tell them that it grew even colder as they journeyed in a southeasterly direction. At night they made colossal fires and slept beside them for the heat. By day they still came across houses that had been burned down. From some of them smoke was still spiralling upward—so recently had they been set alight. And at one of their encampments he, Japie, made himself a bed in a thicket of kreupelhout, so that he had to crawl in on all fours, and was for a brief while enchanted by the dappled green sunshine by day and silvery moonlight by night. For that short space of time he felt sheltered and secure. It was there, too, he remembers it well, that he saw a small cocoon on a branch, the home of some caterpillar or other—surprisingly resistant to damage by wind or weather. It remained attached to a twig until it was ready to emerge as a butterfly. And that made him wonder, that enclosed little insect form, whether the grave is truly the end, or whether the resurrection of the spirit might not be possible after all.

And still Japie continues, taking everyone—at least those who are still listening—along on his descent into hell. He describes how they later used the wood in the deserted houses for firewood, the floorboards as well as the doorjambs, and that he is ashamed to admit that he began to search out these scenes of destruction deliberately—and that he now sees it as a barbaric impulse that drove him, something dark within him that delighted in the devastation.

And he will never forget, he says, as long as he lives, the succession of burned houses along their route. That and the blackened fields in the moonlight he will never forget. They are etched into his memory for ever. And he briefly buries his face in his hands.

In July the exhausted mares had one stillbirth after another, and the war was in effect a curse not only for man but also and especially for the innocent beasts, who had had no part in the decision, and had no control over their fate.

And in this time, during a skirmish with the Khakis, Japie Stilgemoed says, it was clear that a large number of Kaffirs were fighting in the ranks of the enemy, and so it gradually became evident that too many elements were conspiring against the Boers—the odds were too great. The land had been burned, the animals were exhausted, and they were being betrayed—or even worse, murdered—by those from whom a measure of loyalty might have been expected.

Thus a kind of stupor and spiritual dullness gradually came over him, which in a way proved a blessing. And he realised it would never be possible for him to take pleasure in new impressions again. And all that remained, says Japie Stilgemoed, was a longing, an all-encompassing longing to be reunited with his loved ones. And that longing, he says, has remained with him to the present day.

And with these words he pulls his blanket tighter around his shoulders, gets up, wishes everyone a good night, and walks past the large loose boulders that encircle the camp and into the veld.

"Hell," says Reuben, "old Japie with his endless blather. Tries a man's patience."

"Japie's *arse*," says Gert Smal. Heavily intoxicated with weed and liquor.

"My experience was altogether different," Kosie Rijpma suddenly declares, "for before I came here I spent a few months in the concentration camp at Roodespruit."

Ben and Reitz look at him in surprise. It is the first time they have heard him speak.

•

During the night something awakens Reitz with a shock.

Something like a blind, dim urge that breaks through his dreams and his sleeping consciousness.

A dark thing that *strains*, with mothlike furriness and light flutterings.

Something from the outside—or has he been dreaming?

He is wide awake, unable to sleep again.

He lies awake for a long time. Unwelcome thoughts and memories converge on him, seemingly from nowhere. Every thought is painful.

He has no inclination to get up and sit by the cold fire, or to take a walk in the veld. Not at this time of night. Gert Smal would think nothing of it to set the yellow dog on him or even shoot him. From an unpredictable man like Gert Smal one can expect the worst.

He thinks of the geological formations of the surrounding area. As often happens when he is troubled, he tries to summon up his knowledge, for that provides comfort and distraction.

He listens to the night sounds. From somewhere nearby the barn owl screeches: shree-shree. A soft but piercing call.

After a while he falls asleep again.

The next morning he is grateful for daylight. But all day long he feels querulous and touchy.

•

Later that day when they are alone at the river, preparing their lectures, Ben asks sheepishly, out of the blue: "Reitz, did you happen to make a note somewhere of the last time we saw a woman?"

"What do you mean, *saw*?" Reitz asks, his curiosity aroused.

"*Saw*," Ben replies, spreading the fingers of both hands and raising them so that the fingertips are directly in front of his eyes. "Saw with our eyes." Still embarrassed.

"You don't mean in our dreams?" says Reitz.

"No," Ben replies.

"You're not talking about a female skeleton," he asks, teasingly.

"No," says Ben.

"Or a comely woman?" he asks.

"No," says Ben, as if he regrets ever having asked.

"Ben," says Reitz, "what are you implying?"

"I just want to be certain," says Ben, "because according to my calculations it's been so long that it's probably not strange at all that we're beginning to compensate in our dreams."

Ben tosses a pebble into the river.

Reitz looks at him quizzically.

"Reitz," says Ben, still abashed, "I have been visited by a woman the past few nights. This is not strange in itself—given our situation—but what is strange is that it's the same woman every time."

Reitz feels the blood rush to his face. "Does it happen to be a woman," he asks, "with a little feathered hat?"

Ben looks at him, somewhat mystified. "I didn't really notice," he says shamefacedly.

•

Now Kosie Rijpma has also begun to speak around the fire in the evenings, though it is not clear what has occasioned it.

He stares straight ahead while he speaks. His dark eyes are deepset, his voice neutral, not expressing much feeling.

"One day we had to bury Bettie Loots too, wrapped in a blanket," he says.

There is no other sound around the fire. Even Gert Smal and Reuben listen more attentively than usual.

Kosie Rijpma rocks back and forth with his head and upper body while he speaks—the slightest of movements.

"One day we buried Bettie Loots," he repeats, "with whom I had had an animated daily conversation until the day she died. Even though she was so weak and wasted towards the end that it was only with the greatest difficulty that she still managed to speak."

Back and forth, scarcely noticeable.

"The day she died her mother handed me a little volume of Bettie Loots's verses."

His voice betrays no emotion.

"Because she knew or believed it would have more value for me than for her."

Kosie Rijpma closes his eyes.

"Bettie Loots's mother wanted to comfort *me* after her daughter's death."

He opens his eyes. He seems surprised, as if not expecting to find them there.

"I still have it in my possession," says Kosie Rijpma. "I still have

Bettie Loots's book of verses with me."

After this Kosie Rijpma is silent, and Japie Stilgemoed explains that Kosie was a predikant in the concentration camp at Roodespruit for nine months before he ended up here.

"Because he lost his marbles," Gert Smal remarks wryly, picking his teeth with a wooden splinter.

•

For Reitz each night is worse than the one before. His sleep is light and wakeful because he has to defend himself against all that threatens to slip into his sleeping consciousness and get the better of him.

He can see Ben is aware of his restlessness. As soon as they are alone at the river, he questions him cautiously.

"What's biting you, Reitz?"

Reitz cannot really say. Now it is this, now that. It is the place. It is Japie Stilgemoed. It is the whole lot up at camp. They are either too doleful and damaged, or too brutal and rash. In the end he prefers Senekal, the turd.

"You prefer Senekal's brutal rashness?" Ben asks.

"Yes," Reitz replies, "I prefer Senekal's rashness. At least there I knew peace of mind to some degree." He stares straight ahead. Forearms resting on his knees, hands hanging loosely.

"You've forgotten!" Ben exclaims. (A slight rebuke in his voice?)

"No, I haven't forgotten," says Reitz.

"And now?" Ben asks, carefully.

"Now I no longer have it," says Reitz, "I no longer have peace of mind."

"Is it about your wife," asks Ben, even more carefully, "your late wife, of whom you were telling me the other day?"

Reitz seems about to agree, wipes his hand across his face, does not want to admit it; does not *know*.

"Something disturbs my sleep at night," he says, "something constantly trying to worm its way into my deepest sleep."

"Something?" Ben asks. "Something from the outside?"

Reitz is quiet for a long time. He bows his head. He hears the water. The gentle sound of the wind in the leaves. It is peaceful here by day.

"I can't say," he says after a while. "I don't know."

"Reitz," says Ben, "why don't you tell me about her?"

"The worst is," Reitz says, "that I sometimes find I cannot recall her face any more. I find it difficult to remember her the way she was."

He looks at Ben imploringly.

"Sometimes I panic!" he says. "I have nothing to remember her by!"

He buries his face in his hands. "I'm forgetting her," he cries, "despite all my efforts to remember!"

Calm down, Ben says. Calm down. It happens sometimes. It takes him longer to call up the face of his beloved wife too.

"But she's still *alive*!" says Reitz. "When it's all over, you can go back to her!"

Ben says nothing at first. Then he says: "What assurance do I have that she's alive? *Or* the children?"

Reitz looks at Ben briefly and sees on his face an expression he has never seen before.

They are both silent for a while.

Ben occupies himself with the apparent inspection of a plant.

Reitz sits with bowed head for a long time, his forearms resting on his thighs, his hands limp, before saying: "But the worst is that she *knows* it. She knows that her memory is slipping through my fingers like sand."

Suddenly Ben looks at him with greater intensity, and says: "Tell me about her. About your late wife."

"She was a lot younger than me. She was pretty," says Reitz, "but after the death of our child she was never herself again."

He looks at Ben.

"Towards the end she was no longer in her right mind," he says. "And may God forgive me for saying so."

CHAPTER 6

When they return to camp that afternoon, Seun has a high fever and an angry red rash on his body. Someone has to fetch herbs from Oompie immediately—he is also the medicine man. Reitz offers to go, with Ben. (For a moment Ben looks at him strangely. Reitz made the offer without consulting him first.) Initially Gert Smal is unwilling, but given the seriousness of Seun's condition, he gives his grudging permission. (He is clearly worried about Seun, and apparently reluctant to leave him in the care of the others.) But they'd better not try anything, he warns. And they are to make haste. Under no circumstances should they dawdle—the weather looks threatening. (Which indeed it does—a strong gust has risen.) He hurriedly gives them a roll of tobacco for Oompie and shouts a last warning after them.

They set out immediately. Though they hurry, Ben points out a thousand and one things along the way. The soap bush and the hartbees-bos. Cat's tail and bitter bush, snake berry and kriedoring. The kaffir chestnut. A few beetles. A small coral snake—like a necklace—on a rock. The slow trail of a puffadder. Dassies, rock lizards as well as the blue-headed kind.

A hare darts through the grass ahead of them. Ben points out its pale droppings. It is his guess that there are lynxes and even servals in the vicinity. Also the bat-eared jackal, and the more timid maned jackal. There are certainly leopards in the kloof, if there are baboons.

As they walk, Ben asks about the classification system for igneous rock. Reitz explains that to date no satisfactory system has been devised. In the meantime classification still depends on origin. Though some are classified according to the chemical composition of the rock, Reitz says, based on its internal structure—for example how siliceous it is.

A while later Ben goes on his haunches before an aardvark hole beside a very large ant hill. It's bound to be inhabited by a maned jackal—an aardwolf—he says. Look at the tracks, he points. The mane on its back rises when the animal takes fright. Because its teeth are poorly developed, its diet consists mainly of insects, Ben says. They continue on their way. He points out buck droppings, a single mountain tortoise, and a black eagle high overhead.

They must go to the waterfall sometime, says Ben—when they hear the rushing of water in the distance, deeper into the kloof—no doubt they'll find a wealth of insects and plants there.

After about an hour's walk, when they are still some distance from his hut, they come across Oompie. He approaches from the direction of the waterfall. He wears his raincoat and holds a sturdy walking stick in his hand. A leather bag is slung over his shoulder.

They fall in step with him for the last leg of their journey and explain why they have come. The old man walks so fast that they find it difficult to keep up.

When they arrive at the hut, he offers them a drink of sour milk from the clay pot covered by a cloth, just like the previous time. Reitz wonders whether the pot was a gift from one of his brides. He looks around, expecting to find further signs of Oompie's unusual attachments. The hut is cool and shady inside. Again the milk sticks in Reitz's throat, despite his considerable thirst.

Oompie questions them about Seun's symptoms. They explain as best they can. According to Gert Smal the boy was hale and hearty earlier that morning, but towards noon he suddenly became feverish and broke out in a fiery rash.

Amid the conversation Oompie busies himself with various things. He seems to be moving around pots and containers on the stove randomly. Occasionally, however, he fixes them with his small, light blue eyes. Oompie's fleshy face suddenly reminds Reitz of the old president, though Oom Paul's face is heavier, more indomitable. Could Oompie be related to the old president? Reitz wonders what the old man is thinking, for he scarcely seems to be paying them any attention.

When they have told him as much as they know, Oompie, apparently in no great hurry, goes into the small anteroom. His shuffling gait hardly resembles his energetic tread of a while ago, when they could barely keep up with him on their way up the mountain.

They do not speak in his absence. Silently they sit at the table. The two mugs of sour milk half empty on the big, rough wooden surface in front of them. Reitz looks around. He sniffs the strange air hesitantly. He does not want to inhale deeply. He does not trust the unidentifiable mixture of smells.

After a while Oompie returns with two pouches. He indicates how the remedies should be taken and applied.

Reitz is nervous. Their time is running out.

When they are about to take their leave, Oompie suddenly says: "That's not all. Something else has brought you here." He busies himself at the stove again, his back to them.

Reitz and Ben both keep silent. Reitz feels his face flush. He has no idea how to broach the subject, how to make the best use of the opportunity.

"You want to know when the war will be over," Oompie says.

Ben nods slowly, in wonder. Oompie keeps his back to them.

"And one of you is troubled," he continues. "It is a disquiet that is consuming him slowly. That grants him no rest."

Ben gives Reitz a quick sidelong glance. Reitz feels his colour deepen. He avoids Ben's eyes.

Oompie moves towards the door leading into the next room.

"Come with me," he says.

They follow him into the adjoining room. Hesitating slightly as they cross the threshold—uncertain of what they will find there, nervous because they have to make haste with Seun's medicine.

It is even darker here; the ceiling is lower. In the middle of the room stands a table. There are shelves of roughly hewn timber on the walls. On the shelves are glass jars of all sizes, with lids. In the jars are objects, fluids, solid matter—hard to identify these contents in the poor light. There is the smell of dust, the soapy smell of dry bones, the medicinal smell of formalin. The air is cool and musty, fungous. In a corner stand tin trunks and cardboard boxes. High on a shelf there are skulls: the skull of a horse and a baboon, something resembling the skull of a warthog; a large number of smaller skulls probably belonging to mongooses and moles.

Ben approaches the glass jars on the shelves closest to him with interest, wanting to take a closer look at their contents. But Oompie instructs them firmly to take a seat at the table—a smaller table than the one in the other room, with a finer, smoother surface.

"Don't worry about the boy," he sets their minds at rest, "he'll recover soon enough."

He takes down a jar from one of the shelves and places it on the table in front of them.

Reitz recoils slightly from its startling contents.

Inside the bottle the head of a snake—big and pale yellow, with barely any pigment—floats in formalin.

"Thought the old rascal might grab your attention," says Oompie.

"Albino python," Ben whispers in amazement. He inspects it with great interest.

Oompie takes down another jar.

A pale and scaly creature, something between a frog and a lizard, is suspended in the water.

"Salamander," Ben says. "Unusual for this area. A hermaphroditic animal."

Oompie nods curtly in agreement.

He turns to the shelves again, for a while moving the jars and other objects around in the semidark before he takes down a third jar, placing it on the table in front of them as well.

"My faithful old ally," he says.

The jar is considerably larger than the others. Reitz calls out involuntarily—something between a sigh and a cry.

Inside the jar is a head. The head of a person. The eyes are half closed. The features slightly squashed against the sides of the jar.

Reitz feels a flush of warm blood rushing violently into his face.

A black cloudiness that billowed up from the murky bottom when the bottle was moved, gradually begins to settle again. The head is pale black, the hair unmistakably negroid, the features slightly flattened as they press against the sides of the jar; one eye is very slightly open. Around the mouth there is the faintest trace of a smile, or a grimace. There is something cold and saprophytic about the head, like a gigantic pale black fungus.

"Ask him," says Oompie. "Ask him what you want to know."

Ben and Reitz are both speechless.

Oompie touches the bottle lightly, pushing it slightly towards them. They draw back in their seats. The liquid laps lightly at the glass. A black cloud, stirred up again, murky as coal ash, settles slowly after a while.

Ben's expressive nostrils are nervously dilated; as if he fears he may catch a putrid whiff of decay.

"It only seems as if he's asleep," Oompie says. "He's listening. He's waiting."

Carefully he joins them at the table. Reitz glances at him in disbelief. Oompie's pupils are tiny knifesharp dots.

"Ask him!" Oompie urges. "Whisper in his ear! He's listening!"

Reitz's face is burning. His ears are glowing. He gives Ben a beseeching look.

Slowly Ben moves forward. He moves his head closer to the bottle, bringing his mouth as close as possible to the ear.

"When," he asks, "will the war be over?" He speaks softly.

They wait. Reitz's heart is pounding so hard that he feels his pulse hammering in his temples.

Once again the black soot rises slowly from the bottom. Bubbles appear in the proximity of the mouth—a quaking and churning like a small whirlpool. These bubbles fill the entire jar like boiling water.

Oompie comes forward slowly, holds his ear against the jar. He listens. He listens long and attentively. He closes his eyes. When he opens them, they roll back slightly, the whites visible. While he is listening, it appears to Reitz as if Oompie's already swarthy complexion becomes a shade darker. His skin glistens greasily as if it has been rubbed with oil.

When at last he begins to speak, his voice is strangely disembodied.

"My friends," he says, "the war has never been as close to being over as it is at this moment. No more than two months. End of May, beginning of July it will all be over."

Ben nods. Reitz's mouth is dry.

"The war is nearly over," says Oompie—his eyes glazed over, his voice hardly recognisable, "but it's not the end of the struggle by far. The struggle will not be over in your lifetime, nor in your children's lifetime, nor in the lifetime of your children's children."

"Has the struggle been in vain then?" asks Ben. His voice is gruff.

Suddenly Oompie sits up straight. His ear no longer held to the jar.

"Yes," he says in his normal voice, "the struggle has been in vain."

Gradually the bubbles subside. The black substance sinks back to the bottom. All three of them sit in silence.

Reitz dare not meet Ben's eye.

Oompie rises and carefully replaces the three jars on the shelf. One by one. First the head. Then the pale salamander. Then the scaly snake.

He motions for them to get up. Reitz's legs feel unsteady.

Back in the larger room Oompie suddenly asks: "You didn't happen to bring an old man something nice?" He has reverted to being a shifty, shambling old man.

Ben takes the roll of tobacco from his pocket.

Oompie thanks them and shows them out.

When they look over their shoulders one last time, he is standing in the doorway, his arms extended as if in blessing.

•

On their way back they do not talk much. Mercy, Reitz mutters a few times. They make haste: they leap, run, lose their footing. Merciful heavens, Reitz says. Blasted *hell*. The sky is dark and threatening, the wind is growing stronger. They stumble over small ant hills, slip on loose stones, thorny shrubs tear at their clothing.

Shortly before sunset they reach the camp. The sky is dark but no rain has fallen yet. Gert Smal takes the two pouches from them. He does not thank them for their trouble. He merely asks if Ben has seen a ghost.

Yes, Ben answers laconically. He hopes they didn't cause any shit along the way, Gert Smal says.

Ezekiel is instructed to stoke the fire and boil water in a large pot. A fomentation of Oompie's herbs (it resembles steaming cowdung) is placed on Seun's chest. The boy is made—against his will—to swallow the second mixture with hot water. Gert Smal shouts orders left, right and centre, but ministers to Seun himself with the greatest care.

Willem leads the evening devotions. He reads from Luke, chapter eighteen, verse thirty-five, about the blind man of Jericho whose faith saved him. Gert Smal glowers, the heavy horizontal fold above his eyebrows deeper than usual. In the middle of the hymn he jumps up and goes to Seun.

Gert Smal has faith only in Oompie's mixtures, Reitz says to Ben in an undertone.

There is little conversation around the fire.

Only Kosie Rijpma, who broke his silence the day before, is holding forth tonight. Like Japie Stilgemoed, he addresses no one in particular when he speaks, never looks anyone directly in the eye. He speaks as if he is barely aware of an audience.

There were days when there were nine funerals, he says. Always with many people attending. They had nothing better to do. It was a way of passing the time.

A small crowd would often gather around the tent to gawk at the person dying inside. Time and again, with loathing in his heart, he has to admit, he forced his way through the onlookers and chased them away to grant the dying person a last few moments of peace.

He often admonished the crowd sternly. Whence came this horrible attraction to a deathbed? Where did it spring from? he asked them. But always they simply looked at him in silence. He never got an answer. To this day he still doesn't understand it, and he never will.

"With loathing," says Kosie Rijpma, "with loathing in my heart and with contempt for the depravity of human nature—that is how I regarded them."

He stares fixedly into the fire, his dark eyes deep in their sockets.

"And sometimes I wondered," he says, "who was more sinful—these people with their beastly attraction to the suffering of others, or I in my extreme contempt for them."

Reitz's face feels flushed, as if he too has a fever. Though he is moved by Kosie Rijpma's tale, his thoughts keep wandering, returning time and again to their visit to Oompie. He has a resolve, and it makes him restless.

Late that night Seun's fever abates, the rash on his skin clears up almost completely, and he is able to sleep peacefully.

CHAPTER 7

A day or two later Reitz decides to return to Oompie without Ben. He makes his intention known to Ben, and pays no heed to Ben's misgivings about the benefit of such a visit. He tells Ben he believes Oompie has extraordinary powers, and that he may help him find peace of mind. Ben seems unconvinced of that too. Extraordinary powers, perhaps, but not necessarily beneficial powers, he says. He restored Seun's health soon enough, says Reitz. Seun had a fever, Ben replies. It's easy enough to restore the body if one has knowledge of medicinal herbs.

I have a fever too, Reitz thinks. A fever likely to consume me in time.

They leave for the river together and from there Reitz goes on alone, through the drift where the sheer cliff plunges sharply down, and then up the steep incline of the kloof.

Although he feels bound to undertake this mission alone, he misses Ben's company. Ben would have pointed out a great many things along the way, distracting him. He is tense; he does not know how to order his thoughts. He does not know how to explain his problem to Oompie.

When Reitz arrives about two hours later, Oompie is sitting on the stone bench outside his hut.

"I've been expecting to see you any day now," the old man says.

He gets up and shuffles into the hut. He is still clad in the worn raincoat and leather sandals. He motions for Reitz to sit at the table, and pours the inevitable mug of sour milk from the black clay pot. He busies himself about the stove as usual, his back to Reitz.

"You may talk," says Oompie.

Reitz hesitates. Then he asks Oompie to help him get in touch with his late wife.

Oompie stops bustling at the stove for a moment before turning to Reitz. He looks him squarely in the eye. The small pale eyes are narrowed appraisingly; the pupils tiny black specks.

"It can be done," says Oompie, "but there's a price to be paid."

At first Reitz understands that he will have to pay Oompie. In cash? In kind? With a wife perhaps? Which he'll find *where*—cash or kind or woman? These thoughts flit through his mind before Oompie makes himself clear.

Reitz must realise, Oompie says, that sometimes you get in touch with the dead at a hellish price. Because the dead should best be left undisturbed in the realm of shadow.

In the realm of shadow, Reitz thinks.

Oompie gives him a penetrating look with his small eyes and inscrutable gaze.

"It calls for sacrifice," he says, "and even then the encounter may not be satisfactory."

The encounter. Reitz nods. His mouth is dry. His face burning.

Oompie shuffles to the doorway of the second room. (Like the previous time, Reitz wonders where the energetic stride he displayed in the veld has disappeared to.) He looks over his shoulder, his hand on the doorknob, motioning for Reitz to follow. For a moment Reitz pauses, reluctant to enter the room that contains the preserved head in the glass jar.

When he rises, he feels slightly dizzy. He enters the semidark room. Again Oompie makes him sit at the table. Reitz's hands and the back of his knees are damp with perspiration; there is an unpleasant prickling sensation in his armpits; low in his gut he feels an urgent need to relieve himself. He stares straight ahead.

Oompie takes a glass jar from the shelf, places it on the table carefully. The content this time seems no worse than a fine black powdery mixture—mercifully it contains no recognisable object. When he removes the glass stopper, a sharp unidentifiable smell escapes from the bottle. Wearily Oompie takes another jar from the shelf—equally dusty as the one before. The mixture inside is coarser; it looks like pulped plant matter; it smells of grass and flowers, with a hint of animal decay.

Does Reitz have a handkerchief on his person?

A handkerchief? For a moment Reitz must seem surprised. No, he hasn't owned a handkerchief for a long time. No more handkerchiefs were to be had after the first year of the war. They came to fulfil such diverse functions that in due course there was no recognisable handkerchief to be found anywhere.

Oompie searches on the shelf behind him and produces a small tobacco pouch. Using a spoon and working carefully and with deliberation, he measures a small scoop of each jar's contents into the pouch before closing the jars tightly and replacing them on the shelf.

He sits down at the table, facing Reitz.

In the confined space of the room the smell Oompie emits is even stronger. Reitz keeps his breathing shallow, to protect himself. Does Oompie rub his skin with fat or rancid butter? In the dim light it resembles the glistening, oiled pelt of an animal that spends long periods underwater.

Listen carefully, says Oompie. It is important for Reitz to follow the instructions scrupulously. Every evening at dusk he must go to a place where no one will disturb him. This is of the utmost importance. He is to take a small amount of the mixture and roll it in paper and smoke it. While doing this, he must think of his late wife. He must think of her the way he would like to see her. Then he must wait. He must make no sudden or unexpected movement. This frightens the dead away. He must not display excessive emotion. The dead do not know how to deal with it. It makes them uneasy, spiteful even, depending on where they find themselves. We, and Oompie points (fleshy hands, pointed fingertips) at the proximity of his chest, we have what they no longer have, and some of them cannot accept that.

Reitz nods wordlessly. He takes the pouch from Oompie.

"But of the greatest importance," Oompie says, "is that you do not repeat the procedure more than three nights in a row. Bury what remains of the mixture."

Reitz nods again. Oompie gets up with difficulty. Leads the way, shuffling, into the next room.

Reitz does not want to stay longer. He thanks Oompie and leaves at once. He must get down the mountain as quickly as possible, the weather looks threatening.

Halfway down the mountainside he squats behind a bush, lowers his trousers, and evacuates the steaming contents of his intestines with urgent relief.

•

To Ben Reitz simply mentions that he has received something from Oompie which will help him. Nothing more. He has to remain at the river for a while at dusk and he wants Ben to placate Gert Smal should he become agitated. Reitz doesn't know how much time he will need, but if he isn't back within an hour—and he smiles wryly—perhaps Ben should come and look for him. Ben does not look at all happy with the situation, but asks no further questions.

To Gert Smal Reitz says that he needs to do a survey for his lecture, as instructed by the general. At this time of day? Gert Smal asks suspiciously. Yes, at this time of day. It has to do with the position of the setting sun, and he has to do it three days in a row, Reitz answers. Gert Smal seems impressed with this information in spite of himself.

For want of paper, Reitz tears a page from his journal carefully, dividing it into three equal pieces. He takes the paper and the tobacco pouch down to the river.

The threatening storm clouds disperse slightly towards sunset. The cliff face is a deep, gleaming, rosy gold; the sky behind it purple and glowing; the stacked clouds are dark in their centres and glittering at the edges; the overhanging branches already darkly etched against the water.

Reitz sits down on a large rock beside the river, some distance from where he and Ben usually occupy themselves by day. He rolls the precious mixture in the paper. He lights it with an ember he has smuggled along in a tin mug.

He draws the mixture deep into his lungs. It is so potent that he is racked by a violent fit of coughing. It leaves a bitter aftertaste in his mouth.

He smokes the cigarette slowly until only the butt remains. While he smokes, he thinks of her—of his late wife. His dead wife. The wife whose features he can no longer clearly recall. He closes his eyes. He waits.

The mixture shakes him like a sudden fierce gust buffeting a shrub.

A chill creeps up his spine all the way to his neck. His limbs grow heavy. His heartbeat slows. His eyes feel cold and dry. His eyelids feel swollen, his scalp ice-cold. He gazes fixedly ahead, at a tree hanging far over the water.

In the foreground, in front of the moving branches, a thin, vaporous haze forms.

And inside this glow, or radiance, he perceives the outline of a female figure taking shape. It grows more substantial, but never solid. The face remains at first without any discernible features, before gradually taking on the almost recognisable shape of his beloved, his dead wife's face. Half recognisable, half formed. Vague, indistinct.

For a moment he buries his face in his hands. His cheeks are ice-cold.

Then he speaks her name: softly, hesitantly.

She seems about to assume a more tangible form, about to look in his direction.

Instinctively he holds out his arms, and sighs.

A ripple passes through her figure, as if her surface is water.

He tries to speak to her, but something is holding him back.

For a few moments her face takes on a firmer shape and he sees her the way she used to be, but as on a blurred photograph.

His eyes feel cold. His tongue thick.

Then she begins to fade; the density of her figure and outline diminishes, becomes more wavering, and dissolves.

He cries out. He wants to call her back. But the hazy spot from which she emerged remains visible for only a few more moments before it vanishes suddenly. The branches, hanging low over the surface of the water, are dark.

The sun has set. The night sky is bright, the first stars visible. The moon has not yet risen. He becomes aware of a chill rising up from the riverbed.

He does not know how long he sits there. There is a roaring in his ears and he is thirsty. There is a pain in the pit of his stomach that is steadily growing worse.

After a while he gets up and begins to make his way slowly back to camp. He moves slowly, and at times he has to scramble up the incline, losing his footing on the loose stones. He has never noticed before how steep the way back to camp is.

Though he is almost doubled up by the pain in his stomach, he forces himself upright when he approaches the camp. Ben welcomes him with concern, but asks no questions. Reitz is grateful for the warmth of the fire, for his face and limbs are cold as ice.

•

And so they roamed here and there, Japie Stilgemoed continues that evening around the fire, crossing ahead of and behind the ranks of the Khakis, and by day they patched their clothing because it was mostly in rags, much worse than now. And when the weather permitted, they boiled their clothes to get rid of the lice. And here everyone agrees—in a chorus like a rushing waterfall—that on commando the lice are a much greater problem than the Khakis.

To this day, Reuben says, he is much more afraid of a louse than of a Khaki. For a Khaki you can shoot in the head, but when your friend the louse has made himself at home and settled in, there is no way to get rid of him.

Japie Stilgemoed glances briefly in Reuben's direction, nods in agreement, and continues. When the weather cleared up temporarily— for it was the time of the great, unrelenting rains, late March almost a year ago—the youngsters pelted one another with the softened earth of ant hills. And when the rain came down again, everyone took shelter in their tents as best they could. In the mornings they cooked por- ridge, and during the day they did their daily chores, did what the day required: gathered firewood, cooked meals, tended to the oxen, posted sentries.

And he, Japie, thought that the reward for the manly endurance of suffering and discomfort would surely be immeasurably great. He could only hope that this would strengthen his spirit—refining and purifying it of superficial values. But, he also knew that—and Japie tosses another log onto the fire, his eyes black and his hair bristling—if the Creator in his omnipotence never reunited him with his loved ones again, then all of it, the struggle too, would have been in vain.

At the thought tears spring to his eyes.

"For it still remains uncertain," says Japie Stilgemoed, "whether we will ever see our loved ones gathered around us again."

What is the man talking about? Reitz wonders. Which loved ones is he referring to? His annoyance with Japie Stilgemoed is less than his effort to make sense of Japie's words. Reitz feels as if he is observing everything from across a great distance—as if the distance between him and the others is immeasurably great. In his head there is a feeling of cold, empty space and in his fingers a strange prickling sensation.

Ben sits silently beside him. A palpable silence, Reitz thinks, a silence that seperates Ben from him.

Kosie Rijpma speaks of the day when there were nine funerals, and only eight graves had been dug, and one coffin had to be taken back. Consternation reigned; women fainted. That day he thought that, if the fruit of our belief is forbearance, then that kind of forbearance was no longer possible for him.

He too throws a log onto the fire. It flares and sends tremendous sparks into the air.

No, Kosie Rijpma continues, he could not find it *then*—not in the face of the endless suffering of women and children—and he still has not found it.

Reitz strains to make coherent sense of Kosie's words as well.

Where there should be resignation and forbearance, says Kosie Rijpma, a bitter defiance rages inside him. He does not think he will ever be free from it again.

Ben listens attentively, nodding slowly. Willem, too, seems to consider Kosie Rijpma's words carefully—though it pains him. It is hard to tell whether Japie Stilgemoed is listening to his friend, or whether he is still immersed in his own thoughts. Reitz's physical discomfort, his emotional distress, prevent him from taking in much of what is happening around him.

Gert Smal also tosses a log onto the fire and says: "It's because the Kaffirs took up arms against us. That was the beginning of the end. May God wipe out the entire British nation, and Milner in particular."

Ezekiel sits silently in the shadows.

All the while Reitz tries in vain to affix himself to the image of his wife. The moment he is about to recall her vague image in his mind's eye, she has already eluded him again. Her manifestation had been too fleeting.

∙

The next day Reitz is irritable and restless. Time passes too slowly. He slept fitfully; awakened at intervals by acute but passing stomach cramps. Ben and he go to the river as usual. It is a fine day. The place where he sat yesterday looks different today, and try as he may, he fails to recapture her fleeting image.

Ben asks no questions. He continues to study a beetle he came across the day before.

He shows Reitz the bean weevil—a slightly elongated snout beetle with pale spots on the wings. He explains that it should not be confused with the kaffirbean weevil, which is smaller, almost square, and reddish brown or russet, with larger eyes and white lines on the wings, whose larvae develop in kaffir beans and live on them, but which in all probability is not found in this area. Though he'd hesitate to state it with any certainty.

Reitz is distracted; listens with half an ear. He gazes long and absent-mindedly at the surface of the water—at the way the shadows of the branches create ever-changing patterns on it.

Once or twice Reitz notices Ben watching him, but he looks away as soon as he realises Reitz is aware of his gaze.

Back at camp, Kosie Rijpma joins them when they have their afternoon coffee. He is shorter than Reitz by more than a head. It is the

93

first time he has voluntarily struck up a conversation with them. He inquires timidly whether they would be interested in reading Bettie Loots's verses.

For a few moments Reitz stares at him perplexed before he remembers who Bettie Loots is. Ben answers instantly that it would be their pleasure to do so. Reitz makes no reply. Kosie fetches the verses. He hands them to Ben, who thanks him warmly.

Reitz notices that Ben does not show him the verses immediately and thinks: It's better this way.

In the late afternoon, at the same time as the day before, Reitz returns to the river on his own, carrying with him the piece of paper, the tobacco pouch and the glowing coal in the tin mug.

·

Again he shakes like a wispy shrub in a sudden strong gust of wind when the mixture takes hold of him.

Again it is as if a coolness creeps up his spine, but this time with greater intensity, and with it comes the feeling of a gradual loss of bodily warmth.

His heartbeat slows down again; it is as if every sensation takes longer to reach his consciousness.

And once again, in more or less the same place as the previous day, a haze forms gradually, and from this haze comes a glow, and in this glow the outline of a woman takes shape.

But today her form is more substantial, more recognisable; he can begin to see it is she; he recognises her, though her features are strangely fluid, and one half of her face is slightly dented—as if she has been lying on her side for a long time.

He cries out; he hears himself groan as if his voice belongs to someone else.

She looks at him, with no expression, nor any sign of recognition.

In his mouth is a musty taste; in his forehead the sensation of a cold, empty space.

He speaks her name.

She looks at him but seems not to see him. She seems day-blind.

Her arms hang woodenly at her sides. She shudders slightly, as if she remembers something.

"Beloved . . ." he stammers, as if someone else is speaking in his stead.

A movement passes through her body—*over* her body—as if she is no more than a shadow upon water.

"Oh God," he groans. There is an intense burning pain in his insides; in his genitals a painful pressure.

He sinks to his knees; waits for her to recognise him.

"Do you still know me?" he asks softly.

She looks at him, still with no expression, no sign of acknowledgement.

He remains on his knees, his eyes ice-cold, his tongue thick.

Gradually her image begins to fade, until she slips back into the haze from which she emerged.

"Oh God," he hears himself say, "oh God."

Gradually he becomes aware of his surroundings. The coolness of the riverbed, the sound of the water. Night sounds. The empty, bleak, cloudless night sky.

He begins to shiver, spasms pass through his body; an almost unbearable pain in his stomach forces him to crouch down.

He sits like this for a long time before he begins to crawl slowly up the stony rise.

•

Concerned, Ben comes to meet him.

"What is going *on* with you?" he asks—clearly despite his best intentions not to interfere. "Look at you!" he exclaims.

Reitz does not care in the least what he looks like. He cares even less that the others are giving him strange looks. He has to find warmth. He is freezing.

Ben makes him sit at the fire. He wraps a frayed blanket around his shoulders.

"Must be a hell of an effort, this survey," Gert Smal remarks in passing.

"Stay out of it!" Ben snaps, and it crosses Reitz's mind vaguely that he has never heard Ben speak to anyone in that tone of voice before.

Gradually the warmth creeps back into his limbs and he starts to calm down. He takes a sip of water. He has no appetite.

One by one the others come to sit at the fire. They eat, they talk. As on the previous night, Reitz feels as if he is observing everything from across an immeasurable distance.

Japie Stilgemoed speaks, and Kosie Rijpma has some tale to tell about children who were the spitting image of mice—the same large eyes and scrawny limbs. But tonight Reitz finds it an even greater effort to follow any conversation. From time to time he is overcome by acute stomach cramps, the pain even more intense than the night before.

That night he dreams of Bettie Loots. She is agreeably fetching, and she invites him to have intimate relations with her. But nothing comes of her lewd proposal, for its consummation is prevented time and again by the appearance of all kinds of undesirable persons.

•

"Don't you think you'd better tell me, Reitz," Ben asks the next day when they are alone at the river. They have been sitting in silence for a long time before Ben speaks.

It is the third day; today is the last time he can meet her.

Reitz is sitting on a rock in the shade of a tree. He sits with his arms around his knees, legs pulled up, hands folded in front of him, head bent. He has been staring at a single spot for a long time. The musty, mildewy taste is still in his mouth, and there is an unpleasant trembling in his limbs.

Ben sits some distance away, studying a cocoon, making sketches of it in his journal.

"Today is the last day," Reitz says. "I loved her and she is lost to me forever. I have never been as certain of it as I am today."

He does not look up while he speaks.

"Tell me about her," Ben says softly.

"I have lost her," says Reitz, "and now I have to resort to sorcery to get her back for only a few moments."

He is alarmed by his own bitterness, frightened by the implications of his words.

Ben looks upset.

"*Leave* it," he says, "*leave* it, Reitz! Nothing good can come of it! Leave the dead in peace; that's how it's meant to be—the dead don't belong with us any more!"

He looks closely at the open page in front of him.

"However badly we may miss them," he continues, "we have to learn to let them go."

Reitz makes no reply, and they speak no further.

•

In the late afternoon Reitz returns to the river alone for the third time. Ben holds his peace, as does Gert Smal—who has realised by this time that something is amiss.

Today the spectacle of the setting sun is even more impressive than the preceding days; the sky all gold and glory. The cliff face is bathed in the deepest rose-coloured glow. All is gleam and sparkle; the slight breeze keeps every surface in perpetual reflecting, shimmering motion.

Yet there is a leaden feeling in Reitz's chest.

For the third time he draws the mixture deep into his lungs, deeper than before, and doubles over with the force of it. He holds the smoke inside for as long as possible before letting it out.

He thinks of her. With all the strength of his heart and soul he directs himself at her. Not in any detail—for that has escaped him—but opening himself to her, so as to give her a space wherein she can reveal herself to him.

He gives a soft hiccup when the force of the mixture grabs hold of him.

Again he feels the deep chill come upon him—the sudden loss of his precious body heat; again he feels his heartbeat slow down, his eyes grow cold, his tongue heavy, the space in his forehead icy and strangely extended.

Again there is a haze, again a glow, and again her outline takes shape out of the glow.

Now he sees her the way she was. Now he recognises her, his beloved wife, now her features take on their familiar aspect. Now it is she—but it is also not she, for one side of her face is flattened, and her eyes are devoid of expression.

He hears himself moan, like a soul in torment.

He speaks her name, pleadingly.

A ripple passes over her face, like wind on the surface of water. Though her features are strangely fluid, her face is impassive. She looks at him, but does not see him.

"Can you *hear* me?" he asks.

She looks at him. Her head moves slightly, as if she is struggling to pick up the sound of his words.

"Can you *see* me?" he asks, more urgently.

Again the rippling over her face; her lips appear to be struggling to form words.

He sinks to his knees.

"I beg of you!" he says.

Her features move unsteadily. She casts her gaze on him as if there is a great distance between them.

She sees him. But her gaze lacks all knowledge that there was ever any intimacy between them.

Her glance is without recognition, without imputation, without longing, without claim.

The distress that washes over her face comes from a different source.

"My dearest wife," he says, "can you forgive me?"

Again there is the pressure in his groin, in the proximity of his genitals. He feels that his seed is about to gush from his body with painful intensity.

His eyes are ice-cold, his tongue swollen.

Her features fade, her outline softens, she slips back into the haze whence she emerged.

He falls forward on the ground. His face is contorted, his cheeks wet.

He remains prostrate for a long time, his body cold and sweaty. The sun has set. He hears frogs and the sound of water.

The first wave of pain hits him in the pit of his stomach. It is much worse than on the previous two occasions. His body goes into a spasm; he gasps for breath. He curls up in a foetal position, waits until the pain has abated slightly. Then, painstakingly, on hands and knees, he crawls up the rocky ridge.

"Damnation!" he shouts. "Damn this place!"

Halfway up the ridge the next surge of pain overwhelms him.

Ben comes slithering down the slope, slipping on the loose stones. Reitz can scarcely stand—he can barely move. Ben makes him lie down on his side. He puts his jacket under Reitz's head to make him more comfortable. He wants to fetch help. Reitz shakes his head. He lies on his side until the worst pain has subsided.

Then he rises with great difficulty. Ben holds on to his arm, supporting him as much as he is able.

Reitz makes an effort to take the last few steps to camp on his own. The others, already seated around the fire, stare openly. Again Gert Smal makes no comment; continues to pick his teeth with a piece of wood.

Reitz sits beside the fire until his body heat is more or less restored. He says nothing, he eats nothing, he hears scarcely a word that is being said.

The others understand from Ben's expression that they are not to ask questions.

During the night a woman with red hair presses her body against Reitz wantonly. When he reaches out to embrace her, she suddenly changes. She is clad in black, horribly emaciated, and hugging something to her scrawny chest, something resembling a child, but small and flat, like a pack of playing cards or a threadbare little book.

•

Early the next morning he goes to the river alone. He wants to get away from camp; he wishes to avoid the others. He feels weak; at times during the descent his legs can barely carry his weight. He avoids the place where his encounters with her took place. He rinses his underclothing, soaked in perspiration, in the river. He bathes in the icy water; it almost knocks the breath from his body. He sits on a rock, shivering in the feeble early-morning sun. The cold revives him, for during the night he developed a fever, after he had recovered from his chilled state.

Later in the morning Ben comes to look for him.

He was worried, he says. Reitz must tell him if he'd rather be alone.

No, it's fine, Reitz says. He has no objection to Ben's company.

The sun climbs higher, grows hotter. Baboons bark on the opposite cliff. Cicadas strike up their song. Reitz can hardly distinguish their shrill sound from the droning in his head. Dragonflies skitter across the surface of the water. Ben seems engrossed in his task of documenting a beetle or cocoon. From time to time he makes a desultory remark without seeming to expect a reaction. Though they do not speak, Reitz is grateful for Ben's presence. Left to his own devices, he thinks, he would have entered a place of darkness today from which he would not have been able to escape on his own.

They eat food that Ben has brought along. They drink water.

Later they return to camp.

At twilight Reitz grows restless. Oompie's instructions were clear: no more than three consecutive days. There is still some of the mixture in the pouch—bury what is left, Oompie said. He no longer cares. He has nothing to lose.

He takes the mixture and a glowing coal and tells Ben he is going for a walk in the veld—the camp makes him feel restricted. Ben does not believe him; he is angry and worried. Are you sure you're doing the right thing? he asks. Reitz shrugs. Ben says: I'll come for you in an hour. For God's sake, be careful.

Slowly Reitz moves down to the river; his calf muscles feel sore and stiff.

He draws the mixture deep into his lungs; he closes his eyes; please, he says, please. Just this *once*. He makes room for her to move in. He hiccups when the mixture hits him—not in the lungs but in the pit of his stomach, like a kick that leaves one winded. His ears buzz. He feels the blood drain swiftly from his face. He finds it difficult to stand on his feet.

This time she emerges from the haze more promptly.

An intense pain shoots up his spine, from his tailbone to the back of his head.

It is as if a coolness descends upon the landscape, a darkness such as occurs during a lunar eclipse.

A cool, poisonous mist rises in his head. He is aware of a cold frothing in his intestines. Involuntary spasms rack his body.

She stands in front of him, clearer, closer than before. Her outline is more defined, her features more distinct. But her body has no solidity—small ripples move across her surface continuously—as if her image is reflected on water. As if she lacks a crucial dimension.

Her gaze is fixed on him, but makes no claim.

His tongue feels lame, his eyeballs freezing in their sockets. His lungs burn like fire. In his groin he feels the familiar painful pressure.

He wants to reach out his hand to her.

Again her face appears slightly flattened, her lips unusually dark.

"Speak to me," he says.

Her eyelids flicker slightly; her lips move.

"In God's name," he implores, "speak to me."

Her black lips form the words hesitantly.

"I hunger for the light," she says.

Did he hear her? Was it her voice? He does not know. There is a pain at the back of his skull.

The landscape grows darker, colder, as if cascades of cloud are scudding across it at great speed. She appears agitated. Her features flicker, become distorted. He can no longer see her clearly.

"Forgive me!" he hears himself crying.

"The light," she says, scarcely audible.

He falls to his knees. When he looks up, it appears as if she is being rapidly drawn into a twilit darkness.

He remains prostrate on the ground. His limbs are ice-cold and stiff. He calls out when the pain hits him in the stomach. His neck jerks back in a spasm.

He has no idea how long he has been lying there before he hears Ben's voice.

Ben is accompanied by Ezekiel. Ben hauls him into a sitting position, tries to force him to drink some brandy.

They virtually have to drag him up the slope. At camp Ezekiel stokes the fire. They dig a hollow beside the fire for him to lie in. For he is ice-cold, as cold as death.

•

The next day he sits in the sun in front of his shelter all day, grateful for the heat. He can scarcely eat. He feels giddy and nauseous. From time to time he is overcome by almost unbearable stomach cramps. He feels too weak to accompany Ben to the river. Ben does not go either; he hovers nearby, ostensibly writing in his journal. Gert Smal keeps a scornful distance. Only once, when Ben is not near, does he address Reitz in an undertone: Must be a hard job, this survey! Reitz ignores him. He could not care less what Gert Smal or anyone else has to say about his condition.

But in the late afternoon a restlessness comes over him again.

He thinks: I don't give a damn.

He is beset by a fierce recklessness, a chilling death wish, the likes of which he has never experienced in any battle situation.

He thinks: If it means the end of me, so be it.

He gets up shakily, drinks a mug of coffee with the others, though he has difficulty getting it down.

Ben seems aware of his plan, for he says: "Let me go with you."

"I'm going on my own," Reitz says curtly.

With trembling hands he tears a page from his journal; takes the pouch with the rest of the mixture and the ember.

"Let me at least go with you as far as the river," Ben says. Reitz agrees to let him go halfway. Gert Smal gives them a meaningful look, as if he wants to say: I'm giving you rope; go ahead, hang yourself. By this time the others are also aware that something strange is afoot, for Japie Stilgemoed and Kosie Rijpma in particular look worried, and earlier Willem took Ben aside and spoke to him earnestly.

Reitz negotiates the steep descent with great difficulty, his muscles stiff and aching. They move slowly. They do not speak. Only once does Ben implore quietly: In God's name, won't you leave it be? It's the last time, Reitz replies, the mixture will be finished tonight.

Near the bottom they take leave of each other. Before returning to camp, Ben announces that he will return within the hour. He will bring Ezekiel and Willem. Reitz nods. He watches Ben's departing figure.

When Ben is out of sight, Reitz covers the rest of the distance to the river slowly.

The sun is setting. The rock face is ablaze with gold. A vast and cool sweetness wafts from the ground. It imbues and saturates the air. The earth becomes still. There is no sound but the sound of water, and the occasional soft plop of a frog.

For a long time Reitz sits on the rock breathing in this fullness, this blessing of light and abundance.

He rolls the last of the mixture in the paper and uses the glowing coal to light it. He smokes slowly, drawing the mixture as deeply into his lungs as he is able.

He thinks of her. One last time he requests her presence, opens himself to her. His teeth chatter when the mixture grabs hold of him.

A coolness comes over the earth like the sudden beating of wings. She emerges from the haze more swiftly and more distinctly than before. Pain shoots from the base of his spine to the back of his head. It is she. She looks at him. Her image is surrounded by light. Her expression is grim. She looks at him but shows no sign of recognition.

He calls her name; his tongue is heavy.

She looks at him, and her gaze is fierce. She looks, but without comprehension; in vain she strives. Her eyes and mouth are dark, shadowy. She seems to be forming words. The sides of her face are strangely indented.

He mutters, but nothing coherent comes out.

Her gaze remains fixed on him; she struggles against a nameless force. Her face is distorted; her features unsteady, fluid.

In his forehead is an icy vacuum. His breath is cold.

She strains against something. The side of her face is squashed as if she is pushing against an invisible membrane.

"Forgive me!" he says.

She looks at him, her beloved face powerless against the dark namelessness.

"Forgive me!" he cries.

"The light," she says, her face darkening with exertion.

"I'm sorry," he says, "that I have to do this to you!"

For a few fleeting moments a different expression comes over her face—something like pity; her features soften, the effort flows from them, and the next moment she is drawn violently back into the shadowy haze from which she came.

He cries out.

"Jump," a voice says behind him. It might belong to Oompie.

He turns round. There is no one there.

"Jump," urges the voice. "Jump for the opposite shore."

In his bewilderment he thinks: There is no shore on the opposite side.

"Jump," says Oompie behind him.

He jumps.

When he comes to his senses, he is lying on the riverbank. His chest aches, from coughing up water, it appears. Water and vomit. Ben is wiping his mouth. He is wiping blood from his face and head. Ezekiel is building a fire. Willem stands by anxiously, his eyes paler than river stones, the Bible clutched under his arm. Reitz curls up as a wave of pain hits him in the stomach. He is freezing.

They try to take his wet clothes off, but his limbs are stiff, like the limbs of a corpse. They roll him in blankets. Ezekiel stokes the fire. They make a hollow in the sand. They lay him in it. Only when the worst cold has been dispelled from his body do they carry him back to camp.

•

In the course of the night he suffers acute stomach cramps. He cannot sleep, but lies in a stricken daze. Sometimes he is ice-cold and at other times burning hot. He is delirious and calls out names. Ben stays with him; he makes himself a bed in the entrance of Reitz's shelter.

He spends most of the next day lying curled up against the pain, or sitting hunched in front of his shelter. He has cramps in his arms and legs, and at times severe spasms in his neck. His tongue feels dry and swollen. Ben brings him water; he refuses to eat. He refuses to speak.

Willem sits with him for a while and says: "You can thank the Lord we came to fetch you earlier, or you'd most certainly have drowned yesterday."

CHAPTER 8

Reitz spends the next day sitting in the sun in front of his shelter too. Ben does not go to the river; he tries to hide his concern, but nonetheless remains close to Reitz all day. He sits in front of his own shelter, not far from Reitz's, writing in his journal.

The intensity of the stomach cramps has abated and the spasms in his neck come less frequently, but his limbs still feel rigid, his muscles inflamed and stiff. He is sensitive to the slightest sound; bright light hurts his eyes. His tongue still feels swollen and cold in his mouth. His lungs are painful from the water he swallowed. Ben did his best to clean the gash on his head. Because he moves with difficulty, he can barely do more than sit. He is thankful for the sun's heat, for his heart and intestines feel cold and heavy, his organs painfully bruised.

He thinks, here I sit now, just like Japie Stilgemoed and Kosie Rijpma.

At sunset Reuben takes out his mouth organ and starts to play. A more plaintive tune Reitz can scarcely imagine.

That evening around the fire he drifts in and out of the others' conversations; inside his head the sensation remains of a large, empty space.

Gert Smal chews on a piece of wood. He stares grimly into the fire. "The Boers let important opportunities go by," he says. "At De Aar massive supplies had been stockpiled for the English. The Boers frittered that chance away—they should have cut off Methuen's supplies. They should have chased Methuen to hell and gone into the sea. To hell with Methuen! To hell with the Boers!"

He spits a splinter into the fire. "To hell with De Aar!" he adds.

Ben smiles surreptitiously, but tonight Reitz takes no interest in the Boers' wasted opportunities.

Gert Smal is fired up, his eyes glazed.

"Things went wrong from the very beginning! Right from the word go! At Ladysmith, when Joubert failed to send the men in pursuit of the English. After Colenso Botha should have bloody thrashed the enemy good and solid! He should have wiped Buller off the map, chased the swine all the way to the sea! Cronjé at Magersfontein—gone to pot, too feeble to break through Methuen's lines. Too gutless to cut off Methuen's supplies. Too spineless to crush Methuen. At Mafeking the Boers sat on their arses. When the bastards should have been on the move, they were sitting on their arses!"

Gert Smal stares grimly ahead.

"Their arses, every single one of them," he says. "Piet Joubert's arse. Kock's arse. Louis Botha's arse. Piet Cronjé's arse. Marthinus Prinsloo's arse. The English—their arses too!"

Again he spits into the fire.

"To hell with the English," he says. "To hell with the Boers. To hell with the whole bloody lot of them!"

"With hindsight it's easy to say what should have happened," says Ben.

"What?" shouts Gert Smal. "Where did *you* crawl from?"

"From the same war as you," Ben replies.

"Deserters!" says Gert Smal. "You are deserters, every one of you—but especially *you* and your good friend! You are here under false pretences—busy with underhand activities! Survey," and he glares at Reitz, "my *arse!*"

"Steady," says Ben, a warning note in his voice.

Willem gets up slowly. His face is bright red. His eyes are white, like marbles.

"Call us deserters once more," he says to Gert Smal, "and I'll report you to the general when he comes this way again."

Gert Smal gestures as if brushing away a troublesome fly.

"We were called up in the name of the president just like you and each of us, just like you, has done his duty," says Willem. "If it wasn't for this young man," and he points at young Abraham by his side—motionless and silent like a shadow, "who lost his youth and nearly his mind too in this war, we would still be serving in Commandant Senekal's commando!"

Gert Smal makes the same deprecating gesture.

Japie Stilgemoed looks frightened. Kosie Rijpma is scarcely listening. Seun and Reuben seem unperturbed. Ezekiel sits motionless in the shadows behind Gert Smal; the yellow dog sleeps at his feet. Young Abraham sits silently, his face blank. It is the first time Willem has ever spoken about him in his presence in this manner. If he has heard it and made sense of it, he gives no indication.

·

The wind that came up in the late afternoon blows all night. Reitz sleeps restlessly, his sleep interrupted by periodic stomach cramps and neck spasms, by twitching limbs; by dreams resembling visions and hallucinations.

In the early dawn, before sunrise, it starts raining. Ezekiel has indeed built their shelters with great skill, for they do not leak. (Better shelters, Gert Smal said at the time, you will not find anywhere.) A gentle, soaking rain that softens and veils the landscape and isolates them even further from the outside world.

Ezekiel builds a big fire under the overhanging rock at the entrance of the cave. Some of them have raincoats. Coats of an English manufacture like those worn by General Cronjé and Oompie, except that Oompie's coat is oily, like the pelt of an animal—an aquatic animal—Reitz thinks. Oompie's coat is like a second skin. Reitz lost his coat long ago; Ben's can scarcely be called a raincoat any more, so tattered has it become.

Those without raincoats sit with their blankets around their shoulders, for with the rain the weather is suddenly much cooler. They sit huddled together all day—out of the rain, grateful for the warm coffee and the heat of the fire.

Ezekiel comes and goes; constantly busy with some task or another. He wears a frayed raincoat and the stiff tails glisten like wings as he comes running through the rain, carrying water. He stokes the fire. He cooks the porridge. They hold out their plates to him, eager for the consolation of warm food. Gert Smal apparently shot something for the pot a day or two ago—Ezekiel is cooking it. The smell is intoxicating. Everyone sits silently, waiting. For the first time in many days Reitz feels a craving for food; his mouth waters.

He watches Ezekiel intently while he performs his numerous tasks. Ezekiel is a messenger, he realises, a mediator between the realms of light and shade. The black man never raises his eyes, speaks only when spoken to; when Gert Smal snaps his fingers in his direction, Ezekiel provides him with the missing information: the date of a battle, the name of a general, the numbers of dead and wounded.

The colder it gets as the day progresses, the closer they huddle around the fire. And that evening, isolated from the world by the rain, they speak with greater fervour and urgency.

Gradually Reitz begins to feel better. The stomach cramps become less intense. The lingering cold seeps slowly from his intestines. But his tongue still feels heavy and thick in his mouth, and he still observes everything as if across a distance—as if it is not *he* who is present here.

Japie Stilgemoed continues with his tale and nothing can deter Kosie Rijpma now that he has begun to talk. Gert Smal either maintains a menacing silence, the deep fold between his eyebrows like a solid ridge, or, shaking his fist, he rants against everyone and no one in particular. How much he foams at the mouth and how glazed his eyes become are determined by how much he has already imbibed.

Time and again Kosie Rijpma returns to the emaciated, dying figure of Bettie Loots, who spoke to him even with her dying breath.

"She was eighteen years old," he says. "She was at the beginning of her life. Like a paltry little candle her young life was snuffed out in the most wretched circumstances. Like the lives of so many others. How can I ever forget the hope and resignation in her face?"

He stares fixedly at the flames. "Of the eager, trusting Bettie Loots," he says, "only her little book of verse has remained."

Kosie Rijpma pauses; his dark eyes brim with tears. He presses his arms against his body, hands clasped to his chest, as if he is holding the wasted body of Bettie Loots against him one last time. Overcome with emotion, he is unable to continue.

With a feeling of guilt Reitz remembers the promise of carnal intimacy that Bettie Loots gave him in his dream. He remembers it as if it happened in the distant past, instead of only two or three nights ago.

"The day we buried Bettie Loots wrapped in a blanket," says Kosie Rijpma when he has regained control over his voice, "that day I knew . . ."

He does not complete his sentence; just stares straight ahead.

"What?" Ben inquires gently. "What did you know?"

Kosie Rijpma keeps staring into the distance. He seems to have forgotten what he was saying.

"That day I knew," he resumes after a while, "that I could no longer trust in God."

Japie Stilgemoed shoots Kosie a quick but incisive glance.

Willem colours slightly as he always does when he takes offence. He closes his eyes, shuddering slightly and turning his head as if someone has struck him a blow.

Gert Smal regards Kosie appraisingly as if to say: That must be the day when you lost your mind.

Ben nods slowly: "Poignant verses," he says.

Kosie Rijpma looks at him, nods, but says no more.

Japie Stilgemoed, his face even sharper tonight, more tense than before, his hair bristling energetically to expose his high forehead, describes how, after a brief skirmish with the enemy, he was cut off from his commando and drifted on his own for a while.

Young Abraham is restless. He mutters wordlessly. Willem comforts him gently: Settle down, Abraham, don't be afraid. We're safe here.

In the same way that Kosie Rijpma returns time and again to the death of Bettie Loots, Japie Stilgemoed always comes back to those occasions during his wanderings when his yearning for his loved ones became too great to endure. There were times, he says, when he begged God for deliverance, for peace in the land, for an end, for relief—anything, as long as he could be reunited with his loved ones.

He tells of how he roamed in the Magaliesberg district with a pack-mule. How he begged for flour and porridge. How day after day he lived from hand to mouth. He recounts how he came across Boers encamped in the mountains with their livestock, because the animals were all they had left in the world after their houses had been burned down.

Reitz feels an unpleasant prickling in his hands and feet—like feeling returning to a limb that has been asleep. The sense of emptiness inside his head has diminished, and he notices that his customary irritation with Japie Stilgemoed is gradually reappearing.

Gert Smal, sneering, chewing on a bit of wood, spits a piece into the fire. He will blame the Boers for every missed opportunity and bad tactical decision to the end of his days. He will keep ranting and raving. He will shake his fist and curse, shouting his futile curses at the leaden sky.

For two days they sit huddled like that while the rain comes down in heavy sheets, and Reitz gradually regains both his strength and his normal perception.

On the third day the rain stops suddenly, the day breaks glorious and bright, with the chirruping of birds and insects and a fanfare of light, and in the late morning the general arrives with a group of his men. This time no one is caught unawares, for Seun came to warn them that riders were coming and at camp they heard the sound of horses' hooves and saw the men approaching.

This time the general's company is bigger. Apart from the two officers, Blackpiet Petoors and Sagrys Skeel, who accompanied him the previous time, there are five other men as well as the Bushman agterryer belonging to Petoors.

When the general greets Reitz and Ben, he says: "Ready to enlighten the uninformed?"

It makes no difference to Reitz whether it is intended ironically or derisively, but Ben looks uncomfortable, and his nostrils flare nervously.

•

While the general and his men dismount, drink coffee and exchange news, Ben calls Reitz aside urgently. There's no more time, says Ben, the moment has arrived. Damn, says Reitz. Thank God, Ben says (wryly), that the general didn't arrive two or three days ago. Yes, Reitz replies, and wipes his hand across his face, thank God. His eyelids feel heavy. His head is full of loose threads. He knows very well, with an icy dismay, that in due course other feelings will come pouring in to take the place of the unnatural emptiness in his heart, for nature does not tolerate a vacuum. He knows this well enough from his knowledge of natural forces. Unbearable feelings, those will be.

He does not tell Ben he has no idea where to start; he does not want to burden him even more. Lately Ben has had more than enough anxiety on his behalf.

He accompanies Ben to the river listlessly. He avoids the place where he last saw her two days ago. Did he really see her? It was she, yet it was not she. He had been constantly aware of her since they left the farmer's place. She was in and behind everything. It had not been enough for him. Through his evil intervention he drove her away. Now only the silence rings in his ears.

Ben says: "You must talk to me."

Reitz nods, but says nothing. Perhaps he showed too much emotion, he thinks, perhaps it confused her.

They have brought their small trunks and journals along (as they have done every other day). Reitz runs his hand over the cover of his book, as if it he has not seen it for a long time. Gently he rubs across the familiar surface, as if he wants to read something with his fingers that cannot be read inside.

He follows Ben's example, tries to disengage himself, tries to focus on the lecture he has to deliver to the general and his company the following day.

•

Ben and Reitz speak little all day. Reitz is careful not to reveal too much of his restlessness. His concentration is poor. His nerve ends feel raw; there is still an unpleasant prickling sensation in his fingertips and toes; his limbs twitch. In the course of the morning he suffers a few acute stomach cramps.

Only once does he say: My head isn't here, Ben, I'm beyond remedy today, I'm afraid. And Ben nods sympathetically.

When they do speak, he can see that Ben is trying to put his mind at rest. The general is a reasonable man, he's convinced of it, a rational and possibly even an educated man. Reitz must remember most of the fellows here don't have much schooling. He must consider the level of education they have encountered so far. They shouldn't expect much understanding—the Bible is the sole source of knowledge for most of these men.

Reitz nods. He is familiar with the range and scope of prejudice and superstition on commando.

Is Ben trying to ease his own mind? Reitz wonders. Is it a circumspect warning to Reitz to be conservative in his exposition?

Be that as it may. It is too late now. He does not give a damn about what the general and his men may think tomorrow. In the past few days he has passed the point of truly caring about what happens to him.

She is gone. The more he tries to recall her—distorted—image, the more even that eludes him. The greater is his feeling of loss. The loss is exacerbated by remorse. He ruined everything. He sent her even further away than she had been before. She had been here. If only he had been patient. If only he had stood back and allowed her to come to *him*—in her own time and her own way. If he had made room for her in a *different* way. If he had not involved Oompie and his evil machinations. He lost her through his own impatience. Now she has been utterly reclaimed by that darkness from where he called her. Now even the hope of being reunited with her in death is lost.

So his thoughts wander while he is supposed to be ordering and arranging them on the subject of geology. Without enthusiasm he looks at the rocks that have always inspired him. The landscape has lost its geological coherence and attraction.

From time to time he notices Ben's concerned look, but he cannot put his mind at ease. He tries, but Ben knows him too well to be convinced.

Everything is fine, Ben, he says, we're going to tell the general and his men a thing or two.

Ben laughs, but his eyes remain troubled, and his nostrils threaten to flare nervously. He seems suddenly older and greyer to Reitz, more subdued, the furrows across his wide brow deeper, and Reitz wonders whether this, too, is on his account, or whether he has simply not noticed it before.

They have to get away from here. They have to get away from this place; here he is bound to succumb to feelings of loss. Even if the general decides (as Ben maintains) that they are still fit for battle and sends them on some or other mission, even that will be preferable.

By late afternoon, when they have stowed their journals in their trunks, Reitz feels uncommonly irritable.

From time to time on their way back to camp they catch sight of Seun behind some loose boulders, probably hunting for small mammals or birds. Reitz moves with difficulty; his muscles cramp; he is breathless. He realises he has not yet fully regained his strength.

When they have almost reached the top, he is unexpectedly struck on the head by a clod. It can only have been Seun. But it must have been unintentional, for Seun stands up from behind a nearby boulder and regards them with a dumbfounded look on his face—mouth slightly agape.

Reitz, once he has recovered from the shock, rushes at Seun, grabs him by the arm, and strikes him hard against the head.

"You stupid fool!" he shouts.

He grabs him by the shoulders and shakes him so that the boy's teeth rattle before he strikes him another blow to the head.

Ben seizes Reitz forcefully by the arm.

"What the hell is going on with you?" he demands.

Bewildered, Seun scuttles away across the stones; keeps looking at them over his shoulder, blubbering.

"You retarded harelip!" Reitz shouts after him.

"Stop it!" says Ben in a low voice. "For God's sake, get a grip on yourself!"

Reitz stands, his heart racing. He is forced to sit down. It takes a while before he manages to calm down. He motions for Ben to go ahead. Wearily he runs his trembling hand across his face. Ben sits down on a large boulder some distance away. After a while they walk back to camp in silence.

When they arrive, Seun is sitting beside the fire Ezekiel is building. Gert Smal, though not particularly friendly, seems no more hostile than usual. Reitz knows how protective Gert is towards Seun. No mention is made of the incident. Seun sits hidden in the shadows all evening, and Reitz finds it hard to look at him.

Around the fire, in the company of the general and his men, Reitz and Ben do not get an opportunity to talk. Only once, running his hand wearily across his face, does Reitz remark in an undertone: "I'm in a quandary, Ben. I can hardly bear up."

But he dare not tell Ben what intense gratification—almost to the point of physical pleasure—he experienced earlier when he struck the child those two blows.

•

The general has produced more than one bottle of fine Cape brandy. Spoils of war? Reitz wonders.

The men are noisy, boisterous, even. By the looks of it they could not have been enduring much of the hardships of war. They drink the brandy and eat the rhebok they have brought along. Shot for the pot by Blackpiet, cut up by the Bushman agterryer and expertly cooked on the coals by Blackpiet and Red Herman.

Reitz feels light-headed, and when he is hit by an intense stomach cramp he bends over as imperceptibly as possible until it passes. But he is reluctant to leave the fire, afraid to miss anything of importance.

He observes the general and his company closely—as closely as his physical discomfort allows. These men will be their audience tomorrow. Their immediate fate is in the hands of the general.

Reitz guesses that none of the younger men can be much older than thirty. Gif Luttig is an unattractive fellow—thin, freckly and irascible, with hollow cheeks and a heavy jaw. Red Herman Hundt has a red beard and hair, a broad face, a milky complexion, and an air of indifference, as if nothing in the world could hope to impress him. Jannie Neethling carries his head hunched between his shoulders; he wears glasses, his beard is shaggy, his hair is long and wavy, his teeth small and pointed, and his mouth hangs open slightly like a child engrossed in play. He makes a less hostile impression on Reitz than the other two.

Reitz judges the three older men to be in their forties, more or less the same age as Ben and he. From the word go—since he arrived here with the general the first time—Reitz took a dislike to the dark, bearded Blackpiet Petoors with his ashen complexion (like volcanic ash beneath the skin), pale green eyes, flat head and arrogant attitude. He likewise finds the moth-eaten Sagrys Skeel—one slightly squint, drifting little eye—an unacceptable fellow, but he is mostly a bungler and an idiot. Jakobus Wagenaer is a big man with a sharp profile, clearly a man of exceptional physical prowess, as is apparent from his hands and forearms. He moves slowly and rather hesitantly, sideways almost, like a crab. He seldom joins in the conversation, but rises every now and then and walks into the night by himself.

There are also two older men, two belligerent old fellows: Oom Mannes and Oom Honne. Clearly the blood of seasoned fighters courses through their veins. They appear as vigorous and ready for action as youngsters.

With the exception of the Neethling fellow and Jakobus Wagenaer, the group does not make a particularly favourable impression on Reitz. Can this be the general's entire company—the hand-picked little commando with which he carries out his punitive expeditions and thrashes the English? Reitz wonders. If this is the case, if this is his chosen band, then it does not reflect well on the general. And Reitz's faltering courage sinks even lower.

Finally there is Blackpiet Petoors's agterryer—a little Bushman of indeterminate age—all smiles and eager to please. Petoors addresses him as Stofman.

The general looks as dapper as ever—military uniform groomed to the last button and buckle, boots buffed to a high gloss. Broad in the upper jaw, broad across the shoulder, broad across the palm of the hand; eyes narrowed appraisingly and focused on a point somewhere behind the shoulder of the one being spoken to.

Reitz still feels uneasy in the presence of the man. Ben has said repeatedly that he takes the general to be a reasonable man, and Reitz hopes Ben is right, for he has no defence against lack of reason and good sense at the moment. His own judgment feels too shaky and his senses too unreliable.

The talk around the fire this evening is mainly about the war. Some experiences are told first-hand, others are reported from hearsay. From their stories and remarks Reitz concludes that most of the men served in other commandos in the Transvaal and the Free State before joining General Bergh.

Reitz finds it hard to follow the conversation as closely as he would like to, for he is sporadically overcome by stomach cramps or momentary dizziness. This makes him even more irritable and defensive.

Blackpiet holds forth about the Khakis who thought they would get no opposition from the Boers. Buller at Colenso; Gatacre at Stormberg, who had never fought anyone but savages and cannibals before, and couldn't wait to use the sabre on the backs of the Boers. "He thought he could drive them out of the Cape Colony with one mighty sweep, but he was mistaken," says Blackpiet. "*Sorely* mistaken," and he grins maliciously. "Old George White with the gammy leg. Three weeks in the country and he thought he knew how to deal with the Boers. At Ladysmith he soon discovered he wasn't in India, or fighting some heathen nation."

"The fate of our fellow-burghers at Elandslaagte still weighs heavily on our minds," Oom Honne says. "To think General Kock had to suffer the fatal wound in his side there, and so soon. An honourable man," says Oom Honne, "a fearless fighter."

"Elandslaagte," Blackpiet says bitterly.

"The Boers were gored like *pigs*," Sagrys Skeel says in a low voice.

"They begged for mercy," says Gif Luttig, "begged to be shot rather than stabbed with lances, but the English had their orders: no prisoners."

"The dirty *swine*," says Blackpiet. "May the *dogs* devour their dead! May they never be shown any mercy."

"And the survivors of Kock's commando," says Oom Honne, "forced to march through the streets of Ladysmith and taunted by Kaffirs."

"The bitter humiliation," Oom Mannes says softly.

Reitz remembers hearing shortly after the incident that it meant the demise of the Johannesburg commando.

Oom Mannes subsequently speaks of the death of General Kock, who prayed that the Lord deliver him from imprisonment by the English, because he had no friend left who could help him to escape. And he describes how death clouded Kock's amiable, noble features before he passed away early one morning in his sixty-fourth year.

Willem and Reuben are clearly moved by the tale and Oom Honne says: "In truth, we lost a *worthy* leader there."

Gert Smal makes no attempt to contradict him, despite having expressed his thoughts on General Kock's shortcomings in no uncertain terms in the past.

"Yes, yes," Oom Mannes says pensively, "we picked them off—the English—one by one, and still the end is not in sight."

"And we lost many a friend, and many a family member," Oom Honne muses. "And many a time we were outraged at the bloodshed and slaughter of the battlefield."

"After a while one becomes indifferent," says Red Herman.

The others make no reply. Blackpiet throws something into the fire.

"But our faithful God has always been our strength," says Oom Mannes.

"We have paid dearly for our cause. For our beloved country. God will still bestow His mercy on us. That day will come," Oom Honne says.

"Man is insignificant; God disposes in everything—our lives are in His hands!" Willem says with conviction.

"Our hearts are heavy when we remember our brothers in exile," says Oom Honne. "Poor General Piet Cronjé and his men. Marthinus Prinsloo and his men. Men who had to suffer the indignity of surrender."

At the mention of Paardeberg a momentary silence falls upon the company, as if they are gathered around an open grave.

Oom Mannes and Oom Honne shake their grey heads.

Reitz notices that Gert Smal's face is red and the vein in his forehead is throbbing dangerously as he tries to restrain himself. But he does manage to refrain from shaking his fist in his usual manner and cursing Cronjé all the way to hell and back.

Young Abraham, to everyone's surprise, suddenly covers his ears with his hands and begins to screech shrilly and unintelligibly. The others look on in surprise while Willem jumps to his feet anxiously and leads the youngster away to his shelter. Gert Smal points at his head and says: "Shell shock."

"His brother died in his arms at the battle of Droogleegte," Ben explains.

"Heard about Droogleegte," Red Herman says.

"They say an English colonel was hit by a shell fragment there," Gif Luttig says. "He pulled himself to his knees with great difficulty, folded his hands, prayed and fell over backwards, stone dead."

"English vermin," says Blackpiet. "To whom and for what had he been praying?"

Droogleegte. Neither Reitz nor Ben mentions the battle. Even though Reitz recalls clearly the demented jabbering of a burgher who was hit by a shell fragment right beside him, exposing his brain and tearing out his eyes. And young Abraham's brother. Droogleegte was the final incentive for leaving Senekal's commando.

They discuss the ignominious circumstances around the death of the commander-in-chief of the Free State, Ignaas Ferreira. Accidentally shot by one of his own men. In the chest, point-blank. Killed instantly. A great leader, says Oom Honne. A heavy loss, says Oom Mannes. A soldier who could still have meant a great deal to his people, says Oom Honne. He and Danie Theron. We lost two of the best, says Red Herman.

"Fortunately God has been holding Generals De Wet and De la Rey in His hand," says Oom Honne, "for their unwavering courage and great tactical skill serve as edification and example to every burgher in the field."

His words are endorsed enthusiastically by most of the others. The general says nothing, lights his pipe, rises and walks away from the fire.

They speak of De la Rey's recent success at Ysterspruit and the glory of Tweebosch—where Methuen was wounded and taken prisoner.

They speak of the disgrace of Derdepoort in the Groot Marico. Oom Honne describes how the Khama Kaffirs—in alliance with the English and under leadership of an English officer—launched a surprise attack on the town early one morning, and how the women were dishonoured. "One poor girl was held down by four Kaffirs while nine Khakis concluded their dastardly business," Oom Honne says.

"Unforgivable," says Willem, "that a Christian woman should have to endure that."

"Kaffir savagery," says Oom Mannes.

"English cowardice," says Sagrys Skeel.

"English scum," says Blackpiet Petoors. Those bastards can count themselves lucky they didn't have *him* to deal with. He'd personally have seen to it that each of them got a taste of his Joseph Rogers. Where it hurt most. Upon which Red Herman guffaws and slaps his thigh.

"Nine men murdered that day, one severely wounded, two hundred oxen stolen. And the bodies of the dead Boers disfigured by vultures," says Oom Honne.

"But in the end they were given a Christian burial," says Oom Mannes. "Two hundred burghers under the command of Commandant Casper du Plessis attacked the Kaffir laager from the west and torched their village."

"They say the young Boers feasted on the little fattened chickens they found left behind in the deserted Kaffir kraals," says Red Herman, smirking.

Gert Smal does not say much. There is no sign this evening of his usual stream of invective. He contradicts no one. He goes to great lengths to impress the general and especially Blackpiet Petoors. But when the conversation turns to traitors and deserters, he shoots a meaningful look at Ben and Reitz.

Reitz suspects there is the occasional veiled reference to the group's own movements, for sometimes there is laughter and plenty of insinuating bantering about apparently minor incidents. Especially among Blackpiet Petoors, Gif Luttig and Red Herman. Sagrys Skeel complains about something or other and Blackpiet says—much to the amusement of the others: "Been riding the pommel too much, old man!" As the evening progresses Reitz finds that neither his sense of humour nor his favourable expectation of what the following day will bring seems to improve.

In the course of the evening both Ben and he sound out the men cautiously for recent news. (If they cannot get it here—where can they get it?)

"We're still beating the hell out of the Khakis, Neef," says Oom Mannes.

"Khakis and handsuppers," says Oom Honne.

"We don't trifle with Kaffirs who betray us and fight for the English either," says Oom Mannes.

"Just so, Neef, just so," Oom Honne concurs, and lovingly strokes the bandolier around his waist.

"We don't stand for it," Blackpiet Petoors adds. "We have no mercy for Kaffirs or members of their families who cooperate with the Khakis."

"We kill them on sight—if it's called for," says Gif Luttig. "Man, woman and child. Burn down their huts, destroy their villages."

Upon which Blackpiet and he exchange a meaningful sidelong glance which does not escape Reitz.

And in the rest of the country—apart from Methuen who was captured at Tweebosch?

It seems General Smuts is still active in the Cape Colony. Lötter was executed at Middelburg in the Cape Colony on a charge of treason. Gideon Scheepers was captured in October and executed in January. Kritzinger was captured in December. The English are continuing with the nocturnal incursions they started in November. In February the entire Harrismith commando were taken prisoner at Langverwacht. The Khakis are still hot on De Wet's trail, but he succeeds in giving them the slip time and again. He is too clever for them, Blackpiet says with satisfaction.

The general himself barely reacts to anything that is said, and does not join in the conversation. He smokes his pipe, gazes into the fire, gets up often and walks a short distance into the veld.

Stofman, Blackpiet Petoors's little Bushman agterryer, has been scurrying about since early evening: fetching things, preparing sleeping places, carrying armfuls of grass bedding, tending to the horses, bringing hot coals for Blackpiet's pipe.

It's Stofman here and Stofman there—and as the evening progresses it becomes Kinderpiel and Perskie-oor—because his ear resembles a dried peach, Blackpiet says. And indeed, Reitz notices, his ear is small and crumpled like a dried peach. The men laugh heartily when Blackpiet addresses him like that.

The little Bushman submits willingly to the chores and the name-calling. Ezekiel, too, does what is expected of him. With downcast eyes he silently performs his numerous tasks before retreating into the shadows again. He steps into the firelight only when called upon.

Reitz notices that Gert Smal does not show off Ezekiel's extraordinary skills tonight. He refrains from snapping his fingers in Ezekiel's direction when it happens on more than one occasion that a date or a name eludes someone.

Later the two elderly men doze around the fire. Jakobus Wagenaer has not yet returned from his walk in the veld. Japie Stilgemoed and Kosie Rijpma withdrew to their respective shelters early, as is their habit.

Later still there is singing. Folk songs and bawdy songs and the anthems of the republics of the Transvaal and the Free State. This lasts until one by one the men topple over onto the grass beds that have been prepared for them in a wide circle around the fire.

Finally, when the laughing and talking have subsided, when the two belligerent old men are snoring in their grass beds, and only Ben, Reitz and Willem are still sitting around the fire, the general begins to speak.

The general, who has by now also partaken vigorously of the brandy, sits with bowed head, elbows resting on his knees. At times he gazes over their shoulders into the night.

"Milner," he says. "This war is on his conscience, more than anyone else's."

He stares into the fire.

"Milner," he continues. "The old Cambridge boy. He wanted his war, and he got his war. No one was a match for him. Behind him the mighty imperial machine and Rhodes's money."

With unseeing eyes the general stares over Reitz's shoulder into the dark night until Reitz begins to feel uncomfortable.

"None of our people was equal to the task," says the general, and Reitz is unsure exactly what he is referring to—Milner, or the imperial machine and Rhodes's money, or all of it together.

"Not Louis Botha, nor Jannie Smuts with all his book learning and distinctions," says the general. "Not De Wet either. De Wet is a shrewd fighter, but naïve. To De Wet the war is a matter of faith—a holy war—that's why he will never grasp the motives of the enemy."

He takes a large swig from his tin mug.

"Kitchener is merely Milner's hand puppet. Milner has been wanting to get rid of him for a long time, I'll stake my life on it. What do you expect of a man who gets excited about china and orchids and takes his lapdog to the battlefield? A man who can't control his emotions and carries on like a woman? He's been an embarrassment to Milner for a long time. Because Milner has been blowing in his neck, Kitchener has become a desperate man resorting to desperate measures, for he's incompetent. He isn't a strategist's backside. He has no conscience. He has no loyalty, not even to his own men. He won't stop at anything. He'll use the Kaffirs against us. He'll have suspects shot without further ado. He'll murder woman and child alike. He's the kind of man who, when it's all over, will take home as much of the spoils as he is able."

"God grant that the English won't get away with it," says Willem.

"England *will* get away with it," says the general, not sparing Willem a glance. "God doesn't have much of a say in it."

Willem looks deeply shocked. He holds up his large hands entreatingly, palms facing forward.

"If we can't appeal to God," he says, "what hope do we have?"

The general glances at him briefly, but makes no reply.

A moment later he gets up, and it is the signal for everyone to turn in.

CHAPTER 9

The next morning—a morning fresh as a young bride—everyone gathers round to listen to Reitz and Ben's lectures.

But first they pose for a group photograph beside the cave mouth under the overhanging rock, with the rock face in the background.

The camera is set up by the general, since it belongs to him. Everyone is told where to position themselves. The camera has a timing mechanism, and when everyone is ready, the general sets the timer, takes up his position and orders them not to move and to look directly at the camera.

He takes a seat on a low rock in the centre of the group. To his right stands Captain Blackpiet Petoors with a riding crop in his hand; to his left Captain Sagrys Skeel, his foot on a rock and his hand on his thigh. To the left and right on either side stand Oom Mannes and Oom Honne, each with a rifle firmly planted on the ground at his feet. Gif Luttig, Red Herman Hundt, Jannie Neethling and Jakobus Wagenaer are seated in the foreground. Red Herman is in a semireclining, horizontal position; Gif Luttig sits tense and erect, like a ramrod. On the ground, almost out of the picture, the little Bushman squats on his haunches.

Next to Oom Mannes poses Gert Smal, with hands behind his back. Proud and defiant, he gazes into the distance. At his side stands Seun, looking sheepish—not sure what is taking place. Between them is the dog with the yellow eyes (Gert Smal is brusquely trying to make her sit). Next to the dog crouches Ezekiel.

In the back row, their backs against the rock face, stand Japie Stilgemoed, Kosie Rijpma, Reuben, Reitz, Ben, Willem and young Abraham. Willem has his arm protectively around Abraham's thin shoulders.

The general and his deputation are spruced up this morning, wearing polished boots and trim riding breeches, or decent velskoens and waistcoats. And swanky hats. They are all posing with rifles and bandoliers. The group from the camp, however, are trying their best to hide their patched, threadbare clothing from view.

Complete silence falls.

From above comes the call of a rock kestrel: kek-kek-kek. The shutter makes a loud clicking sound. The photograph has been taken. Their image has been recorded for posterity.

The group dissolves. The lectures can commence. But first the general asks Oom Mannes (the oldest amongst them) to open with Scripture reading and prayer.

In ringing tones, though stumbling somewhat over the words, Oom Mannes reads from Exodus. He reads about the Israelites' victory over Amalek in Rephidim. Then he prays long and earnestly for the Lord to help them eradicate the English from this beautiful land. He prays that the Lord may give them strength and endurance and, above all, the upper hand over the enemy.

On this soft, mild autumn day at the beginning of April in the last year of the war, with the general and the two belligerent old men on camp stools and the rest of the group seated on a variety of loose rocks and wooden stumps, Ben and Reitz give the men—fit as well as unfit for battle—a brief overview of the range covered by their respective fields of study.

The air is crisp and clear. The light has that particular autumnal shimmering that prompts thoughts on the fleetingness of human life. The scent of the surrounding veld hints at the abatement of summer's ferocity, and at the advancing sadness of winter.

Reitz begins by saying that geology is the science that sets out to describe the structure of the earth's crust and its various layers, as well as its history.

When we look at the hills and mountains, the rivers and plains around us, Reitz says, they seem unchanging. And indeed, in contrast with the transient impermanence of our lives, this is true.

And yet, says Reitz, if we pay careful attention, we'll see that there are constant changes in the appearance of our environment. Small changes of which the cumulative effect in time will alter the aspect of the landscape completely. Thus land and sea change places over thousands—millions—of years, rivers change their course, mountain peaks are chiselled, valleys scooped and plains extended.

"How many millions of years?" Red Herman demands challengingly.

Here it comes, Reitz thinks. Unavoidable.

He will give an indication of the ages of the various geological periods presently, he says.

He continues. Geology studies the history of the earth, he says, and the soil and the rock formations under our feet are the records that reveal the chronology of that history. Every variation of rock and stone has its own distinctive place on the surface of the earth. It is the task of the geologist, he says, to interpret these records and to document the sequence of changes that have occurred from the earliest times up to the present day. The earth is old, so old that its crust has eroded in places. Rock formations, he says, are the building blocks of the earth's crust, and they all consist of one or more minerals. He explains how the three kinds, namely sedimentary, metamorphic and igneous or eruptive rock are formed. He keeps his explanations succinct. He has decided to make his lecture no longer than necessary.

Thus and in that vein Reitz informs his—at times restless—audience about the broad principles of geology.

General Bergh listens attentively, though his gaze is fixed somewhere in the distance. (It is therefore entirely possible that he is contemplating prospective military strategies.)

Willem sits with his large eyes clear as pebbles and it appears as if the mere mention of all these things evokes a great and nameless sorrow inside him. Young Abraham sits motionless, with a vacant expression—impossible to determine how much he grasps or assimilates. Seun scratches restlessly at the soil with a stone, and after a while he takes off.

Kosie Rijpma listens distractedly; from time to time his attention appears to wander. Gert Smal is chewing on a splinter, his expression varying between annoyance and scorn. Reuben smokes his pipe and whittles intermittently at a wooden object.

Jakobus Wagenaer sits hunched forward, his face averted; it is hard to tell whether he is listening. Right from the start Blackpiet Petoors, Sagrys Skeel, Red Herman and the lean Gif Luttig listen with barely concealed misgiving. Why this should be so, Reitz is not sure, although it does not altogether come as a surprise.

Oom Mannes and Oom Honne sit on camp stools, with legs crossed, still wearing their bandoliers and keeping a firm hold on their rifles, as if they are expecting the enemy in their midst at any moment.

Ezekiel crouches behind them in the shade of a large boulder, with the little Bushman agterryer some distance behind him.

Only Japie Stilgemoed and Jannie Neethling listen with undivided attention.

A study of the present, Reitz continues, supplies us with the key to unlock the mysteries of the past. To describe the changes that are taking place, he says, it is, however, also necessary to have knowledge of natural powers that affect the surface of the earth, like rain and wind, ice and snow.

But, says Reitz (he feels light-headed, his face warm and his hands cold), if the history of the earth was merely a history of dead, inert material, of sand and rock formations, of solidified lava and granite, it would be of little interest to us. Fortunately this history also preserves the records of successive generations of plants and animals that have populated land and sea since the earliest times.

"Since God created the earth," Willem declares firmly.

It's difficult to imagine, Reitz continues, when we look at the dry plains that surround us here, that there was a time when the climate of this region was very different and, instead of veld, there were marshes and lakes. We now know that this environment, in the murky prehistoric past, used to be part of a huge lake that was fed by a great river coursing through the land from the north.

"What's wrong with the Orange?" Red Herman cries. The others laugh.

Thousands of reptiles—large and small—lived and left their bones here. Giants from another world, extinct creatures that we know today only from the scattered remains of their bones all around us. Reptiles of wondrous appearance and gigantic dimensions, says Reitz.

"Never come across anything around here except the bones of horses and oxen," Blackpiet Petoors declares.

Reitz continues. He ignores all comments. Over vast stretches of time the climate changed here, he says, the mud turned into shale, and the bones became as hard as rock. These petrified prehistoric remains we call fossils.

Do we ever ask ourselves, asks Reitz, what happened to flowers, trees, insects, birds and animals over a period of thousands of years? All those forms of life that have disappeared without leaving a trace?

"Like the Khakis when we've finished with them," says Blackpiet Petoors, and everyone laughs.

"Now why would an insect want to leave a trace?" Oom Mannes asks, and everyone laughs again.

Of some animals and even certain insects traces are found, says Reitz. We find these fossil remains in selected places, like the alluvial terraces of rivers, or in briny deposits at the bottoms of lakes, or on the floors of underground caves, or in peat bogs. These early forms give us an indication of how they differed from their present forms and where they were found earlier. In this way we can form a picture of what life looked like in primordial times.

"Before or after the flood?" Blackpiet Petoors asks.

"Before *and* after the flood," Reitz says deliberately. He feels a growing irritation take hold of him.

Don't interrupt the man, the general admonishes.

Reitz continues by explaining that geology does not concern itself only with what we can see with the naked eye—the hills and mountains, rocks and stones. Neither does it study only those layers in which *old* bones are found—forms of life that lived and died out long before us. Or those layers of the earth's crust in which *no* forms of life are found at present except a record of the fierce creative forces of the earth. Geology also concerns itself with the deepest, invisible layer—the red-hot centre of the earth—that in some places has already erupted in the form of volcanoes, and is still threatening to do so. These volcanic eruptions make an important contribution to the changes and the shape of the earth's crust.

"You're right there, Neef!" says Blackpiet Petoors. "We all know hell is a warm place!"

"And day after day Satan does his evil work on earth," says Oom Mannes.

Geology is a science of observation, says Reitz, emphatically. Once we've become aware of our geological environment, it's difficult not to see some geological process or another taking place daily—or evidence of one that ran its course many years ago.

Reitz ends his talk by briefly pointing out a few distinctive attributes of their immediate surroundings. He points out the sedimentary layers in the red ridges, the harder sandstone that takes longer to erode than the softer rock layers—the mudstone and the shale. But it is actually the so-called Karoo dolerites that are responsible for the most prominent features of this area, he explains—the iron-hard igneous rock that has penetrated the sedimentary rock everywhere. He points at the large, loose boulders all around them—igneous rock that was forced in molten form through the crust of the earth from deep within by volcanic eruptions.

But Red Herman interrupts again.

"How old would you say the earth actually is, Neef?" he asks. The most vindictive and cleverest of them all, thinks Reitz.

To hell with it, he thinks. He is irritable; he has cramps in his stomach.

The science of geology, he says, teaches us that the earth is much older than we have always thought. Some of the fossils that have survived are millions of years old. The oldest geological period—the Archaean—long before the Paleozoic, the period of ancient life—is estimated to have been more than four thousand million years ago.

General pandemonium erupts.

"Now you're talking shit, Neef!" Red Herman shouts. "Just the other day I read that the earth is three thousand years old."

"Four thousand and four years," Gif Luttig declares with conviction. "I heard it from a reliable source before the war."

"Then it must be four thousand and seven years now," Blackpiet says promptly.

"It's inconsistent with the Bible." Willem is dismayed. He can scarcely be heard, for everyone is speaking at the same time.

Reitz indicates to the general that his lecture is over. The general nods politely, and calms the men down. With a gesture of the hand he shows that it is Ben's turn.

Reitz sits down. He feels even more light-headed. He has made it difficult for Ben, for it is clear some of the men are now openly ready to challenge every word that is said.

But Ben does not seem in the least flustered. In fact—unlike Reitz—he seems to delight in the prospect of sharing his knowledge with his audience.

He starts by saying that he works in the field of natural history, a discipline that concerns itself with the characterisation and description of various types of plants and insects and sometimes also smaller mammals, as well as with their distribution and adaptation.

Ben explains that all kinds—or species, as they are called—were classified in the eighteenth century by one Carolus Linnaeus, and that in due course this classification was refined. The classification is an orderly system, by means of which plants and animals are divided according to type—a useful and important system, he says.

As Ben speaks, his enthusiam for his subject grows. The natural world, he says, is astonishing in its abundance and variety. To someone who is interested, nature is an endless source of information, fascination and variation. A huge, inexhaustible field of study!

Think of the abundance of the plant kingdom to begin with, he says. The various algae and mosses, the ferns and conifers, the gymnosperms, the cycads, the jointed pines, the flowering plants—each order with its numerous types testifies to the abundance and variation of nature!

And the animal kingdom with all *its* branches. If we consider the shapes and variety found in living organisms, in insects, birds and fishes—not to mention the different kinds of animals—that have populated the earth since the earliest days, then we cannot but be filled with wonder at the bounty of the natural world, Ben says. The plant and animal kingdoms are an inexhaustible field, he says. Even the tiniest organism is worthy of being studied—from the simplest sponge in the ocean to the great whale, from the humblest insect to man with his exceptional talents, every type or species is worthy of our interest and attention.

Does he understand correctly, Gif Luttig interrupts, that Ben says man is part of the animal kingdom?

That's correct, Ben replies (slightly taken aback); in the animal kingdom man belongs to the class Mammalia and the order Primates. With a piece of charcoal—that he specifically prepared for the purpose—he sketches a simplified diagram of Linnaeus's classification on the rock face behind him.

The men regard the diagram with clear mistrust. Some shift restlessly and voice their dismay in furtive murmurs. The general listens with a neutral expression, young Abraham remains rigid, Kosie Rijpma seems immersed in his own thoughts and Japie Stilgemoed and Jannie Neethling nod at regular intervals to affirm their interest and agreement.

"The Bible says," Gif Luttig proclaims threateningly, "that man is the pinnacle of creation."

"And has dominion over the animals," Blackpiet adds.

"But man himself is no animal," says Sagrys Skeel.

"Nor is he related to the ape," says Red Herman, his eyes narrowed menacingly. "I know where this is going."

Again the general decrees that the speaker should not be interrupted. There will be an opportunity to ask questions at the end. The men are to hold their queries until then.

The natural world, Ben continues, just like the geological world—as his friend Reitz has explained—is changing all the time. But we are not referring here to those changes that we notice as time goes by, or observe during our lifetime, but to gradual changes over almost unimaginably long periods.

As nature changes, the various forms of birds and fish, animals and insects must also change to adapt to their new surroundings.

Let's take the horse as an example, Ben says with enthusiasm. The earliest prehistoric ancestor of the horse we know today did not always inhabit grass plains. When this ancestor moved out of the jungle and the wooded areas, certain changes took place to help it adapt to its changing environment. Its teeth changed to enable it to eat coarser grass; its limbs became longer so that it might run faster. It became bigger and stronger. And Ben explains how the toes gradually changed into hooves.

Thus the horse did not always look the way it does today, Ben says. In countless fossil remains we have seen that the ancestor or forerunner of today's horse—*Eohippus*—was the size of a smallish dog a few million years ago.

General laughter and badgering erupt. Reuben laughs so much he almost chokes on his tobacco.

"God Almighty," Oom Mannes shouts, "never!"

"*Your* horse, perhaps, not mine!" Blackpiet Petoors cries.

"If your horse's grandfather was the size of a dog, it's *your* problem!" Sagrys Skeel jeers.

Red Herman says: "Yes, and I'm sure we could win the war—on horses the size of dogs!"

"Yes," says Gif Luttig, "we could even teach them to hunt!"

Again the general warns them to calm down.

But we mustn't make the mistake, Ben repeats (unperturbed, but emphatically), to think these changes happen overnight. That wouldn't be possible. All these adaptations take place over long periods—much longer than we humans, with our limited lifespan, can ever imagine. And, what is more, much longer periods than have always been believed. These adaptations and changes—like the geological changes they have just heard of—probably occur over millions of years.

"Millions of years!" Red Herman cries. "Millions of years, my arse!"

"What about the ark?" Reuben shouts.

Ben is clearly not going to be driven off course today, neither will he allow his enthusiasm to be dampened, Reitz notices.

If an animal or insect type cannot adapt to its changing circumstances, Ben continues, it becomes extinct. Numerous species of animals and insects, birds and fish, that once inhabited the earth do not exist any more. The trilobites and ammonites—early marine arthropods—have died out . . .

"The Amalekites and the Philistines," Blackpiet Petoors interrupts, "now you're talking, Neef—they've all died out!"

General laughter ensues.

Undisturbed, Ben continues. The woolly rhinoceros and the mammoth have died out. The sabre-toothed tiger, the ichthyosaurus and the pterosaurus—large sea lizards and flying reptiles—have all died out. And of course the dinosaurs—giant reptiles from the prehistoric world. All extinct. The only proof we have that these vanished forms ever existed is fossils that have survived—as Reitz has already indicated—fossils and ancient bones.

"What you are claiming, Neef," says Willem, his face red with agitation, "is in conflict with the Bible. God created man and beast, and that's how they have remained, unchanged. That's what the Bible teaches us."

"Yes, what about the ark?" Reuben cries again.

Some of the others seem about to step in, their indignation rising like an ominous groundswell, but the general makes a stern gesture.

It was believed for a long time, Ben answers, that everything has remained unchanged since creation. But lately new information has come to the fore—the discovery of fossils and bones, new facts and insights and concepts in natural history that have considerably changed our views of the history of the earth and the living organisms that populate it.

Willem shuts his eyes as if this is more than he can endure, even out of loyalty to Ben and Reitz.

We know, Ben continues, that some forms have been in existence much longer than others. The arthropods longer than the amphibians, the fishes longer than the reptiles, the first birds and reptile-like mammals longer than the true mammals—of which man is an example.

This is going to get ugly, Reitz thinks.

But those that have survived, says Ben, are wonderful examples of ingenious adaptation taking place over a long time. Take the frog and the spider, the cockroach and the dragonfly. Unassuming forms, but eminently adapted for survival. Much better adapted than the extinct mammoth, the woolly rhinoceros and the sabre-toothed tiger.

There is muttering among the men but, driven by the courage of his convictions, inspired by his enthusiasm, unwilling to give an inch, Ben carries on. Reitz thinks, here they're confronted with the unshakeability of Ben's convictions—where facts are at stake, he will make no amicable compromise.

All elements of the environment, Ben continues, climate, vegetation, location—have an influence on the changes species undergo. The individuals of a species that are able to adapt effectively have the best chance to survive. Groups that are less adaptable become extinct. In this way, says Ben, all living things are remarkably well adapted to their environment and connected in the intricate web of life of which they are all part. Life on earth, says Ben, is a struggle for survival, and only the fittest survive—those that adapt best to their changed surroundings.

"It's *us*," says Blackpiet Petoors (sidetracked for the moment), "it's *us* who will survive."

"Fit or unfit," Red Herman remarks, "if you happen to get in the way of a Khaki bullet, you're dead."

That's how new species are formed over thousands of years, says Ben. Those that are better adapted survive, and those that are less well adapted are eliminated.

"It's not consistent with the Bible," Willem repeats quietly, visibly upset.

"You're right, Neef Willem," says Sagrys Skeel. "God made all things the way they are, and they look the same today as they did then. That's what the Bible says. And man after His own image."

"Don't let this fellow mislead us today," Oom Honne warns, "with his outlandish drivel."

Again the general bids them calm down, but it takes a while before the worst grumbling abates.

Reitz can see Ben will not let it go.

In the field of natural history we know today, Ben says, it is accepted that all forms of life are connected, because in the course of millions of years all forms have developed from a shared primordial source, and the differences that exist have their origins in deviations from that source. Life on earth, says Ben, started in the ocean, with organisms so small that they could barely be seen with the naked eye.

"But will you stop this bull about millions of years, man!" Oom Honne shouts.

"And about things in the sea," Oom Mannes adds.

"Aha!" Gif Luttig cries suddenly, as if he has caught Ben cheating at cards. "Now you're going to tell us man didn't look the way he does today either—just like the horse!"

"A good deduction," says Ben, unperturbed.

Oh wilfulness, Reitz thinks.

"I know!" Red Herman cries, red in the face, red with the dark blood that is starting to boil in his veins. "You're going to say man started off as an ape! I've heard that story, I know your type! I saw it coming!"

Now there's going to be shit, Reitz thinks.

But Ben, he notices, will not budge. He is white around the nostrils and at the corners of his mouth—as if he is in the heat of battle—but he does not give an inch. He sticks to his guns. He is not going to compromise for the sake of peace. From the evidence, Ben says, obtained from excavations and fossils, it is accepted in natural history at present that all life originated in the sea, and although man (Reitz's head feels ice-cold and the size of a pea) is the culmination of millions of years of developing life, his family tree reaches back through the apes of the ancient world, through the mammals, the amphibians, to that common primeval source from which all life originated.

"I *knew* he was going to fuck with our heads!" Red Herman cries triumphantly.

"Fuck," says young Abraham tonelessly in the shocked silence that precedes the next outburst of indignation.

"No, God Almighty!" Oom Mannes cries.

"I won't be insulted like this by a deserter!" Oom Honne's voice rises above the tumult.

Exclamations of disapproval and outrage as well as insults are flung at Ben. Some men find it hard to restrain themselves—Blackpiet Petoors and Sagrys Skeel do not even try to hide their hostility.

"Double blasphemy!" Sagrys Skeel cries out.

"*Your* damned grandfather was an ape," shouts Oom Mannes belligerently, "and you are one too!"

"No, man," cries Red Herman, "his grandfather was an ape long ago—when the world was still young!"

"*Before* creation," says Gif Luttig, "when the earth was barren and wild!"

Willem holds up his hands, his face averted. "Enough!" he cries. "You have scoffed at the Bible enough!"

When the laughter has died down, Gif Luttig adds: "Not to mention his mother."

"He's no more than a vagabond and a tramp," Oom Honne says in an undertone. "I could *see* this fellow was going to cause trouble."

Ben says nothing, but Reitz thinks he detects a hint of triumph in the ever so slight twitch at the corners of his mouth.

Willem's face is ashen, with a glowing red spot on either cheek. He is clearly torn between his view of the truth and his feelings of friendship and loyalty. "*One* day after the fishes," he says. "The fishes and fowl on the fifth day—the beasts of the earth and man on the sixth day."

Blackpiet Petoors cries: "Yes! Blasphemy! Man was created on the sixth day to have dominion over the animals!"

"In the likeness of God," Willem says softly.

"God Almighty, no!" Oom Mannes says indignantly, and knocks on the ground with his rifle butt.

Oom Honne says: "I refuse to listen to this tripe a moment longer. I won't be insulted like this."

"I haven't heard this much rot in a single day for a long time," Oom Mannes says, lovingly stroking his rifle.

Today's the day they shoot us here like dogs, Reitz thinks.

The general holds up his hand. Silence, he commands. Reluctantly the men fall silent, but nonetheless Reitz is grateful to see that the word of the general—a reasonable man if ever he has prayed for one—still commands the necessary authority.

When everyone has more or less settled down, Oom Mannes says: "The next thing you'll probably be telling me, Neef, is that there's no difference between a Kaffir and myself."

Ben hesitates for a moment before saying: "I wasn't planning to touch on that subject in my discussion, but seeing that you've brought it up—yes, I'm convinced there's no difference between black and white as far as inherent capabilities are concerned."

All hell bursts loose. Reitz thinks: Now we've had it. This is the end.

The general roars for silence. They can debate this in a civilised manner on another occasion, he says, this is neither the time nor the place for it. Today's discussion is not about the Native question.

Oom Mannes is temporarily dumbstruck, but the others cannot wait to have their say—despite the general's prohibition.

"You've gone too far now, Neef," says Blackpiet Petoors. "I could still laugh at all the other shit, but now you've gone too far."

"If my horse could speak, it would be more intelligent than a Kaffir!" says Red Herman.

"A creature—that's what the Bible says," Willem says agitatedly, "never meant to be the white man's equal!"

At this point Kosie Rijpma (who has up to now not taken much notice of the discussion and seemed distracted all the while) gets up. He states clearly and unequivocally that he agrees with Ben. That white man and Kaffir are equal not only in the eyes of God, but in every other way as well.

"And he calls himself a predikant!" Reuben exclaims.

"He's been off his head for a long time," Gert Smal jeers, violently spitting out a splinter of wood. "When he arrived, he was crazy, and he's worse than ever now!"

Japie Stilgemoed, agitated, jumps up and says he believes that the Native does have a lot of ground to make up, but has never been given the opportunity to do so.

Blackpiet Petoors also leaps to his feet—ready to strike Kosie Rijpma, but the general intervenes and once more forbids them to carry on with the conversation. Random comments are no longer permitted, he says. There will now be an opportunity to ask questions, and it will take place in an orderly fashion.

Upon this the general himself asks the first question to Reitz about the formation of diamonds.

When Reitz has replied, Blackpiet Petoors gets to his feet. Questions he doesn't have, he says—he just wants to state again that he doesn't believe a single word of all that's been said. It's not the way it's written in the Bible. He can't believe that responsible burghers like themselves should have had to listen to such rubbish! He's not going to say anything more about the Kaffir question, though of everything that was dished up here today, that may well have been the biggest load of shit. If this is what comes of education, then he'd rather remain uneducated.

A chorus of approval goes up.

"Yes," says Oom Mannes, "more shameful and improper talk, more disgraceful shit I haven't heard in a single day for a long time."

"Filthy blasphemy," Oom Honne adds. To think that they as Christians, dignified and honourable fighters, have had to listen to it.

"Yes," says Oom Mannes, "as Christians we would be neglecting our patriotic duty if we didn't object strongly to such false and heathenly notions." And he grasps his rifle in a firmer, more loving grip.

"Newfangled nonsense. Inflammatory lies," mutters Oom Honne. "And this thing about Kaffirs' equality . . ." He shakes his head.

Yes, and what's more, Sagrys Skeel adds—it borders on blasphemy, as he mentioned before. The Bible speaks of clean and unclean beasts.

"Cattle, creeping things and beasts of the field, each after his kind," Willem corrects him.

"The Bible says man will bruise the head of the snake, not put its name on a list," says Sagrys Skeel, "and the Bible mentions explicitly the descendants of Ham—hewers of wood and drawers of water."

"The snake is a creeping beast," says Reuben.

"Yes," Blackpiet Petoors adds, "Noah took all the animals into the ark in accordance with God's command, and those that drowned during the Deluge, the Lord—and this you may believe—did not deem worthy of rescue."

Jannie Neethling challenges him: "The Bible is no longer our only source of knowledge—by which I'm not saying we should hold the Bible in contempt."

"Who's this *we*, I'd like to know?" Gif Luttig inquires.

Blackpiet Petoors insists: In the beginning the earth was wild and empty, then came the Deluge, and they can say what they like, but after the flood the earth underwent no further changes, and no newfangled bullshit will make him believe otherwise.

"Everything the Lord ever made was in the ark," Reuben declares.

"And God created the mountains the way they are today," says Red Herman.

"And man to have dominion over the beasts, and the white man over the Kaffir," says Sagrys Skeel.

Before long they are once more drowning each other out. Only Jakobus Wagenaer smokes his pipe calmly and stares silently into the distance. Gert Smal's face is red with annoyance; now and then he adds or disputes something. He is in his element. "Never mind the Bible!" he says angrily. "Why do you have eyes in your head if you can't see for yourself how things fit together? Why come with all this outlandish shit?" and he glares at Reitz and Ben.

"Yes," Blackpiet Petoors cries, "that's what it is—outlandish *shit!*"

"Unpatriotic, treasonous, outlandish shit," Sagrys Skeel adds.

"And everyone knows the mess this outlandish rubbish has landed us in," says Gif Luttig.

Reitz and Ben wait patiently, for it is hardly expected of them to take part in the noisy discussion.

"Ben, what have we got here now?" Reitz asks surreptitiously, and Ben replies softly: "It's no more than we expected."

The general raises his hand to put an end to the uproar.

Reuben jumps to his feet, ready to put the matter to the vote. The others want to vote too. This isn't something that will be voted on, says the general, it's new knowledge, and they can accept it or they can ignore it. (Reitz finds the general's position exceptionally reasonable.) The men grumble—they want to vote; they want to prove it is all stuff and nonsense.

With that the lectures are over. Blackpiet Petoors and Sagrys Skeel make a point of turning their backs on Ben and Reitz. Gert Smal wears a triumphant expression, as if he is thankful that they have undeniably, once and for all in the eyes of everyone, especially the general, proved themselves to be good-for-nothing deserters and, above all, irresponsible burghers—if not traitors to the nation. Reitz suspects they might have been assaulted were it not for the presence of the general. Or summarily executed.

"Reitz," Ben says laconically, "I think we may have made a few enemies today."

Only Jannie Neethling, with his pointed teeth and steamed-up spectacles, comes to tell them as unobtrusively as possible that he found the lectures interesting, that he is interested in the natural world too, and that he hopes to qualify as an engineer after the war. And Japie Stilgemoed says he is grateful that they have given him food for thought; there is much for them still to discuss.

Willem lays a hand on their shoulders as if to show that, despite everything, he still considers them his loyal friends.

And Jakobus Wagenaer, pipe in hand, asks Reitz after long deliberation: "Neef, what would you say, what is the force holding all these things together in their wonderful variety? The earth in her abundance and the planets in their orbits, the mountains and the rocks—so that everything doesn't simply scatter and vanish into infinity?"

Shortly after lunch the general and his company depart, but not before he has pored at length over a number of maps with Gert Smal and his men.

When he takes leave of Reitz and Ben, he gazes over their shoulders into the unfamiliar and unfathomable distance and says curtly that they have done a good job. He can see they have not been wasting their time on commando. He plans to use their expertise in the field shortly.

But it does not appear as if the general has any intention of allowing them to accompany Willem and young Abraham anywhere in the near future.

•

That evening around the fire Gert Smal is in an exultant mood—Reitz and Ben have showed their true colours. He has Ezekiel build an extra big fire and he brings out another bottle of brandy as well as a flask of honey in the comb from the back of the cave. (Honey from Oompie's bees?)

Everyone is expected to toast Reitz and Ben's defeat—so it seems—including themselves. But not before Willem has read from the Bible at length and with great emphasis. First from Genesis, then from Job.

From Genesis he reads chapters one and two up to verse three: God who blessed the seventh day and sanctified it, because He rested then from all His work that He had made.

And deeply moved, and with greater emphasis, Willem reads verses twenty-six and twenty-seven again: God who made man in His image, after His likeness, to have dominion over the fish of the sea, and the fowl of the air, and over all the earth and over every creeping thing that creeps upon the earth. And God who created man in His own image, who created male and female.

Willem refuses to be hurried along, in spite of Gert Smal's impatience. He reads from Job, chapters thirty-eight and thirty-nine. He reads how the Lord answered Job from the whirlwind, how He asked Job where he was when He laid the foundations of the earth. Does the rain have a father, Willem reads. Who had begotten the drops of dew, out of whose womb came the ice, who had gendered the hoary frost of heaven, he reads. Can you bind the sweet influences of the Pleiades, or loose the bands of Orion, bring forth Mazzaroth in his season and guide Arcturus with his sons, he reads. And finally, with great emphasis, Willem reads how God asked Job whether *he* knew the ordinances of heaven.

Despite his mood Reitz is stirred by Willem's reading. Gert Smal can barely keep his impatience in check—he wants to start drinking. With each verse Reuben nods in agreement. Kosie Rijpma sits with averted face. Seun, with his bulbous head and harelip, breathing through his mouth, as usual, probably does not hear a single word, and young Abraham sits motionless, as is his wont.

Finally they sing a hymn—with Ezekiel leading them as on every evening in his deep, pleasant voice, and only then does Gert Smal get the opportunity to fill their mugs and propose an insinuating toast to everyone's health (in other words, to Reitz and Ben's defeat).

Ben accepts Gert Smal's exuberance with good grace and Reitz is too distracted to pay Gert Smal any heed.

He thinks: We must get away from here, Ben and I. Everything here charges me for being rash and foolish.

CHAPTER 10

The next morning at the river Reitz says: We must get away from here, Ben, I can't take it any longer.

"Where will we go?" Ben asks. "The war isn't over, we aren't neutral burghers. You either fight for the Boers or you fight for the English—neither side has sympathy with deserters! At least we have temporary asylum here until Bergh sees fit to apply us. We might as well use our time well until it happens."

Reitz makes no reply. It is true. Everything Ben says is true. He has always been able to rely on Ben's sober judgment.

"What's hounding you?" Ben asks.

Reitz maintains a stubborn silence.

"Is it the thing with your wife?" Ben asks, more sympathetically.

"That I don't know," says Reitz, running his hand over his face.

"Reitz," says Ben, "while the war is still on it won't be better any-where—not for us and not for young Abraham."

Reitz rubs his face wearily. "The thing—with her—has changed everything," he says.

"How?" Ben asks.

"It has made this place unbearable for me," he says.

"Reitz," says Ben, and he fixes his clear, reasonable gaze on Reitz, more gravely than usual. "If we are to believe Oompie and that dreadful head—and I'm inclined to do so, don't ask me why—then the war is almost over. There are other signs too. It's in the air. If we can wait it out *here*, if the general should even forget about us for a while, then at least we'll have no further part in the bloodshed, in the exhausting futility of commando life. Think about *that*."

Reitz nods. Grateful for Ben's friendship. Grateful for his insight and sound judgment at a time when his own troubled mind does not see things clearly.

Ben says: "Give it time. The unpleasant incident is still fresh in your memory."

For a while they work in silence. Reitz feels as if he has not done any field work for months, though it has only been a couple of days.

After a while he asks Ben: "What about your wife and children?"

Now it is Ben's turn to be silent.

"I'll have to make a plan," he says. "Sooner rather than later. I'm ashamed of the way I keep putting it off. Perhaps I could ask Bergh's permission to go."

"There hasn't really been an opportunity so far," Reitz comforts him half-heartedly.

"I try not to think about them," says Ben. "The idea that something might have happened to them I find almost unbearable!"

The unusual agitation in Ben's voice catches Reitz unawares. He is at a loss how to ease Ben's mind.

They carry on in silence. Ben is studying a plant.

"I dreamed last night," he says after a while.

Instantly Reitz is more acutely aware of the heavy autumnal sweetness in the air, like honey. In the cliffs behind them he hears the muted twittering of swifts preparing to migrate. Further along the bank finches are buzzing like bees and the endless zik-zik of the yellow weavers is audible in the background.

"I dreamed," says Ben, "of a woman."

Reitz is keen to hear and yet he does not want to hear. Ben's tone makes the hair in his neck stand on end. A damselfly hovers motionlessly above the surface of the water, upon which light and shadow glimmer in slow, alternating patterns.

"I dreamed," says Ben, hunched over the plant, "of a woman wearing a kind of feathered hat."

There is a prickling sensation in Reitz's armpits.

"I got the impression," says Ben, "that she was a kind of messenger."

"What kind of woman?" Reitz inquires cautiously.

"An ordinary woman," says Ben, "but when I embraced her, her body turned black. Burnished black. Black like ebony."

"I see," Reitz replies uncertainly.

"I'm rather ashamed," says Ben, taking care to keep his voice neutral, "to have to tell you what happened next. For when I entered that woman's body, it was blissful."

Involuntarily Reitz thinks of his dream of Bettie Loots.

"But that's not all," says Ben, still busying himself with the plant, not looking up. "For though the body of the woman was blissful, it was like the body of death. It was like entering death."

Reitz gives a muted cry.

"It was a temptation, Reitz, as I've never experienced before."

"What do you mean?" Reitz asks.

"It was a temptation to surrender to death. As if death was an escape and a release."

"Oh God," Reitz says softly.

For a while they both continue with their work. Ben is making a careful sketch of the root system of the plant—a Kaffir thistle—in his journal, and Reitz is contemplating the usefulness of the topographical notes with which he began a while ago.

He finds it difficult to concentrate. Ben's dream has upset him.

After a while he inquires bashfully: "The feathered hat of the woman in your dream, did the feathers shimmer in the sun—like the wings of a bird? Was it a little like the hat the farmer had seen in the dream he described to us?"

For the first time Ben looks up. There is an astonished look on his face.

"Yes," he says, "yes, it was!"

•

That evening around the fire Japie Stilgemoed says: "We have all learned a lot from this war."

"Learned, my *arse*!" says Gert Smal, "those who needed to learn something, didn't learn a thing! And those who *did* learn something," he continues bitterly, "are all dead: Danie Theron, Ignaas Ferreira, Isaac Malherbe, Gideon Scheepers. Good men. All dead."

"Kock is dead too, and Piet Joubert," Ben remarks laconically.

Gert Smal gives him a withering look.

"Time and again I was amazed by the duality of human nature," Japie Stilgemoed continues. "On one hand I longed desperately for an end to our suffering on commando, and on the other hand I was grateful that the war had given me experiences that normally wouldn't have crossed my path."

Reitz thinks: He speaks of the war as if it belongs to the distant past.

"I am grateful to God for subjecting me to these experiences," says Japie Stilgemoed. "My natural inclination is toward an orderly and calm existence, and God has deemed it necessary to cast me into a life for which I have no bent. To make of me a better, more tolerant person."

Japie Stilgemoed gazes at the flames intently. His dark eyes are wide, his hair bristles vigorously.

Kosie Rijpma sits with his head averted. His sombre eyes have none of the intensity of Japie Stilgemoed's gaze. He seems to remember things about which he would rather not elaborate. Reitz thinks: Of this man I know nothing, except that he treasures some verses written by a young woman called Bettie Loots.

Gert Smal tosses a log onto the fire and says: "Who learned anything? Did Kock learn anything at Elandslaagte? Did Piet Joubert learn anything? Did Cronjé, the turd, learn anything? Lukas Meyer at Talana? Snyman at Donkerhoek? Prinsloo in the Brandwater basin? My *arse*! They didn't learn a *thing*! Perhaps old Maroela Erasmus and his brother learned something once they were forced to return to the field as ordinary burghers!" he adds scornfully.

No one makes any reply. Reitz recalls having seen Maroela with his swarthy complexion fleetingly at the beginning of the war. Clad in a black tailcoat and tophat.

"Everyone makes mistakes, Neef Gert," Willem says. "But in God's great plan nothing happens without a purpose."

"God's plan," Kosie Rijpma says bitterly. "I have yet to be convinced that God is the benevolent Father we think He is, who cares about the fate of each earthly creature."

"Neef Kosie!" Willem cries, distraught. "Mind what you are saying! We dare not judge God from our flawed human perspective!"

But Kosie just looks at him, and makes no effort to reply.

Reuben sits smoking his pipe. Seun's mouth hangs open as he sits beside Gert Smal, staring into the fire. Gert Smal is picking ticks from the coat of the dog at his feet and tossing them into the fire with a hissing sound. Young Abraham sits motionless as always, huddled close to Willem. Ezekiel crouches in the shadows. Now and again he steps forward to tend to the fire. Always on the alert in the shadows, ready to answer Gert Smal's questions.

"I'm a bitter man today," says Kosie Rijpma, "and I'll die a bitter man. I have seen things for which I cannot forgive God and my fellow-man."

A nightjar calls. A shooting star streaks across the sky. They are surrounded by the night, vast and aromatic.

Willem raises his hands as if to ward off danger. "Please, don't ever say those words in my presence again!" he cries.

●

The month of April. Winter is approaching. The veld has less of a joyous aspect. Darkness falls earlier and in the mornings day breaks later. The shadows stretch longer during the day, their colour more suffused. The grass yellows gradually; early in the morning it is heavy and wet with dew. Down at the river the deciduous poplars and willows are shedding their leaves. There is an imminent languor; the earth is spinning more slowly around her axis, Japie Stilgemoed remarks one morning.

That night Reitz dreams someone has died. Oom Sakkie? Tell me again, he says. Say it slowly. Repeat the names more slowly—it's confusing, I can't hear you, he says in his dream. He? And he too? All of them? How is that possible?

His uncle, Oom Sakkie, too. But his Oom Sakkie passed away long before the war, he remembers when he wakes.

The next morning at the river he tells Ben that he thinks Japie Stilgemoed is right when he says books have been his salvation. In their case, says Reitz, their salvation has been in their field work and their journals. If not for those, he says, he would have lost his mind long ago. And Ben says: Yes, it is true, the journals have sustained us. And each continues with what he is doing—Ben studying a cocoon and Reitz drawing a small topographical map of their immediate surroundings, on which he has already begun to indicate the most distinctive geological features. He works at it when he is not hunting for fossils lower down the riverbank.

After they have worked in silence for a while, Reitz remarks that today, for some reason, his thoughts keep turning to everything they have experienced so far. He asks whether Ben remembers the day Daan Verhoef's son died. Ben remembers. That day he knew he never wanted to hear a man cry like that again, says Reitz.

They agree that Allesverloren and Skeurbuikhoogte were dreadful, but that they hope never again to experience a battle like the one at Droogleegte.

"If the course of the war could have been foreseen—how many of us would have decided that the price was too high?" Ben asks thoughtfully. "Apart from the diehards, of course—those for whom no price is ever too high."

"There are images I cannot banish from my thoughts today," says Reitz. "Things I have not thought of for months."

Ben, the little cocoon in his hand, stares fixedly ahead.

"All the dead," says Reitz. "Who could have imagined the extent of the slaughter?" he continues, half in wonderment. "My good friend Frikkie Mostert bayoneted at Elandslaagte. Frank Oosthuizen with a bullet through the heart at Donkerhoek, Wynand de Lange with a bullet through both lungs. Dewald Retief also died that day. I'll never forget how Jan Jokes Willemse rocked back and forth, his head on his knees, before he died. And Theo Vos's prolonged suffering at Allesverloren."

Ben has remained so motionless that Reitz cries out: "Your wife and children! Your brothers! Oh Lord, Ben," he cries full of remorse, "It wasn't my intention to make it harder for you!"

After a while Ben says: "We mustn't lose hope." His face looks older, broader, milder. "Even if it should all have been in vain." He looks at the cocoon he is studying. "And I believe it has been," he says. "I believe it has all been in vain. And today I regret," he says, "not laying down arms and swearing the British oath. At least I would have been assured of my family's safety."

•

That evening around the fire Japie Stilgemoed also speaks pensively about those who have died and the horror of the battlefield.

He tells the story of two burghers who drowned one freezing night when they had to cross the Skeerpoort River in haste. Their absence was noted only the following morning. Some of the men returned and found their bodies washed up on the riverbank. Those two dead were different from those killed on the battlefield, he says.

"They lay there so rigidly," says Japie Stilgemoed, "so cold and indifferent. So devoid of pity."

"Pity for whom?" Ben asks softly.

"For the living," Japie Stilgemoed replies.

Reitz remembers an evening when they laid the day's casualties on the sand of a riverbed, placed the wounded on their horses so that they could get away, and hollowed out the earth to sleep. He cannot remember exactly where it was.

For the first time Reuben speaks about the battle of Dwarsleersbos, where he lost his leg. The pain was bad, he says, but the thirst he suffered that day was worse. "God Almighty," he says, "pain is one thing, but thirst is the real devil of the battlefield. Never in my life will I forget the hell of that thirst." His rough, angular face seems more vulnerable to Reitz today than ever before.

For young Abraham's sake Willem, Ben and Reitz keep silent about Droogleegte—the last battle the four of them fought in together—where Abraham's brother died in his arms, his face and chest blown away.

But though Droogleegte is not mentioned directly, young Abraham seems disturbed by the talk, for he stirs restlessly and begins to utter incoherent words and phrases.

Betock, says young Abraham. Beworth, he says. And bibble, bobble. Prinking roost bequit. And betwiddle, he says. And gock, and guck, and groddle.

There now, Willem says soothingly. Steady, boy, there's nothing to fear. But Abraham's distress increases and Willem is forced to lead him away from the fire to his own shelter.

Gert Smal is so unusually quiet tonight that Reitz wonders if one or more unrepeatable episodes might not be the reason for his silence. He never speaks of his own life. Perhaps he, too, used to be part of the general's little commando?

And again Reitz wonders what lies behind the intensity of Kosie Rijpma's profound silence—what the source of that intensity could be. Though it is clear that Bettie Loots was a turning point for him, it must be *more* than Bettie Loots. It seems as if the thoughts awakened in him tonight might silence him for the rest of his life.

After everyone has gone to sleep, Reitz remains behind. He walks into the veld, away from camp. He is afraid that here in the night, under the radiant moon, he may not be able to ward off the emotions that are threatening to overwhelm him. He makes up his mind that he will go the next day. At nightfall he will return to the place where he lost her for good through his rash, foolish behaviour.

•

The next morning at the river Ben is quiet. He does not become engrossed in the study of some or other plant or insect the way he usually does. He sits with bowed head, his hands lying loosely in his lap. Reitz wonders if their conversations of the past two days are to blame.

After a while Ben says: "Since yesterday I've been unable to get the image of my wife and children out of my mind." He is silent for a while before he continues very softly: "I had another dream last night. I'm beginning to fear the worst."

Reitz listens with a heavy heart.

"When I think of the innocence of my children. When I think of my tenderhearted wife. When I think that they may come to harm—in whatever way," Ben says, "then I have to resist my feelings of anger and bitterness, lest they overwhelm and destroy me completely."

Reitz listens, alarmed.

"I have to agree with Kosie Rijpma," says Ben with a laugh. "For heaven knows—I don't know if one can still put one's trust in God."

Reitz says nothing. What can he say?

Two turtledoves call softly in a tree: coo-cuckoo—soft, liquid notes.

After a while Reitz says: "Did you also notice the way everyone spoke about the war as if it's been over for a long time?"

"It *is* over," says Ben.

"How can you be so sure?" Reitz asks.

"I sense it in everyone," says Ben. "No one speaks of what can be gained any more. Everyone speaks of what is at an end."

"What about the general?" Reitz asks.

"The general and his men are ignoring the signs for their own sake. But they know too."

In the late afternoon, just before sunset, Reitz goes to the river alone. He reassures Ben. I have no plans, he says.

He has not returned to the place on the riverbank where he met her since the day he nearly drowned. Seven or eight days ago. It feels like weeks.

The air is cooler here. The shadows deeper and longer. The cliff face glows faintly in the last rays of the setting sun. It is remarkably quiet. No bird calls, no barking baboons. Only a soft splash in the water now and then. There is a desolation about the place which frightens Reitz.

He sits down on the big rock. He looks at the branches of the tree from where she appeared. He gazes at the moving shadows on the water for a long time. Did she speak to him? Did he hear her say: The light? What did he *do* to her?

•

That evening around the fire young Abraham still appears unsettled. He's been like this all day, Willem says. And he still refuses to eat. Something is bothering him. Something has occurred to him.

"Perhaps last night's conversation has something to do with it," Ben says.

Abraham mutters ceaselessly. His eyes appear bewildered.

"Gornut," he says. And: "Beflict."

"Perhaps we should try to make sense of what he says," Ben remarks.

"Crazy. Not unlike a few others I know," Gert Smal observes wryly, spitting out the bit of wood he has been chewing on and staring pointedly into the distance.

Willem speaks soothingly: "There now, boy, we're safe here." He tries to coax Abraham into taking some food, but the young man averts his head resolutely.

Japie Stilgemoed looks on sympathetically, and it is clear from Kosie Rijpma's demeanour that he finds it difficult to look at young Abraham in his present condition.

Gert Smal seems annoyed that his tirade is constantly being interrupted. Tonight—as on every other night—he rages about the opportunities either passed up or bungled by the Boers. They should have had the foresight to cut off the railway lines at the onset of the war. They should have thrashed the Khakis on various occasions and chased them into the sea. They shouldn't have released a single prisoner. They shouldn't have burdened themselves with droves of women and children. That's no way to wage a war, he says.

"If Froneman and the Kaffirs could get away, why couldn't Cronjé? It's because of all those women!"

"I was told by eyewitnesses," begins Willem, "that General Cronjé conducted himself nobly during the battle—even though it resulted in his undoing. They say he sat beside his wife in the dry riverbed, holding her hand and comforting her. He cared for each of those women as if she was his very own sister."

"Women, my arse!" Gert Smal bursts out. "Sisters, my arse! Why were they there in the first place?"

Unperturbed, Willem continues. "They say the good general paused by a dying man to wipe the sweat off his brow. He even pressed a kiss to his lips—with the bullets all the while flying around the stretcher."

"My arse!" Gert Smal shouts. "If he'd paused to use his head instead, there would have been no need for him to go around kissing dying men!" He glares fiercely at the assembled company. "Kiss, my *arse*," he adds.

Willem remains undaunted. "They say he encouraged the hopeless and strengthened the faint-hearted and repeatedly urged the burghers to pray to God."

"My *arse!*" Gert Smal insists. "And did he expect God to clear up his mess?"

"Alas," Willem continues, "the throne of the Almighty was shrouded in darkness that day."

"Cronjé's *head* was shrouded in darkness," says Gert Smal. "Why couldn't one of his men have shot *him* by accident, instead of Ignaas Ferreira!"

"They say it was terrible to behold," says Japie Stilgemoed. "The horses fallen in the crossfire. The oxen prone, lowing pitifully. The wagons going up in flames. The pestilent stench of the rotting carcasses of horses and cattle corrupting the air. And along the entire Modder River, from Rondeval Drift to Paardeberg, under every bush and behind every rock lay the bodies of Khakis, wounded or shot dead, perished of hunger, of thirst or exposure to the icy nightwind."

"Khakis, my arse," is Gert Smal's only reaction.

"It was inhuman of Roberts," Japie Stilgemoed continues, "not to grant Cronjé a ceasefire to bury his dead."

"Roberts can go to hell," says Gert Smal. "His balls in a bully-beef tin."

"Even the bravest among the men must surely have thought the Lord Himself had taken issue with them that day," says Japie Stilgemoed.

"Cronjé," Willem says softly, reverently, "the lion of Africa."

"My arse," says Gert Smal. "The sheep of Africa!"

Upon which he begins to postulate how the Boers let off the English too lightly. No prisoners should have been taken—they should have been shot there and then. Every single bloody one of them. Without further ado. And Milner should have been the first to face the firing squad. And after him Kitchener. Followed by Roberts and French.

Turning at this point to look for Ezekiel in the shadows behind him, Gert Smal inquires: "When was it again that Kitchener proclaimed his devilish policy?"

"It was on the sixteenth of June 1900, Baas Gertjie," Ezekiel replies.

"That was our undoing," Gert Smal says bitterly. "Kitchener was an old wretch," he continues, "but Milner is the *true* devil. They should both," he says, "have been hanged by the balls early on."

"On Church Square in Pretoria," Reitz mutters to Ben.

"We behaved much too decently during this war," Gert Smal declaims.

"Blear," says young Abraham.

"I'm afraid he may not be able to sleep tonight," Willem says worriedly.

"Phlepping phlip," says young Abraham.

The others look at him uneasily.

"Yat," says young Abraham, his eyes rolling back, and: "Guck."

"He's said that before," says Kosie Rijpma, and Ben nods in agreement.

Gert Smal is still harping on about the Boers. It is only De Wet, it seems, who meets with his approval. All the others are cowards and handsuppers. De Wet managed to escape and make contact with De la Rey. De Wet played for time so that Botha and De la Rey could regroup. "De Wet knew when to use the sjambok," he says, looking pointedly in the direction of Reitz and Ben. "He showed deserters no mercy—he knew very well how to deal with them!"

Young Abraham begins to move around more and more restlessly. His arms flap out of control at his sides and his head lolls awkwardly from side to side.

Give him a drink, says Gert Smal impatiently. See if he won't lie down, Japie Stilgemoed suggests. Willem's eyes are pale as marbles; on his cheeks two growing red spots bear witness to his apprehension.

Young Abraham's teeth begin to chatter slightly.

Today we'll have to call on Oompie, God help us, Reitz thinks.

"Come, Ezekiel, come old Kaffir," Gert Smal says impatiently, "bring your potions," and he snaps his fingers at the black man.

Ezekiel emerges from the shadows. He fills a tin mug with water. He crouches beside the fire and takes from the folds of his blanket a small leather pouch. He pours a small quantity of a powdery substance into the mug and stirs the mixture slowly with a spoon.

Then he goes across to Abraham and holds out the mug to him. Head bowed, subservient, he stands before him, the mug in one hand, his other hand supporting the outstretched one.

At first Abraham continues to fidget; he seems unaware of Ezekiel's presence. But after a while he quietens down and looks long and intently at the black man still standing motionlessly before him with downcast eyes. Then he takes the mug and drinks its contents.

Soundlessly Ezekiel returns to his usual place outside the circle of the firelight.

A short while later young Abraham relaxes visibly. His arms hang loose at his sides, the bewildered look vanishes from his eyes. Presently Willem takes him to his shelter, young Abraham making no effort to resist.

"Kaffir medicine," Gert Smal says triumphantly. "But it *works!*"

"Clearly not the first time they've put it to good use," Ben says to Reitz laconically.

Early the next morning, before there is any sign of life or movement in the camp, Reitz is awakened by a strange sound. Like muted cries, like pitiful wailing.

He scrambles out of his shelter, in time to see Gert Smal crawling from his own shelter on all fours, whimpering.

"Gert!" Reitz addresses him. "What's the matter?"

Gert Smal does not recognise him. He is moaning incoherently, rocking back and forth on his knees. His shoulders are hunched, his hands clenched between his thighs.

"Gert!" Reitz addresses him again. "It's *me!*"

Only then does Gert Smal come to his senses. A moment longer he appears dazed before he suddenly recognises Reitz. He seems embarrassed but also relieved. He gets to his feet swiftly, mutters brusquely: "Bad dream," and crawls back into his shelter.

•

Two days later Blackpiet Petoors and Red Herman arrive at camp early in the morning. First they confer with Gert Smal urgently, their heads together conspiratorially. Then Reitz and Ben are summoned. They have brought instructions from the general for the three of them: Reitz, Ben and Gert Smal. Colonel Davenport and his regiment are heading for the Free State from the direction of Middelburg. They will be passing between two solitary koppies about a day's ride from there. The three of them have orders to lie in wait for the English at the first koppie—the taller of the two—and to fire at the English column, creating a diversion. In the ensuing confusion they—General Bergh and his commando— will launch a surprise attack on the Khakis from the opposite koppie. The first koppie is clearly visible—a landmark in the region.

They will be safe on the koppie, Blackpiet Petoors assures them, for the summit is strewn with rocks that afford good shelter. The Khakis will have no idea that they are being observed.

A map showing Davenport's supposed route, the two isolated koppies and the Orange River—northwest from here—is spread on the flat rock. The koppies are close to the Free State border. A while later the two depart.

There you have it, Reitz, says Ben, at last our services are being put to use—but as for our capabilities, of that I'm not so sure.

CHAPTER 11

They depart early the next morning: Ben, Reitz, Gert Smal and the dog with the yellow eyes. Reitz wonders if they should take their journals. Ben says they will probably not get much time for making notes. We'll leave them here, he says. If all goes well, we'll be back tomorrow. Reitz hesitates. Ben says: We'll take the chance.

They shake hands solemnly with everyone at camp. Willem says: God bless and keep you. Japie Stilgemoed says: May you soon be back with us safely. Reitz notices that Gert Smal presses Seun's round head to his chest for a moment.

It is a clear day, with few clouds. They have not been on horseback for a long time. The cool morning air is pleasant on Reitz's cheeks. He is grateful for a chance to get out of camp at last, even for a day or two. The plan is to move in a northwesterly direction for an hour or three before turning sharp west and continuing in that direction until they reach the koppie where they are to wait for Davenport.

They dismount at a clump of trees beside a small stream. They water the horses, rest in the shade. Ben looks around with interest. He points out the kaffir copper butterfly and the scavenger beetle, the sand beetle, the red-breasted jackal buzzard. Somewhere in the distance they hear a quail's protracted cry: keeoo-keeoo. Gert Smal speaks little. He seems nervous. He chews at his thumbnail and studies the map.

During the course of the day they dismount a few more times, in the vicinity of a spring or stream, if possible, to water the horses. Preferably in the shade, for the day is growing progressively hotter.

Reitz and Ben show a keen interest in their surroundings. Gert Smal sits on his own, studies the map, scarcely speaks to them. The dog with the yellow eyes lies beside him in the shade. Where he is able, Reitz inspects the successive soil layers in the banks of rivulets or streams. Wherever he goes, he is always on the lookout for an unusual stone, for unusual rock formations, for fossils. During the battle of Allesverloren he caught sight of a well-preserved fossil as he was lying next to an ant hill. He keeps this in his small trunk. He will send it away for identification as soon as the war is over. He is proud of this discovery; it pleased him greatly to pick it up on the battlefield.

They rest for short periods only. Gert Smal is impatient. He has come along to keep an eye on us, Reitz remarks in an undertone. Or we on him, Ben says. He seems ill at ease, says Reitz.

Gradually the landscape changes. It opens up as rocks and low scrub make way for taller grass and thorn trees, interspersed with rocky outcrops. Ben points out an unusual shrub here, a small mammal there. Guinea fowl in the grass, and even the rare Stanley bustard in the distance. Once the spoor of a jackal. Large ant hills. A blackshouldered kite circling overhead.

"Daggabush," Ben points out, "Gert Smal's favourite weed." They laugh.

"Drift," says Reitz, "place where you cross a river."

"Dog," says Ben, "man's best friend."

"Dearest," says Reitz, "most beloved person."

"Dobba," says Ben, "bitter veld plant."

"Death," says Reitz, "the end of life."

"Death-cup," says Ben, "a poisonous mushroom."

"Dead end," says Reitz, "the end of the road."

"Deathwatch beetle," says Ben, "small beetle that lives in old wood."

"Death shadow," says Reitz, "shadow cast by death."

"Goodness, Reitz," says Ben, "why so sombre today?"

"Dead right," says Reitz, "actually I'm dead right today, Ben." And, indeed, he seems to have shaken off his unease and heavy-heartedness of the recent past.

Gert Smal rides ahead, keeping a distance between them. As the day progresses, he grows more restless, consults the map more often.

Towards afternoon they come to a range of low hills that have been lying ahead of them in a semicircle. As soon as they pass through the narrow gap, they find themselves on a vast, magnificent expanse of grassland scattered with small trees. From here they have a view of the first koppie in the distance—a conspicuous landmark in the area.

As the koppie gradually looms larger, they note that the ascent will be easy, and the rocky summit will afford good shelter. Blackpiet had been right. It does not seem as if their assignment will be met by any hindrances.

When they are about a twenty-minute ride from the koppie, they pass a series of low outcrops to their left—some no more than a pile of loose boulders—with a deep donga directly ahead.

As they approach the donga, Gert Smal starts looking over his shoulder every so often. The dog begins to whine softly. Then, without warning, Gert Smal digs his heels into his horse's flanks. The mare shoots forward; Reitz and Ben have a hard time keeping up—there has been no time for questions.

On the edge of the large donga Gert Smal reins in his horse slightly to negotiate the steep slope. Reitz and Ben are nearly on top of him.

As Gert Smal is about to descend, Reitz hears the first shots. Gert Smal's horse takes a hit, and so does Gert Smal. The next bullet hits Reitz in the thigh. Desperately he tries to steer his horse down the slope in time. Ben is behind him. He hears more shots.

Ahead of Reitz, Gert Smal falls off his horse. The mare tries to scramble up the opposite bank. Blood is spurting from her flank. Halfway up the slope she keels over.

His own horse neighs and staggers to its feet. There is dust and milling about. Ben's horse whinnies as it gallops past Reitz and scales the opposite bank of the donga.

When Reitz looks round, he sees Ben lying on his stomach some way behind him. Ahead of him, halfway up the slope, Gert Smal is lying on his back.

Reitz jumps off his horse. The firing has stopped. There is a deathly silence in the direction from which it came. Apart from the buzzing in his ears, it is suddenly unnaturally quiet.

Ducking and limping, he runs to Ben.

Ben! he cries.

A large pool of blood has started spreading under Ben. Reitz rolls him carefully onto his side. Then onto his back. His pulse is feeble, but Ben is alive. He has been severely wounded in the neck and in the shoulder, just below the collarbone.

Ben! he calls softly. Can you hear me?

Ben shows no reaction. Reitz takes off his jacket, puts it under Ben's head. He takes off his shirt, rips out the sleeves and tears them into strips. With these bandages he tries his best to stop the bleeding. As Ben is bleeding profusely, it is an almost impossible task. He is pale and cold. At the same time Reitz is trying to staunch the bleeding in his own leg.

For the time being Reitz leaves Gert Smal lying on the opposite slope.

The sun is still hot. He has to get Ben into the shade. Higher up the bank is a ledge, with a few sparse shrubs that will offer some shelter. Carefully Reitz places his hands under Ben's arms. Slowly, laboriously, he drags him up the bank.

The ledge is wide enough. He makes Ben as comfortable as possible in the meagre shade. He wipes Ben's face with a piece of cloth. He tries to get him to swallow some tepid water from his drinking bottle. He himself takes only a few sips of the precious liquid.

Ben's eyes are half open. He does not seem to see Reitz. His breathing is shallow and uneven. His brow is cold.

Reitz rips handfuls of dry grass from the tufts that grow on the bank and uses them, along with the bandages torn from his shirt, to try and stop the bleeding.

He watches over Ben. He watches his slightest movement. He talks to him. He tries to make him take some water. From time to time Ben groans softly. The blood is no longer spurting, but the bandages are saturated.

The pain in Reitz's leg is severe. His horse seems to have wandered off along the donga. He has no time to look for it now.

When the sun begins to set, he moves down the slope with difficulty.

There is nothing he can do for Gert Smal on the opposite bank. There is a round bullet hole in the side of his head. His eyes are open but expressionless. His mouth is fixed in a sneer. His upper lip is withdrawn in a grimace exposing the eye teeth. Blood from his nose and mouth have congealed under his head. Blowflies are caked on his face. The day has been hot.

He takes Gert Smal by the feet and drags him a short distance down the slope. He leaves him lying in a natural inlet in the bank, formed by two vertical earth walls. It takes a great effort to retrieve Gert Smal's bandolier. He takes the compass, but cannot find the map. He looks for something to cover Gert Smal's face, for he has nothing with him that he can use. He piles tufts of grass, loose leaves and twigs on the dead man— uncanny to be covering Gert Smal's face like that. Using first his hands and later a sizable rock, he scrapes together loose sand and clods and heaps them over Gert Smal. He tries to cover the body as best he can. It is hard work, for the soil is dry, he is in pain and every now and then he pauses to see if Ben is still lying undisturbed on the opposite bank. It takes Reitz a long time to cover the dead man. Then he collects every large stone in the vicinity that he is able to carry, and stacks it on the scant mound. Anything that will stop scavengers from unearthing the body. Pain and exhaustion cause him to rest frequently. At last the task is completed.

Goodbye, Gert, he says. Rest in peace.

There is no sign of the dog with the yellow eyes.

He leaves the dead horse lying further up the slope.

Vultures are circling in the sky overhead and the crows never let up their brazen clamouring: kraa-kraa.

He is anxious to return to Ben.

The sun goes down. Darkness falls. The first stars appear. The moon rises. A plover calls. Later a jackal howls. Scavengers begin to descend on the dead horse. Ben, says Reitz, don't give up. Ben's eyes look shallow and glazed.

Reitz props himself on the rocky slope beside Ben. It is cold. Should he build a fire? Devise a shelter from the scant branches? He is numb with pain and cold. He does not sleep, but dozes off for brief periods.

There are other night sounds. A major scavenging feast at the horse's carcass higher up.

Ben's eyes are half open, but unseeing. His eyeballs gleam white in the moonlight.

The day has been hot; the night is cold. Reitz puts his jacket over Ben. He presses himself up against the earth wall. He hopes the grass clumps will provide some warmth.

The gluttonous scavenger party on the opposite bank carries on all night.

The earth before sunrise is cold and inhospitable. The opposite bank etched darkly against the blanched sky. In the early hours before dawn tears streak Reitz's cheeks. Damn, he says. Damn it all.

The sun comes up. Ben is restless, delirious. He cannot swallow any water, because of the wound in his neck. Reitz moistens Ben's lips; he carefully pours a little water into the corner of his mouth. His own leg aches unbearably. The day grows hot. There is a continuous stream of ants.

Reitz speaks to Ben ceaselessly, to stop him from slipping away. Ben, he says, it won't be long now. He speaks to Ben of rocks. He speaks of mountains. He grasps at any scrap of information presenting itself, often no more than a mere fancy. Ben shows no reaction; his breathing comes shallow and fast.

The day grows hotter. The nocturnal animals have long since scurried into hiding. There are vultures and crows on the carcass on the other side. For brief moments Reitz drifts off in the soaring heat. He has feverish but lucid dreams. A name comes to him—in wonderment he exclaims: Bettie Loots. On the opposite bank he sees a lion with a huge mane.

Ben's mouth is dry and caked with dust. The bandages are sticky. There are ants and blowflies. Now and then Reitz weeps a little. A few futile, dry tears. Ben, he says.

Reitz thinks he hears Ezekiel's voice. He is overcome with joy. Do you hear it, Ben, he asks—Ezekiel's voice? He thinks he hears Ben say: Ezekiel is the angel of death, is he not?

He is instantly awake. He sits up. Ben? he asks anxiously. He feels Ben's forehead. Ben's limbs are racked with spasms. His hands are ice-cold and clammy. His eyes threaten to roll back. He convulses as if he is having a fit. Reitz moistens his lips and brow with a piece of cloth.

Ben? he says. Ben seems to be struggling for breath. Reitz tries to lift him into a sitting position. His body is rigid and icy.

Please, Lord, Reitz prays, in God's name.

Ben is deathly pale. Blue around the eyes and mouth. From time to time his body stiffens, his limbs jerk, a rattle comes out of his throat.

Reitz holds him in his arms. Please, he prays, please.

He talks to Ben; he moistens his forehead; he talks incessantly. Don't give up, Ben, he says, it won't be long now. We're only a day's journey from camp. Ben! he shouts fearfully. Then he prays: Please, God, please. Ben, he says, we're going back to fetch the journals. Then he prays: God, please send someone.

Towards late afternoon Ben is calmer, his breathing less laboured. Reitz lays him down carefully, placing the jacket under his head. Reitz dozes off for brief moments. He sees Gert Smal stir in his shallow grave on the opposite slope. The earth and the stones move as Gert Smal stirs and turns underneath. Amazed, Reitz says to Ben: I think Gert Smal is trying to tell us something. I think he's trying to warn us.

As the sun begins to set, the eager yelps of scavengers fill the air.

Reitz listens attentively, for he thinks he can hear women's voices.

With great effort, he clambers to the top of the embankment and staggers to his feet.

Some distance away he sees two women sitting in a horse-drawn cart.

He raises his arm and waves. One of the women jumps down, comes running. She shouts something over her shoulder, but her words are lost.

She slithers down the slope on her behind.

With great difficulty Reitz and the two women manage to lift Ben onto the cart. Reitz sits in the front, beside the woman who is holding the reins. In the back of the cart Ben lies with his head in the other woman's lap. She has removed her bonnet; her hair is red.

The woman next to Reitz does not speak to him. He slumps in the seat beside her. Occasionally she glances at him, concerned, or over her shoulder at Ben.

Reitz cannot utter a word. Now and then he has a shivering fit. The woman says: It's not far now. What is she saying? He does not know what she means.

Along the way he throws up twice. Nothing comes out. There is nothing in his stomach.

After what feels like hours they cross a wide, shallow drift. There are high banks on either side.

When they arrive at the homestead, an older woman and two young girls come through the back door.

They help Reitz across the cool threshold. His shoulders shake with cold or emotion, he cannot tell which.

He is made to lie down on a cool bed. The red-haired woman cleans the wound on his leg.

Her eyes are cool as grapes, but he notices a great sadness in them.

It's not my real name, she says, but everyone calls me Niggie.

•

The two women stopped when they saw the vultures circling.

Jeremiah had heard the shots the day before and they went to investigate.

They have not heard of any Khakis in these parts recently.

The Khakis burned down part of the house earlier that year. They were searching for Boers. By the grace of God, Niggie says, a violent thunderstorm erupted and the English left before they could conclude their evil mission. The people on the neighbouring farm weren't so lucky. Everything was razed to the ground. They were taken away, to camp.

For a while the women hid in a kloof nearby before returning to the house. God alone knows how they survived, Niggie says.

The farm belongs to Anna Baines and her husband, Johannes. He is away on commando. Tante is Anna's aunt, her late mother's sister. The two girls are Anna's nieces—Lena is the elder, Sussie the younger. Their mother, Anna's only sister, died recently after a long illness, Niggie tells them. Niggie herself is Anna's second cousin. Niggie, Anna and Tante originally come from the Cape Colony, Johannes is a Free Stater. The only black help on the farm is Jeremiah and his wife, Betta.

Anna and her sister were unreconciled right up to her sister's death, Niggie says. Anna is filled with remorse. She feels she should have been less unyielding.

Anna doesn't think she will ever see her husband again, Niggie says. He is on commando somewhere. God help her. A woman can't live like that. With such uncertainty.

Anna is more or less Reitz's age. She has dark hair and a direct gaze.

Niggie is younger than Anna, possibly in her late thirties.

After a day Reitz is able to sit up and join the women at the supper table. He marvels at Niggie's complexion by candlelight, her rich, gleaming hair, her glistening but sorrowful eyes, and the way in which the light plays upon her frock, shimmering green like water quartz.

By day he watches over Ben when Niggie is busy elsewhere.

For the first few days Ben's condition is critical. Then it seems he will survive, but not without permanent damage.

God help him, says Niggie, it doesn't look as if he'll ever speak again.

CHAPTER 12

During these first days, when Ben's condition is critical, Reitz and Niggie take turns to watch over him. Niggie and Tante treat him with all the remedies available to them. Niggie was trained as a nurse and Tante has knowledge of medicinal herbs, and just as well, for where would they get hold of a doctor in these days? Ben is weak. He has sustained serious injuries to the neck and shoulder. He has lost a lot of blood. He is hardly able to swallow.

It's a wonder he survived at all, Niggie says.

In the evenings, at their devotions, Tante prays for the gravely injured man's speedy recovery. We place his life in Your hands, she prays. Tears come to Reitz's eyes. During the prayer he notices Anna staring straight ahead with stark, open eyes. She is unmoved, Reitz thinks.

By day Reitz sits at Ben's side. Niggie watches over him at night. She tells Reitz: Be sure to sleep. You're going to need all your strength later.

Reitz sits at Ben's bedside in the darkened room and speaks to him softly. Do you know where we are, Ben? he asks. Do you know that we're back in the Free State? Do you know what happened? Ben lies motionless. Niggie enters, or stands at the wash stand with a basin of water in her hands. Don't ask him questions, she says. He can't answer you. Tell him what happened. He'll hear what you're saying.

Little by little, step by step, he covers the difficult terrain with Ben.

He says: Ben, do you remember the morning we left with Gert Smal? We'd received our orders from General Bergh. We were to ambush Colonel Davenport at the first of the two koppies. We were to create a diversion. Red Herman and Blackpiet Petoors had brought the general's message.

Ben's complexion is waxen, like that of a dead man. His throat is bandaged with clean strips torn from sheets; he is swathed like a corpse. Reitz can hardly bear to look at him.

But he cannot stop talking to him. He cannot help himself. He brings his head close to Ben's face and speaks urgently in his ear. In this way he can remain sane. And in this way he keeps Ben alive, so that he does not slip into the nebulous realm.

Niggie says: God help him—the opposite shore is beckoning. I have attended many deathbeds. I can see when someone is struggling.

Reitz continues (with greater urgency): Ben, do you remember the river? You and I went there every day. We're going back. Do you remember the camp? Ezekiel built the fire at night and Japie Stilgemoed spoke at length of all that had befallen him. He almost drove me out of my mind. Ben?

Now and then Ben's eyelids flicker, as if he is on the verge of breaking through to consciousness.

Reitz says: We were led into an ambush. We came under fire. Gert Smal is dead. I thought you were dead too. I was also wounded, but not as seriously as you. I'm grateful that you're alive. The women found us just in time.

One morning Ben opens his eyes. At first he looks at Reitz as if he cannot quite place him, but after he has examined him at length, recognition dawns in his eyes.

Reitz is moved; for a few moments he holds Ben's hand in his own. As if to welcome him back after a long absence.

•

While Reitz's leg is mending, he moves around the house self-consciously. He often sits on the stoep. He is ill at ease in the presence of the women.

The house is large and solid with high wooden ceilings. The floor-boards creak. Reitz sleeps on a narrow bed in a small outside room with a cement floor off the side stoep. The room also contains a wash stand, wash basin and jug. The orderly hand of a woman is evident. Ben's room is inside the house, at the end of the passage, opposite Anna's room. The passage is wide and dark, with family portraits. Reitz dare not look at them.

At the front of the house, on either side of the wide steps leading up to the stoep, stand two giant cypresses. The large front garden—ruined and neglected—ends in a low stone wall. Beyond the stone wall is a long drive flanked by poplars. At the side of the house is the rose garden. This is separated from the large orchard by another low stone wall. At the back, a little way from the house, is a dam.

The pantry, the outside rooms and most of the dairy were damaged by the flames the day the Khakis tried to burn the house. They broke a number of windows—smashed them with their rifle butts, Niggie says, and looted most of the silver and other family heirlooms. They killed what had remained of the poultry. Luckily they left before they could do more damage. The bloody little corporal in charge was jumpy, she says, and to the man they were terrified of the thunderstorm.

They came into the front garden that day, horses and all, trampling everything deliberately, but Anna didn't say a word. By the grace of God, says Niggie, they didn't destroy her rose garden, for she doesn't know what Anna might have done *then*.

The cattle and sheep are long gone—claimed by various commandos and the Khakis. Only two cows are hidden in a copse not far away, near the kloof where they themselves hid for a while after the English had left here. And Anna buried a few of her valuables there a long time ago.

In the meantime Jeremiah has planted a vegetable garden at the first spring; sometimes he shoots something for the pot and by God's grace they still have some flour, and a few bags of mealies that they hid long ago, but there is no more sugar or tea or coffee. But they don't complain, Niggie says, for compared with the poor women in the camps, their situation is still fortunate.

•

After a few more days Ben can sit up in bed. He is still too weak to walk. Anna cooks a thin broth and Niggie feeds Ben one spoonful at a time, but it is a painfully slow process because of the severity of the injuries to his throat. Niggie says repeatedly: It's a wonder he survived. Ben lies with his eyes closed for long periods. Reitz talks to him. He starts at the beginning again. He tells him how they ended up here. He speaks of the camp. He speaks of the river. Ben nods weakly. Reitz tells him how they followed the general's instructions and left with Gert Smal early in the morning. He explains how towards afternoon shots suddenly rang out, and that Gert Smal is dead. Ben frowns—when he hears they were fired upon, he always frowns.

Perhaps he has lost his memory, Niggie says, from the shock.

In his small room Reitz dreams at night with great urgency. He dreams his older brother who died young is waiting for him outside in the veld, his back turned to Reitz. On his head is a strange hat. He dreams he sees his late father—oh, so clearly! He is wearing a grey suit—his Sunday best—and he is sitting proud and erect. But his hands are ice-cold. To his dismay Reitz cannot recall his father's words to him the next morning.

Women come to him in his dreams—Bettie Loots, his late mother, strange women. (But *she* is gone.) At times his dreams are as violent as if he is being flung against a wall, his arms thrust out as if warding off an attack.

In the early morning the birds are audible over a great distance. First the soft, distant call of a dove: coo-cuckoo. As if to circumscribe the expanse surrounding them. Then a bird calls near his window: chirp-chirp, and more shrilly: tirri-tirr.

It is cooler by day, and in the evenings there is a noticeable chill in the air.

Reitz begins to take short walks. If only Ben was well. If only he would recover fully. If only he could speak again.

The women in the camps, Niggie says, God help them.

•

A few days later Ben is on his feet. He is painfully thin and weak; he moves slowly, like an old man. For a short while each day he sits on the front stoep. He sits in silence, for he cannot speak. Reitz and Niggie sit with him. She peels potatoes, or sews, and she talks.

"I've been present at many deathbeds during these past few months," she says. "I've had to witness too much suffering."

When Reitz is alone with Ben, outside on the stoep or sitting beside his bed in the darkened room, he speaks to him incessantly.

Sometimes Ben lies with his eyes closed, sometimes he stares at a spot on the opposite wall, sometimes his gaze is fixed on Reitz. Gradually he begins to react more. He nods slowly, or tries to smile, or sometimes, with great effort, forms soundless words with his mouth. Then Reitz holds his ear close to Ben's lips, but there is no distinguishable sound, for Ben cannot even utter a whisper.

Every time Reitz mentions how they were fired upon, Ben frowns and shakes his head. He clearly has no recollection of it.

Sometimes Reitz sits on the stoep alone, or takes short walks in the garden or the veld—for the time being it is all his injured leg will allow. The landscape is somewhat flatter here, he notices, there is more grass, the rocky outcrops are smaller—more scattered, but geologically the terrain broadly resembles that of the camp.

By day he gradually begins to help with chores in and around the house. He allows himself to take comfort in the women's daily bustle. He keeps wishing, however, that he had his journal. He misses the daily routine of jotting down the details of his surroundings.

In a dream he sees Oompie swim up a waterfall, smooth as an otter. He often dreams of Gert Smal, always performing some or other little task, a sneer on his face, often in the proximity of his own shallow grave. He dreams of different shelters—variations of their shelters at camp. He dreams his teeth crumble in his mouth. A hole appears above his eyebrow, and caves in.

He wakes up very early in the morning. His first thoughts are always: If only Ben could speak again. If only Ben could be himself again.

•

With a chair drawn close to Ben's bed, or seated next to Ben on the stoep, Reitz speaks to him softly and urgently. He feels more at ease when Niggie is not there.

Niggie brings Ben a slate and a piece of chalk.

Reitz asks: "Ben, do you remember anything of what happened?"

Slowly Ben writes: *Gert Smal.*

Reitz says: "Gert Smal is dead, Ben. He was shot. I don't know what happened. I can't get to the bottom of it. There was never any sign of anybody on horseback. There was hardly any cover in the area—it was so open. Gert Smal suddenly galloped ahead. The next moment I heard shots. It was as if *we* had been ambushed—not they: whoever they might have been. It happened so quickly. I saw Gert Smal fall. I was terrified, Ben. I thought you were dead too, the way you lay on your stomach without moving. Gert Smal had been shot in the head. Poor fellow."

Ben frowns. He nods slowly. He stares straight ahead for a long time before he turns his gaze back to Reitz.

Reitz continues. "I buried him later," he says. "Actually, I heaped stones on top of him. I had nothing to wrap him in. Not even something to cover his face. So I used leaves and grass. It was strange to have to throw clods on him like that. Poor Gert Smal. Poor bugger."

Ben frowns. He rocks slowly back and forth. As if the rhythmic movement might help him remember.

"I saw Gert Smal stir in his grave in the clear light of day," Reitz says with a little laugh. "I must have been delirious, for I saw him pushing up the soil like a mole. I thought he was trying to tell us something. Perhaps he was—perhaps he knew who had been lying in wait for us. Whoever it had been, fortunately they didn't come back. Merciful heavens, Ben, I don't *understand*! We'll probably never know who it was."

Niggie comes to see if everything is in order. When she has left, they sit in silence for a while.

"At night they feasted on his horse—the scavengers," Reitz says after a while. "Jackal and such, I couldn't really see in the dark—you would have been able to identify them. They made an unearthly racket." Reitz shudders; a shiver runs through him at the memory.

"I feared for your life all the time, Ben," he says. "I thought you weren't going to make it. If it hadn't been for the women. I don't even want to think about it. That a beautiful day like that could take such an appalling turn!"

Ben rocks slowly and rhythmically—pensively—and looks at Reitz as if he does not completely understand what had caused the appalling nature of the day.

"But thank God, Ben," says Reitz, "you're alive! You will recover, you'll see. We're going back to camp—our journals are still there. It's a good thing we didn't bring them along—our horses would have gone off with them."

He has second thoughts. Perhaps he should not have mentioned the journals at this point. He lowers his voice: "Ben, don't lose hope. The women are looking after us well. It seems they too have suffered."

Ben nods. As if he believes Reitz, without knowing what he is talking about. Reitz talks. He talks for both of them. He talks to ward off his own painful feelings. He talks because he is afraid of Ben's amiable but defeated silence. To see Ben like this—without speech, without resolve, without defences!

Sometimes Niggie comes out and stands on the stoep. She gazes at the garden for a long time without speaking. Or she stands in the bedroom doorway. Even in the darkened room her eyes glimmer a transparent green. At times it looks as if she has been crying. Come, she says, let Ben rest for a while. It will help him recover sooner.

She holds the door for him and Reitz moves past her akwardly.

Every day it surprises him anew how far they were removed from the healing sphere of women.

·

In the evenings around the table it is mainly Niggie who does the talking. Tante listens politely and makes a comment now and then. She is a smallish woman with an attractive, sympathetic face. It is mostly she who sees to the children's needs; she treats them both with a caring tenderness. Especially Sussie, the youngest, is clearly greatly attached to Tante.

By candlelight Niggie's hair is a reddish bronze. Her skin is like thick white milk. Under her skin the rich blue veins are clearly visible. When she laughs, her small white teeth show in a slightly rounded curve. Her body is firm, her breasts full, her movements languorous. The sadness in her eyes is emphasised by the slight downward pull of their outer corners.

Some evenings Niggie wears a frock the colour of watermelon or ripe sweet melon, at other times the one that shimmers like water quartz in the flickering light. Her eyes glimmer and her skin glows, and although the frocks are not new, they do not detract from her appearance. She laughs and talks with animated gestures. Anna looks on, mostly in silence, but always indulgently.

Anna is slighter, smaller than Niggie. Her cheeks are pale. She is usually dressed in black. Her heavy dark hair shows traces of grey. She does not talk much, but when she does speak, it is always considered and to the point. Her eyes are dark; there are deep lines around her mouth. Her gaze is steady and appraising.

Reitz finds the girls touching. He marvels at the bright innocence of their eyes, the softness of their skins, their vulnerability.

The little one is able to show her feelings, Niggie says (sitting on the stoep with Reitz and Ben), but the older one, God help her—she has terrible nightmares; she tries too hard not to show her feelings. And their mother so recently dead.

Anna has no children, Niggie continues. She lost two young children. She never talks about it, but it's a great sadness in her life.

Jeremiah and Betta attend the family's evening devotions. They sit on the floor in a corner of the dining room. Jeremiah has a broad, grave face. Betta always keeps her eyes averted. In her youth she must have been a strong, good-looking woman.

The blacks have lost everything, Niggie tells them. They are the only two left on the farm. Their sons went on commando with the men. Their youngest child died last year. The poor people. Where can they go? she asks. And they are loyal unto death.

At times during the day when Reitz sees Jeremiah in the distance, he thinks for a moment that it is Ezekiel. Then his heart leaps with glad recognition. He tries to find out from Jeremiah whether he knows Ezekiel. But no matter how carefully he describes and explains, Jeremiah shakes his head long before Reitz has finished. He knows only the people on the neighbouring farms, he says. Reitz does not know whether Jeremiah is hostile by nature or whether he is simply unwilling to speak to some-one he does not know and whom he regards as a stranger.

Reitz uses a small calendar that belongs to Niggie to keep track of the days since he and Ben left the camp. On the first page of his journal was his own handwritten calendar, on which he used to mark off all the tedious, dragging days, weeks and months of the war. But the journal and the tin trunk were left behind at the camp.

They left the camp on the tenth of April. They have been here for nearly ten days.

CHAPTER 13

By day Reitz and Niggie sit on the front stoep with Ben. They look out over the ruined front garden at the low ridges on the horizon.

Niggie speaks; they listen. "Anna has always taken great pride in her garden," she says, "but after the Khakis trampled it that day, she turned her back on it. Now she never sits on the stoep any more. She doesn't even tend her roses."

Niggie bends over the sewing in her lap. She bites through a thread. Outside on the stoep her hair is a reddish blonde, with less of a coppery glow than in the evenings by candlelight.

"God keep us from melancholy and loss of faith—these past years have not been easy for anyone. We from the Cape Colony—it's not even our war, and yet it's a scourge to the entire nation."

Ben stares silently ahead.

The minute Niggie gets up to do something inside, Reitz speaks to Ben.

"Ben," he says, "don't give up. You're going to recover completely. Soon we'll go out into the veld again. There's bound to be interesting things around here."

Ben looks at him, touches the bandages around his throat, smiles slightly as if to put Reitz's mind at rest.

Reitz says: "You and I have a lot to talk about."

On the slate Ben writes: *Our journals.*

Reitz says: "We're going back to the camp as soon as you're better. The journals are safe—Willem will look after them."

Ben nods. For a long time he gazes into the distance. Then he writes on the slate: *Your wife.*

Reitz looks away, caught unawares by the unexpected inquiry.

"She is dead, Ben. She died before the war," he says.

Ben looks at him intently, as if he wants to read something more in Reitz's face.

"She died almost a year before the war broke out," says Reitz. "She never got over the death of our child. I think she died of a broken heart," he adds softly.

Ben is still watching him intently. He shakes his head slowly, as if something is clear to him now that he did not understand before. But how can Reitz know? He can no longer say with any certainty what is going through Ben's mind. The thought makes the blood rush to his face.

Niggie comes through the door. She takes up her sewing and sits down with a sigh.

"Anna is upset today," she says. "And for good reason, for she's in touch with the dead."

That evening at supper Reitz regards Anna with greater interest. A woman in touch with the dead. He watches her, as if to determine from her conduct the nature of the contact.

•

The next morning Anna wants to ride to the second spring to see whether it is still flowing strongly. Niggie does not want to go. She has had a bad night. Lain awake until the early hours. She feels tired and listless. Ask Reitz to go along, she says, we have a man around the place again, after all. Reitz blushes.

They set out in the cart—the same one in which the women brought Ben and him to the farm.

It is a clear morning. Anna has asked Reitz to bring his rifle along. One must be prepared for every possibility, she says. Reitz knows this only too well.

Reitz is nervous, though he tries to hide it from her. He feels exposed in the open veld. He is constantly expecting a surprise attack. He is aware of every rustle and movement in the grass. It is the first time he has been out in the veld since the day they left camp in the company of Gert Smal.

The river lies between them and Spitskop, Anna says. (Spitskop, Reitz now knows, is the name of the first koppie, where they were heading that day.)

Closer to the river the vegetation is denser—with taller grass and a greater number of thorn trees. They stop a short distance from the river's edge, tie up the horse, walk the rest of the way. Reitz notices that Anna is also cautious and on guard.

When they crossed the river before, he did not realise it was the Orange. The stream is broad, but the water level is low. The banks are wide, with many hollowed-out swallow's nests in the steep cliffs on either side.

Concealed behind the dense foliage, they stand watching the opposite bank. It's taken the river thousands of years to carve out the banks like this, Reitz says. He scans the bank nervously. Does he expect to see their attackers hiding there? he wonders.

From the other side, Anna says, you have a view of Spitskop in the distance.

Cautiously they make their way back to the cart. They head away from the river, in a northwesterly direction. The second spring is surrounded by a shady grove of wild olives, not far from a smaller tributary of the big river.

At the spring Anna sinks to her knees on a large, flat stone. She clears the area with her hands. The water flows strongly. Before the war they planned to sink a well here, she says. She has long, narrow hands. The nails are tapered. The bottom joints of the three middle fingers are straight but the top two joints angle away from one another. It gives her hands a childlike awkwardness that is not evident in either her gaze or her bearing.

He stands beside her. He looks down at her. A woman with narrow hands who is in contact with the dead. He would not know what to say to her.

At the small nearby stream they sit down on a rocky ledge in the shade of a willow tree. The water is cool and clear. Reitz washes his burning face. His thoughts are in turmoil. Despite the clear day and the beautiful surroundings, he would prefer to be elsewhere.

He thinks of Ben today—Ben recovered, the way he used to be. Ben and he doing field work. He finds it painful to have to think of Ben like that—as if he is dishonouring him. Ben is alive, Ben has survived. Ben was right when back at the camp he said that they could be in a worse position.

On the way back Anna is more talkative. She points out things: the ravaged fields, the poplar copse where they keep the two cows, the direction of the first spring where Jeremiah has planted a vegetable garden, the kloof where they went into hiding after the English attempted to burn the farmhouse. She points out a nest with plover eggs. The female cries shrilly from afar to divert their attention. The English killed everything on the farm that day, she says, and destroyed and looted a lot of things from the house, but it could have been much worse.

Reitz refrains from asking how.

That night Reitz dreams that he meets Kosie Rijpma, who tells him: I love her. It is not clear whom Kosie means, for there is a woman in a dark frock on a wagon, who might be Anna, but might also, on the other hand, be Bettie Loots. She has painfully thin arms. Later Kosie Rijpma takes Bettie out of a small box, and she scurries away in the manner of a cricket-like insect. Then Kosie Rijpma raises one of the floorboards and motions for Reitz to take a look, but Reitz lacks the courage to do so.

•

The next morning Reitz tells Ben that he wants to return to Oompie as soon as he can properly use his leg. He wants to find out who fired at them.

Ben frowns. He seems puzzled.

"Oompie," says Reitz. "Oompie, who gave me the mixture. Where we saw the bottled head," he adds in a low voice.

Ben frowns again, a troubled expression on his face.

Patiently Reitz starts at the beginning. "Senekal," he says. "Commandant Senekal's wagon laager." Ben nods. He nods slowly as if he is calling to mind with great clarity the precise duration of their lengthy stay there.

"Willem," Reitz continues, "Willem and young Abraham. We left Senekal to take Abraham to his mother in Ladybrand."

Ben nods to show that he understands.

"We journeyed for a few days before reaching General Bergh's camp. Gert Smal and Ezekiel came upon us and took us there. It was just before nightfall. We were hungry."

Again Ben nods in agreement.

"At the camp we met Japie Stilgemoed and Kosie Rijpma. Japie Stilgemoed almost drove me mad, Ben. I found it hard to endure his endless tales."

Ben smiles, slightly uncertain.

"Reuben and Seun were also there. Seun with the cleft palate." A wave of guilt washes over Reitz; still ashamed of the pleasure it gave him to strike the child.

"In the mornings we went down to the river," he continues. "Gert Smal had no objection, as long as we went on foot. We did field work in the vicinity; we took our journals."

Ben nods slowly, reflectively.

"Those were good times, Ben," says Reitz, and Ben nods again, his gaze averted from Reitz's face.

"We'll go back," says Reitz, "as soon as you're completely recovered. Our journals are waiting there. You were right when you said we could have had it much worse."

He is not certain why Ben shakes his head in denial.

"I wanted to get away from there after trying to get in touch with her," Reitz continues in a low voice, "with my late wife."

He rubs his hands across his face.

"Oompie helped me. He gave me a mixture. I took it for five successive days. The last time I thought I heard him telling me to jump. If you hadn't found me, I would have drowned."

Ben looks at Reitz in dismay. Slowly he nods.

"Do you remember?" Reitz asks softly.

On the slate Ben writes: *I remember.*

They sit in silence for a while.

"I want to go to Oompie," says Reitz. "I want to know who shot at us. It's the kind of thing he's bound to know."

Ben closes his eyes, shakes his head vehemently, motions with his hands: No.

Niggie comes out on the stoep. She is wearing a light green dress, the colour of her eyes. Her eyes are clear, with a sorrowful expression.

"Don't talk too much," she tells Reitz. "He's regaining his strength gradually. It's better if he doesn't remember everything as yet."

•

Niggie trims Ben's beard. She works painstakingly, taking care not to hurt him. Ben closes his eyes while she is busy. Reitz thinks: It's a miracle that Ben survived that appalling day.

Niggie burned their torn, blood-soaked clothing on the first day. Nothing to save there, she replied when Reitz inquired about the clothes. Anna gave them new clothes—clothes belonging to Johannes, Niggie informed him. Reitz was reluctant to wear the clothes. Don't be silly, Niggie said, in a war you've no choice. But she laughed when the trouser legs and shirtsleeves were too short. Anna also smiled, and Reitz insisted that Niggie lengthen them. Well, aren't you vain, she mocked, and Reitz made no reply.

Reitz walks in the garden alone, at first only to the end of the orchard, but he soon ventures further afield. He keeps his eyes open for cocoons and beetles, for anything that might arouse Ben's interest. Niggie gave him a few precious sheets of paper. He begins to document the topography of the area, to serve as a foundation for a geological description. However, without his instruments he cannot achieve much. These— spirit level, tripod, cartographic board—he left in his trunk back at camp.

At night he is cold, but he dare not ask for more blankets. He dreams. He ponders over all that has happened recently.

He always thinks of their friend Willem first, and of young Abraham.

He hopes Willem isn't too troubled by their disappearance. He hopes Abraham's condition has improved in the meantime.

He thinks of Bettie Loots. Of all the deaths Kosie Rijpma witnessed daily in the women's camp, the death of Bettie Loots had been the turning point for him. What was it about Bettie Loots that moved him like that? Had he loved her? Had he loved her and deemed it inappropriate?

He thinks of Japie Stilgemoed. Japie's protracted tale, his endless yearning to be reunited with his loved ones, irked and exasperated him. He has a clear picture of Japie in his mind—holding forth, his hair wild and bristling, his dark eyes smouldering.

What would camp life be like now—with Gert Smal dead? Would the little group in camp even be *aware* of Gert Smal's death? Would the general know by now?

He is beginning to think—and he longs to be able to discuss it with Ben—that it is possible they weren't ambushed by the Khakis. Not by the general either. Could Blackpiet Petoors and Red Herman Hundt have planned it of their own accord? But what could their motive have been to get rid of Gert Smal? Doing away with Ben and himself because they were seen as traitors and underminers on the basis of their lectures, that was possible, though unlikely. But Gert Smal? Gert Smal hadn't done them any harm.

It is the kind of thing Oompie would know. Provided he isn't hand in glove with Petoors and Red Herman. Should he go on his own, as soon as his leg is healed? He can't wait for Ben—Ben's recovery is too slow. He must return to camp. He must put Willem's mind at rest. He must fetch the journals. To hold his journal in his hand will give Ben's spirits an enormous lift.

Every time he reminds himself of the calamitous day that Gert Smal died, he thinks: Ben could have been dead. That Ben is alive should be all that matters. But it is not enough. He wants Ben restored to his former self.

•

In the evenings around the table Niggie does most of the talking. She describes her youth in the Cape Colony. She tells stories and anecdotes about friends and family. She is an animated and engaging raconteur. As she talks, Reitz cannot keep his eyes off her shapely wrists, her lovely hands, her hair, her white skin, the rich blue veins at her throat.

Niggie says: "In the Cape Colony we wouldn't become embroiled in such a barbaric struggle so easily—not even for the sake of the freedom of our people."

Tante says: "My child, people are the same everywhere."

Reitz has little desire to engage in talk at the table. Initially he is overwhelmed by the appointment of the meals—the white tablecloths and cutlery, the serving dishes. Though scant, the meals represent something civilised and refined, something that had been lost on commando. He is also overwhelmed by the presence of the women. He looks in wonder at the light gleaming on their hair and skin. At their gestures. Such a prolonged time that they have been cut off from the company of women.

Though it is apparently not expected of him to say much, Tante sometimes speaks to him. She asks where he is from, about his studies abroad. About commando and camp life.

Anna listens attentively, mostly without comment. Niggie is impatient, interrupting often.

He tells them how they met up with Senekal in the Cape Colony. He tells them about Willem and young Abraham. He tells of the battle of Droogleegte and how they subsequently decided to get Abraham away from Senekal's laager. Tante shakes her head and says: What a shame, the poor youth. Niggie says: Yes, yes, many a young life has been destroyed by the war. It has also been my experience. Anna is silent. The girls listen wide-eyed. The eldest flushes deeply with distress on hearing young Abraham's story.

Reitz makes cautious inquiries about Oompie. He wonders whether they have heard of him. He explains that Oompie lives up the kloof some distance from camp and that he is the camp's bee man. He says no more for the time being.

"So," Niggie says, "you had honey?"

Reitz tells them of General Bergh. They know about him. He comes from the same town in the Cape Colony as Anna's parents. Tante remembers him as a young boy. Clever, she says. Sharp. They heard that he makes short work of the Khakis, and of traitors, but they have never come across him or his commando here.

Niggie is affectionate towards the girls. She often embraces them and says: Poor lambs, losing your mother at such a young age. Especially the youngest then nestles close to Niggie, pressing her small frame to her as if to find in Niggie's embrace again the touch of her dead mother. The eldest finds it harder to express her emotions.

Anna touches the girls only briefly. She lays a hand on their heads, or strokes their cheeks or shoulders. A brief, passing touch, as if she is unwilling to allow herself anything more.

Niggie tells Reitz: Unlike me, Anna finds it difficult to show her feelings.

Sometimes Tante and the girls join Ben, Reitz and Niggie on the stoep for a while. The little one plays with a doll, the bigger one stares aloofly into the distance, or, lost in thought, keeps her face averted—her expression dark with undefined longing. Niggie says: Anna doesn't like to sit on the stoep. She can't stand the sight of her ruined garden.

A strong resolve grows in Reitz to fetch the journals. First he must get to where they were ambushed. From there he will find his way back—he has Gert Smal's compass and a keen sense of direction. But it would help if he could also find Gert Smal's map, perhaps in the vicinity of his grave. He should have looked in the saddlebag of the dead horse that day, but he had been in no condition for it.

He asks Niggie whether she has a map of the area. Lord, no, why would I have one? she replies. He asks her to take him to the place where the two of them were found that day. Why? she asks. He wants to see if he can find the map. He wants to fetch their journals from the camp. He must reassure Willem that they're alive. He can't wait any longer for Ben to recover, it's taking too long. Fine, Niggie agrees, she will take him.

Reitz has a dream in which Willem has a strawberry birthmark on his face and his eyes are like white lights. Between them stands a stranger in a threatening pose.

CHAPTER 14

In the afternoons Niggie joins Ben and Reitz on the stoep. Bent over her sewing, she talks. Sometimes the sewing lies forgotten in her lap while she looks out over the neglected garden at the low hills on the horizon.

She bites through a thread.

"God knows," she says, "I've lost everything that I valued and loved. My parents lie buried in the Boland. I've no brothers and sisters left. The family farm was sold from underneath us. I am dependent on others for my daily bread."

She threads the needle with care. A dove calls drowsily: coo-cuckoo.

"For a while I was a nurse in the Bethulie camp. There I saw how the women suffered," she says. "There was no reprieve—not for the elderly, not for woman nor child. And yet most of the women wanted their menfolk to persevere in the struggle. I thought: God help them—they are bringing this upon their own heads."

Niggie picks up her sewing and works with meticulous, fine stitches.

"I was present at many a deathbed while I was in camp," she says. "Before and afterwards as well. People began to rely on me to be there. I sat with Marta, Anna's sister, too. She died in my arms and I laid her out myself. And where was Anna? To the end of her days she'll regret not having been there. She never mentions it, but I know how she feels."

Reitz and Ben listen without comment.

Niggie lays her sewing in her lap.

"God help us," she says, "to take from life whatever little we can get. It all goes so swiftly."

She puts the sewing on the chair beside her, gets up and enters the house.

•

On the twelfth day after their arrival, Reitz finds Anna, Tante and Niggie in the kitchen early one morning. Anna is visibly upset. She is busy at the stove. Tante and Niggie are seated at the table.

"I have a feeling I won't see Johannes again," she says.

"My child," Tante says, "you know you can't always trust these feelings."

"Not always, but mostly," Niggie says.

Tante turns and gives Niggie a reproving look, but says nothing.

Anna says: "I had a feeling about Marta and three weeks later she was dead."

"We all knew she was ill," Tante says.

"We didn't know she was dying," Niggie retorts.

"Anna," says Tante, "you shouldn't be so heedful of these things—they're often no more than premonitions."

"I knew from the beginning I'd never see him again," says Anna. She still has her back to them.

"You must learn not to pay so much attention to these feelings," Tante says.

"Did you dream?" Niggie asks.

"Yes," Anna replies, "I dreamed."

"What did you dream?" Niggie asks, glancing knowingly at Reitz.

"I dreamed Marta was sitting on a wagon. The wagon was on its way to the graveyard. Johannes stood beside the wagon. He wanted to climb aboard. The wagon stopped for him."

"My child," Tante says, "Marta's death is still fresh in your memory."

When Anna turns round, Reitz is startled. She seems alluring today. An alluring mediator between the living and the dead.

Shortly after lunch, when everyone is resting, there is the sound of approaching hooves in the distance, and not long afterwards in the yard. Reitz, alarmed, is uncertain whether Ben and he should hide, and he is relieved when he hears from the shouts outside that it is not the English. He goes out immediately. There are two burghers on horseback, and the first one addresses Tante: "We have a dead man with us, Tante, on a wagon. Could you identify him? We heard he was from around here."

Tante nods.

The two men dismount. They stand next to their horses, hats clasped to their chests, waiting for the wagon to arrive.

They huddle at the back door in complete silence—Tante, Anna, Niggie, Reitz and the two girls. The wagon, drawn by a mule, enters the yard slowly, the dead man covered by an old blanket. It is so breathlessly quiet that Reitz hears his own heart beating in his ears.

When the wagon comes to a halt, Anna turns to Tante and says softly, almost entreatingly: "I don't think I can do this."

"My child," says Tante, "sometimes we don't have a choice."

Anna goes up to the wagon. She pulls back the blanket. She stands looking for a long time.

Then she draws the blanket up over the body and turns.

"It's not him. It's Nettie's Sarel," she says, walking past them and into the house.

•

Tante and Niggie wash the corpse and lay it out.

The three burghers, Reitz and Jeremiah take turns to dig the grave. It is hard work, for the ground is hard and dry. They do not lay the body to rest in the family graveyard, but under a tree some distance from the house.

Reitz questions the men carefully. What news do they have of the war? Nothing good, says Jan Buys—the oldest of the three. More and more commandos are surrendering. Only De Wet is still holding out. The men are tired, says Jan Buys. They've had enough. Look at us. Look how patched and ragged we are. (Reitz blushes in his borrowed clothes.) Do you call these shoes? Buys asks. On his feet are bundles of rags tied up with riempies. Look at my teeth. He points at his mouth. Broken stumps, gaps where the teeth should be, Reitz sees. Drought and locusts, says Jan Buys. What is there for the horses to feed on? I have seen men carry their saddles to spare their horses. Two weeks ago the slaughter took place at Rooiwal in the Transvaal. The Free State is rotten with Khakis. At Sannaspos and Mosterdhoek there was still hope, but now we don't stand a chance any more. And the Kaffirs are getting out of hand too, he adds softly.

The men appear bedraggled indeed. We had to throw away our clothes when we arrived here, Reitz explains apologetically. He tells them how they came to be there.

Especially the two younger men look used up, dazed. They are young, no more than seventeen, eighteen. Young and defeated. They do not say much; Jan Buys does most of the talking.

Reitz asks him to explain exactly where they are. Jan Buys picks up a stick and draws a map on the ground. Here is the Orange. This is where Davenport passed through a few days ago. Here they engaged with him. This is where the dead man (and he points at the house where the corpse is being laid out) fell. A few days ago? Reitz asks. Yes, says Jan Buys, and uses the stick to trace Colonel Davenport's movements all the way from Beaufort West. Here is the Skeurberg, here the Koueberg. Here is Middelburg. Here Aliwal North. Here Bethulie. Here's Colesberg. Here are the concentration camps. Here are the areas of greatest devastation. The English are here, and *here*.

Reitz thinks he is beginning to get a clear picture of where they are, also in relation to General Bergh's camp in the Cape Colony.

In the meantime General Meth came marching from the direction of Middelburg with reinforcements, Jan Buys explains, but he was intercepted by a commando and apparently turned tail before he could cross the Orange, so that he was unable to join up with Davenport, which had presumably been the plan.

When it is his turn to help dig the grave, it strikes Reitz that the ground is as hard as the day he had to cover up Gert Smal. God grant, he thinks, that the animals of the veld have not dragged him from that shallow grave by now.

In the afternoon they bury the dead man, wrapped in the blanket which covered him on the wagon.

Tante reads from the Bible and prays. They sing a hymn. Everyone except Ben is there. Sussie, the youngest child, stands huddled against Tante. She is overcome by tears and buries her face in Tante's bosom. Lena stands bravely on her own, but later she allows Niggie to put her arm around her protectively.

Poor lambs, Niggie says, their mother's death still so fresh in their memory.

It is a fine day, and the afternoon coolness settles imperceptibly on their brows. A dove keeps up an incessant cooing and a profound peace descends on the surroundings. The moon is in her first quarter: a pale disc in the sky.

The men have supper with them before they depart. They are impatient to rejoin their commando and prefer not to travel by day.

God help the poor woman, says Niggie of Nettie—the dead man's mother—her house has been burned down, she and the younger children are in camp, her husband and sons are on commando, and now her youngest son has been killed.

During the meal Reitz tries to question the men about the Boers' movements, but Niggie continually interrupts him. She is wearing a pale frock, and its satiny surface shimmers with her slightest movement-like a milky, opaque liquid. Her hair has a deep coppery sheen. Her eyes are as cool as minerals tonight. Her skin is like marble. Every gesture she makes shows off the shapeliness of her hands and wrists.

Reitz notices that Jan Buys is less willing to answer his questions than that afternoon because he and the two younger men find it hard to keep their eyes off Niggie. The two youngsters sit in a daze—overwhelmed by the candlelight, the steaming dishes, the women, and especially by Niggie's dark ardour.

Finally Reitz asks Jan Buys whether he has any idea how long the war will continue.

Jan Buys replies—hesitantly—that, according to their information, peace talks have already commenced in Pretoria. Before the end of May, he says, some rumours have it.

Oh, says Niggie, Anna predicted it long ago; it won't be a day later than end of May.

Anna says nothing. She looks everyone in the eye—as is her habit, and gives a slight shrug. Tante looks at Niggie reproachfully. Reitz wonders why Niggie has never mentioned it to Ben and him before. The men are uncertain how to react. Jan Buys gives a deprecating little smile.

Soon afterwards the three men depart with horses and wagon into the night. Reitz stands watching as they leave.

"A bedraggled little group," says Niggie when they are gone.

"My child," Tante says reproachfully, "do you think it's by choice? It's their patriotic duty. Those poor boys. They might be doing it for the sake of their own freedom, but in the end it may well be for the benefit of all our people."

"They may be our people," says Niggie, "but it's not our war."

"We must respect the ideals of freedom that our compatriots hold dear—even if they differ from our own," says Tante.

"Respect is one thing," Niggie says, "but to suffer because of their bloody war, is another."

"My *child*," Tante says, and shakes her head.

Niggie shrugs.

"The two of you were no less bedraggled when we found you," she remarks to Reitz, "and look how handsome you've turned out."

Anna turns where she has been standing in front of the stove, and looks at Reitz, as if to verify Niggie's statement with her own eyes. Reitz blushes. He hurries off to his room.

He looks at the little calendar Niggie gave him. April the twenty-third. He must get to their former camp urgently. He must let Willem know they are alive. He must fetch their journals.

It is what Oompie said too—Oompie, or perhaps the abhorrent pickled head: the end of May, and the struggle will have been in vain.

In the night he steps out onto the desolate farmyard. The moon has risen. She is waxing. Imperious, she bathes the wide desolation in her silvery light.

•

Early the next morning Reitz finds Anna in the kitchen alone. He slept badly because of the cold, plagued by restless dreams. He was thankful when day broke, and is thankful now for the warmth of the kitchen.

Like the day before she is busy at the stove. He sits down at the table.

"Niggie said that you have contact with the dead," he says—surprised by his own temerity.

Anna stands still for a moment before she answers: "Niggie often speaks out of turn."

She stirs the fire.

"Sometimes I have a premonition," she says, "and sometimes I dream, but it can't always be trusted—like yesterday."

She pours them each a cup of weak coffee, brewed from ground mealie kernels. She sits down at the opposite side of the table and looks him in the eye. He has always thought her eyes to be brown. Now he sees they are a murky greenish grey, like serpentine, or chrysoprase.

"What is your concern with the dead?" she asks.

He averts his eyes. Suddenly embarrassed, caught unawares.

"I don't have any particular concern with them," he says softly.

She sits before him with both hands wrapped around her cup and her steady gaze fixed upon him.

"My wife died shortly before the war," he says. "I began to feel her presence after we had left General Senekal's laager. Oompie gave me a mixture because I wanted to get in touch with her. I saw her. It was she and yet it wasn't she. I shouldn't have done it. After the last time I knew I had lost her for good."

Anna sits before him in silence.

"I loved her," he says, "and I didn't have a chance to take leave of her properly the first time."

Anna—not a woman to be easily moved, in his eyes—says: "It must have been very hard for you."

Wordlessly they gaze at each other across the table. Then she gets up, turns to the fire, and says: "If you had any hope that I can put you in touch with your wife again—I have no connection with the dead. To my relief *and* to my sorrow."

•

Later that day, in the late afternoon, when Reitz, Ben and Niggie are sitting on the stoep, the sky begins to change colour. Heavy, dark cloud masses are forming in the north, but hold no promise of rain.

"That poor youth," says Niggie, "lying under the tree over there. As we were laying him out I was struck again by his tender age."

Instinctively all three of them look in the direction of the tree. The slanting rays of the sun light up the branches with a radiance so brilliant that it is impossible to look for longer than a few seconds.

A large bird of prey circles overhead. Reitz hopes that Ben will show interest but Ben gives no sign that he has noticed.

Reitz tells him that according to Jan Buys there are rumours that peace talks have commenced in Pretoria, and that the commandos are surrendering one after the other.

Ben stares straight ahead, shakes his head slowly.

"From my own life I am deeply familiar with a sense of hopelessness," says Niggie. "One morning you wake up and you think: God knows, there's nothing left for me here."

From the corner of his eye Reitz sees how motionlessly Ben sits. He thinks: I cannot look at Ben. He thinks how little he knows of what has been going through Ben's mind since the shooting. How difficult it must be for him to be unable to express his thoughts. How anxious he must be about the welfare of his wife and children.

"I'm a terrible person," says Niggie. "Once I've turned against someone, I never look back. Sometimes you discover things about yourself that aren't pleasant. But what can you do? It's part of life."

Suddenly she lays her sewing in her lap.

"I had such a rare dream last night," she says, "about this decrepit, doddering bloody old fool of a fellow, sitting in a kind of scotch-cart contraption. It was like a dream taking place in another lifetime."

She picks up her sewing, continues working.

"Maybe it had something to do with Anna's dream of the other day.

She had a bad fright yesterday. She was convinced the dead man was Johannes. She firmly believes that they'll bring him here in the same way. If not this time, then next time."

Ben looks puzzled. Niggie tells him about Anna's dream.

"Anna is stubborn," she continues. "She believes what she believes. And she hasn't had an easy life, even though they are prosperous. As prosperous as the likes of us have never been and never will be either. But that was before the war. It's plain to see that they were well-to-do. Before the Khakis wrecked the place and killed the livestock. Before the damned Khakis forced us into hiding in the kloofs."

She lays down the sewing again.

"It was too much for Anna so soon after her sister's death, and with the children so young as well. Poor lambs. Poor orphans—where is their father today? And their brothers? On commando with Johannes, and who knows whether they'll return alive! In the kloof I kept thinking: We're going to be wandering like this till Kingdom come—our bedraggled little group and the two black helpers. There we were, and we felt ourselves as forsaken as God Himself wouldn't want it! Tante was the one who kept us going. Every evening she prayed that God would grant us strength in adversity. Our old Tante is a good woman—she'll go straight to heaven for her unwavering faith."

Niggie bites through a thread.

"Unlike me, Anna can be very *obstinate*. I've had to adapt to many different situations. You've no choice if you eat another man's bread, as I've had to do for years. For years I've had nothing to wear but these threadbare clothes and worn out shoes."

Niggie displays her shoe, and Reitz and Ben—embarrassed—can hardly help noticing the shapely foot and ankle.

"It's hard, God knows, for someone as proud as myself," she says.

The sun has gone down. A cool bleakness comes over the veld, advancing from across the distant horizons.

"When all is considered, on the other hand," Niggie says as she gets up to help with the chores inside, "we still have a great deal to be thankful for."

•

In the days that follow Reitz leaves Ben in Niggie's company for longer periods. She has given him a few more precious sheets of writing paper. He now goes for longer walks in the surrounding area. He tries in vain without his instruments to make topographical observations. He is tense and on the alert. He knows he must go back to the camp as soon as possible to fetch the journals and to put Willem's mind at rest, but he is scared of undertaking the journey on his own. The day he left camp in the company of Ben and Gert Smal he had no sense of foreboding; now he is never without it.

He prefers the veld, for his thoughts are less restricted there. There he feels less invaded by them, finds it less menacing to try and make sense of recent events. Why did Gert Smal take such an intense dislike to Ben and him from the word go? Why did Blackpiet and the others say Colonel Davenport would be advancing from Middelburg, while Jan Buys claims it was Beaufort West? Did they not know, or did they deliberately supply the wrong information? Why is he becoming more and more convinced that it was *not* the English that had fired at them? But what in God's name could they have had against poor Gert Smal, for his death could not have been an accident. Unless they—whoever they may be—were afraid that he would divulge their plans to the general later.

He often thinks of Oompie. Oompie with his raincoat. Gert Smal called him a great sorcerer. Oompie told him to jump. Was it really Oompie?

It may not be such a good idea to return to Oompie in order to find out about the shooting. Better to resist the temptation of Oompie's evil powers. Ben had been distrustful of Oompie since the beginning. If only he'd listened to Ben.

In the veld he moves around cautiously, aware that he may be a target to invisible snipers. He is careful always to take cover—where possible, he stays close to boulders or large ant hills, or an isolated clump of trees or thorny scrub.

But the region is barren; it affords little protection. The landscape here is sparse—more open, more boundless than at camp. It is flatter, the rocky outcrops, trees, thorny shrubs are fewer—and further apart. More dry veld than grass.

He notices that his eyes do not seek out the geological features of the land, but rather the smaller things that would interest Ben: the plants and bushes, the insects, the lairs of small mammals, the pellets and droppings, the trails and tracks. Ben would have identified them all.

It is cold in the early morning. Small shrubs grow amongst bare patches of earth. The wind tugs at them, bites into Reitz's hands, neck and cheeks. He finds small bleached skulls; once he finds the tiny bones of a bird near a hole in the ground. Everywhere signs of occupation, but seldom a living animal or insect. At some of the holes he sees the deep, powerful scratch-marks of the aardvark. When the aardvark abandons the hole, Ben told him, jackal or mongooses inhabit it. He looks at the ant hills closely—some are smashed, others have already been plastered and repaired. Birds circle or soar high overhead. At times the silence is like a presence. The humming silence, the boundless space, and the small, piercing wind.

Sometimes he sees herds of buck in the distance, but the dim outlines and topography of the low hills on the horizon interest him less than usual. He keeps his eyes fixed on the ground at his feet and on his immediate surroundings, his ears cocked for the slightest sound.

·

He sits on the stoep with Ben and Niggie. Niggie is bent over her sewing.

"The older child started this morning," she says.

Reitz and Ben look at her blankly.

"She started her monthlies for the first time this morning," says Niggie. "Poor dear, her own mother dead, not here to instruct her. And what lies ahead for her?"

Niggie bites through a thread and answers her own question: "The pain and pleasure of her life as a woman." She looks at Reitz, and he feels the warm blood rushing to his face.

"Poor little lamb," she says.

Betta does the washing and among the clothes on the line the monthly bandages flutter like banners. Flutter like winding-cloths or wedding sheets. Who can tell what it is like for the child who has become a woman overnight?

That evening at the table the girl is pale and distant. Reitz feels ill at ease. Tante is even more solicitous than usual. Niggie has an excited blush on her cheeks and Anna eats with downcast eyes, a grim expression at the corners of her mouth. Only the gaze of the little one still reflects innocence about the ways of womanhood.

•

The nights are hardest for Reitz. He seldom sleeps through. He is often cold. He feels cooped up in the small outside room. Sometimes he wakes with a fear of suffocation, for his thoughts threaten to cave in on him. Or they cling together, quaking, like clusters of bats. He tries to console himself by thinking of the others, asleep in the house. He tries to imagine the night outside—the expanse of veld in the moonlight. He thinks of morning, of the heat of the kitchen, the comforting presence of the women. These thoughts are his bastion and defence against the dark, desperate clustering and knotting of his feelings.

He names the rocks: blue ironstone, firestone, limestone, red ochre, sandstone, flake graphite, oilstone, ironstone, crystal. Dolomite, feldspar and shale. He calls to mind everything he knows. With all of the knowledge he possesses he shields himself against the night. The names of precious stones he recites: milky quartz and rose quartz, dark lepidolite and pale lepidolite, magnesite, serpentine, grey jasper, brown opal, butter chert, brown and grey granite, green and yellow opaline. Chrysoberyl and chrysolite. Beryl stone and leopard stone. Grey marble.

He thinks of the great age of the universe. He imagines the nebulous cloud from which the solar system emerged—at a time unimaginably far removed from the present; the violent force attracting fragments of matter to one another, until they finally condensed into planets. The coldest outer planets in their icy orbits. The sun, the hot centre of the original nebula.

He thinks of the earth and her ages. The scale almost ungraspable by the human mind. The Cambrian and the Ordovician periods. The Silurian and the Devonian—the age of the fishes. The temperate, humid Carboniferous period, with gigantic tropical jungles and endless marshes. The cooler earth during the Permian period. The conifers and ferns of the Triassic, when the first dinosaurs appeared. The warm Jurassic period, when gigantic herbivorous dinosaurs dominated all life on earth. The soft, calcareous seas of the Cretaceous period. He thinks of seas and lakes forming, mountains and volcanoes. The hot core of the earth—hotter than molten steel. He thinks of the formation of rocks. The gradual sedimentation of organic remains that had sunk to the bottom of the sea. He thinks of the earth and her slow processes, occurring over millions of years. He thinks of an earth the size of a grain of sand in the universe. In this way he tries to comfort and protect himself against the invasion of malevolent thoughts.

He thinks of the giant buffalo *Bubalus bainii* of the Quaternary period, of the aquatic reptile *Lystrosaurus* of the Triassic, and the reptile *Dicynodon* that inhabited the marshes during the Permian period. And the many extinct animals that still have to be discovered, whose bones lie buried under the earth, layer upon layer—all that once lived in this giant, marshy basin.

He tries to remember the names of all the animals and insects Ben documented in his journal, as Ben sometimes read their names to him or pointed them out in the area. The maned jackal and the banded mongoose. The red hare and the Cape hare, the monitor lizard and the porcupine, the blue-headed lizard, the slender-tailed meerkat. Bat-eared fox and serval. Wild cat. Red meerkat. The red-cheeked night owl with its haunting cry on moonlit nights. The caseworm in its cocoon of sticks, artfully camouflaged for survival.

Sometimes he is comforted, soothed by all these names. By the thought of the great variety of forms in nature. The profusion of species. The unimaginably long history of the earth, of which at this moment they form only a bitterly small part. A history infinitely more extensive than the terror of his own restricted fears.

Sometimes he even recalls the names of battles and of those who died, of places they passed through. Pretoria, Lydenburg, Carolina. Donkerhoek, Kimberley and Slangfontein. Beaufort West and Vanrhynsdorp. Hot on Smuts's elusive trail. Langjan Lategan at Donkerhoek. Shot in the head. Gieljam Dekker at Droogleegte. Bullet through both lungs. Jakob Roodt at Boshoek. Fatally wounded in the stomach. Freek de Vos at Skeurbuikhoogte. Shot in the chest.

But sometimes no names, no knowledge, can shield him from the repeated horrors of his dreams, or his feelings of dread and dire foreboding as he lies sleepless in the dark for long hours on end.

His dreams are either lascivious or nightmarish. Bettie Loots comes to him in many different guises. Women make lewd proposals. Gert Smal and the other dead flirt with the living. In his dreams it is by no means clear who has survived and who not.

A dead man with shrivelled and charred limbs, his face covered with a thin wet blue membrane like a birth sac, through which the staring eyes and grim mouth are visible.

Kosie Rijpma tells him: I weep such sorrowful tears. In the dream he holds out a small book to Reitz. I have been dead for a long time, you know, he says, you must tell me what these words mean.

It was never like this in the grass shelter under the stars. It was never as godforsaken there as in this big house with its sleeping inhabitants.

Sometimes he rises and steps out onto the bleak, desolate yard in the bitter cold. It is preferable—that endless desolation—to the gravelike constraint of his cold bed.

·

Of *her* he dare not think at night. She is the only one among the dead who leaves him in peace. When he thinks of her, he is overwhelmed by feelings of remorse.

The outbreak of war overshadowed the shock of her death. The first months of the war occupied his thoughts—there was no chance to mourn. He drove all thought of her from his mind.

It was only after they had left Senekal's laager that he became aware of her presence. She came to *him*. He can see it no differently. He yearned to set things straight between them. The promise of contact—of a reunion after all those months—made him feverish. But he was rash—that is why he failed at it. Because he believed Oompie could help him. What was he thinking—that Oompie could give her back to him through his vile artistry? He knows now that she would have come to him anyway, in her own time, in her own way. He realised it too late.

Now she is gone. It is never she who comes to him in a dream. Always other women. Bettie Loots, or Niggie, or even Anna. It is never she.

He has resigned himself to it. She is gone. He is to be blamed. He failed her. He avoided her before she died because he thought she was no longer herself. Didn't he once even tell Ben that she had been of unsound mind? God forgive him for the injustice he did her.

He loved her, and now he finds it hard to recall her image.

Of this he thinks at night, while he lies sleepless.

CHAPTER 15

Ben recovers gradually. He walks short distances in the yard and in the surrounding veld. He takes his meals at the table with the rest of them. Reitz knows he must fetch the journals, but he keeps putting it off.

Ben tires easily. He struggles to concentrate. Reitz points out a variety of small things in the veld—everything he has taken note of during his own walks. But it seems as if these things no longer hold the same fascination for Ben.

There is a passivity in Ben, a detachment; he is often content simply to sit.

Niggie accompanies them regularly on their short walks. Reitz would prefer her not to. And yet—her presence bridges the silence and makes it more bearable.

Now Reitz is the one who points out things to Ben—insects, plants, tracks and droppings—where before Ben used to point out these things to *him*. Ben looks at each object politely. He picks it up. He holds it in the palm of his hand. He inspects it. But without his former enthusiasm. He gives Reitz an embarrassed smile. Reitz notices that sometimes Ben's hands tremble.

It's exhaustion, Niggie says in an undertone.

That is when Reitz welcomes her presence, for without her he would be at a loss what to do with the lump in his throat and the grief in his heart. He realises that he is talking to Ben less and less.

•

Ben and Niggie and Reitz sit on the stoep. Niggie sews. She tells them anecdotes from her life. She speaks of people they do not know.

Niggie comes in from outside, her face flushed, and Reitz remarks softly to Ben: A beautiful woman. Ben nods, and looks away.

Reitz has little contact with Anna. She keeps to herself. At the table he watches her surreptitiously—someone who dreams significant dreams. They have never spoken to each other alone since the morning of their short conversation in the kitchen.

Out of everyone there he senses that Tante is most sensitive to his situation—despite knowing little about his circumstances. Sometimes he intercepts her glance at the table, and her gaze is always sympathetic, as if she wants to ease his mind.

In the evenings he continues to gaze at the girls in wonder—at their complexions and their hair in the candlelight. Especially the little one— the fine blue veins visible in her neck, on her chin. The soft contours of her unformed child's nose, the corners of her eyes and mouth. The older child's face is already taking on a firmer shape; her body a more feminine form. Reitz can hardly look at her, now that she has become a woman, so painfully moved is he by her blossoming womanhood. And guilty too, because he realises he is looking at her the way a man looks at a woman.

Sometimes he comes across Jeremiah and for a few moments he confuses him with Ezekiel. He is still trying to engage him in conversation; he questions him carefully. Jeremiah always replies with downcast eyes, still unwilling to talk to him.

Betta, too, brushes past him in the kitchen with unseeing eyes. Do they—the servants—think that Ben and he have no right to live in the house, that they are trying to replace Johannes, Anna's husband?

•

One morning Reitz takes Niggie along to search for the place where Gert Smal lies buried. (Where Reitz *hopes* he still lies buried.) He hopes to find something in the vicinity—a map, an indication, anything that will cast light on the matter and will give him the courage to undertake the journey back to camp on his own, for Ben is still not strong enough for a day in the saddle.

Early on the morning of the twenty-ninth of April, eighteen days after they arrived on the farm, Niggie and he depart in the horse-drawn cart.

After they have crossed the Orange at the drift, Reitz realises that he does not recognise much of the environment through which they travelled that day after the women had found them.

"You were in such a state the day we found you," Niggie says, "as God Himself wouldn't want it!"

"It was a dreadful day," Reitz says abstractedly.

Niggie enjoys the outing as if they are undertaking a pleasure jaunt. There is an eager blush on her cheeks. She wears a frock the colour of rose quartz, and the material rustles silkily whenever she moves. The sleeves, Reitz notices, are frayed at the elbows and cuffs. Instead of her usual bonnet, she wears a little feathered hat. The feathers flash archly in the sun, like the feathers of a bird displaying its plumage.

The veld is wintry dry with small bluish grey shrubs; low blue hills with dark patches of vegetation are visible in the distance, and even further away, faint on the horizon, in diminishing swells, the furthermost low mountain ranges. It is a clear day. A day that does not reveal anything of its intent—yet remains utterly transparent. This brings a lump to Reitz's throat.

He keeps a careful watch; feels exposed in the open. He is mindful of the slightest unexpected movement. Beside him sits a woman in a feathered hat. His heart feels small in his breast.

On reaching the large donga, they soon find the place where Niggie and he brought Ben out that day.

Reitz looks around and thinks: This is the place. This is where it happened.

He has an impulse to hide, afraid to be a target of unseen persons again. He looks around anxiously. Keeps his rifle at the ready. There is an unpleasant prickling in his armpits and groin. They slither down the bank, past the spot where Ben had lain on the ledge.

At the bottom there is complete silence. He looks up at the sky.

Cloudless and clear. Not a sound. Only the steep, barren, ochre banks of the donga reaching up on either side of him.

They find Gert Smal's grave without any difficulty. It still looks the way Reitz left it that day, though there are signs of scuffling and digging in the vicinity. There are droppings and tracks left by scavengers.

Reitz thinks: Strange to think that Gert Smal lies here.

Niggie says: "Heaven have pity on the poor departed soul who lies on this barren slope."

They search the surroundings. First they find Gert Smal's broken rifle. Further up the slope lie the bones of his horse, stripped of flesh. The saddle lies to one side, badly damaged and spoiled, torn apart and chewed, but there is no map in the saddlebag, no indication of anything. Reitz will have to do his best to find his way back to the camp from here without help.

Going back, Niggie says: "God help Ben. Even I, who don't know him well, can see that something is weighing on his mind."

Reitz says: "Since our arrival here I have never mentioned his wife and children to him."

Niggie says: "The poor man. His voice gone and perhaps his loved ones too."

A bird calls and a small animal scampers through the scrub. Reitz looks up at the sky. Cloudless and clear.

He says: "Since the two of us have been on commando together, he has discovered two new insect species. All the details are recorded in his journal."

Niggie says: "You have to fetch that journal as soon as possible."

•

That night Reitz hardly sleeps. At daybreak he gets up. As usual, he finds Anna in the kitchen.

She notices the worried look on his face. He says he must return to the camp. He cannot put it off any longer. He must reassure the people there that Ben and he are alive. He must fetch the journals. It might encourage Ben.

She pours coffee. He looks at her narrow hands, at the fingers curving outward, with the knuckle of the middle joint awkward like a child's.

Later that morning he says: "Ben, I'm going to fetch our journals."

Ben nods. He gives a shaky smile. He looks uncertain.

Reitz kneels beside him. "Ben," he says, "don't give up hope."

That night Reitz goes to Anna's room—because he is cold, because he cannot sleep, because he found her hands lovely that morning, and because he thinks he has nothing to lose.

If she is surprised by the unexpected visit, she does not let on. She receives him without false pretence of modesty. But she averts her face when he tries to kiss her on the mouth. I'm still a married woman, she says softly in the dark.

CHAPTER 16

Reitz moves through the landscape like a crab, skittering, hoping to remain inconspicuous. He is unused to the horse; she is scrawny and old; he allows her to rest often. Where possible, he moves from shrub or tree to rocky hill. He is alert and mindful of the slightest movement or sound.

Sometimes, when he approaches a cluster of loose boulders, his heart races and he perspires freely. Who or what may be lying in wait?

All is quiet, however. The terrain is so majestically vast, and the day so still that it causes his head to spin and his ears to ring.

Anna has packed food and water, as well as a blanket.

The day before he drew a rough map based on Jan Buys's information. He has Gert Smal's compass and he has a good sense of direction; his fear is not of losing his way. On the other side of the donga he finds himself back on the sweeping plain with the range of hills lying before him in a semicircle. Shortly after they had passed through the low poort, they were shot at. Behind him Spitskop—where they were heading—is clearly etched against the morning light.

He feels as if eyes are trained on him constantly. He imagines that his back is a target, his chest, his head. He is wet with perspiration, though the day is cool. Early that morning, when he departed, the wind was piercingly cold.

One after another he recognises the landmarks of their outward journey. Here they rested. Here is the stretch dotted with an unusually large number of ant hills. Here Ben pointed out the tracks of the bat-eared fox. At this dry run they dismounted.

It is useful that he registered the changing landscape on that journey carefully, without even being aware of it. Through force of habit his eye measured and took note. The gradual change from the great flat flood-plain of the Orange River to an area with more koppies and hills. In this wide expanse it is easier to see the larger pattern—to correlate the sills from a distance, as they run from one rocky hill to another in a large ellipse, with the shales forming the darker layers between. Marshy in the prehistoric past with an abundance of plant and animal life. Ferny plants and mammal-like reptiles. Now it is barren and dry. Wide and desolate. Instead of giant reptiles, lizards scurry about, the warm-blooded meer-kat and mongoose dart across the veld. He is startled by a leguaan on a stone. A yellow cobra slithers to safety under a loose rock.

May God grant him a safe journey and may he retrieve the journals safely. He can already feel the solid weight of the familiar book in his hands. Through all the uncertain times—the fruitless meandering, the occasional battles, the horror of bloodshed, the boredom and discomfort of their daily existence, the rain, the cold, the dearth of food—his jour-nal was a fixed point, it gave shape to their days, and he knows it was the same for Ben. *That* and his friendship with Ben made it all bearable.

Reitz hopes that Ben will be fortified when he sees his journal, that he will gain strength and take courage if he realises it has not been in vain after all—two and a half years of scrupulous note-taking and two new insect species. God help Ben that it might happen.

In the small trunks where they keep their journals are, besides Reitz's instruments, also rocks, soil samples, fossil remains, insects, plants, vari-ous skulls and bones, everything they collected over time. A good thing, Reitz thinks again, that they didn't bring their trunks and journals along, or the horses would have run off with the lot. (Jeremiah went in search of them, but the horses were never found.)

He picks up a dead beetle for Ben, the bleached skull of a small mam-mal, an empty tortoiseshell. He spots a caseworm on a branch. If Ben had not pointed it out to him once, he would never have noticed it—artfully disguised as a few sticks seemingly glued together. He carefully stows everything in a small flour bag he has brought along for the purpose.

What should I look out for, Ben, he asked when he took leave of Ben.

I'll bring you a new species, he said, and if it's female—he remarked teasingly—we'll call her Niggie. Ben blushed. He motioned with his hands—he seemed confused and upset.

He shook Ben's hand. I'll be cautious, Ben, he assured him. I won't do anything rash or take unnecessary risks. But Ben would not be appeased. Reitz was relieved he could leave him in Niggie's care.

Reitz solemnly took leave of everyone with a handshake early that morning. Of Anna too. They waved as he left. This affected him deeply. Ben on Niggie's arm. When Niggie said goodbye, she said: May God keep you, my friend, it's an important journey you're undertaking. Anna looked into his eyes with her clear, open gaze, without a trace of embarrassment or regret about the night before, and he was overcome, so that his face turned a deep red, and he felt an excited fluttering in his stomach.

As he travels, he thinks of the woman. He felt as if he was being admitted to her very being, the source of her impassive gaze. It was so unexpected, so out of the blue, and she permitted it, though she spoke a warning and kept her head averted.

May God give, may God give, he mutters, without knowing exactly what he wants God to grant him.

But he must also recall the day when Ben and Gert Smal and he made this journey in the opposite direction. Gert Smal consulted the map regularly and chewed on his nails. He was nervous. He spoke little. What did he anticipate? Ben and he, on the other hand, were in high spirits all day. Reitz cannot remember having a single premonition of danger—their instructions were simple enough, and they did not expect to come face to face with the Khakis.

He found the day beautiful, Reitz recalls, the veld was beautiful; he was happy to undertake the excursion with Ben. His head seemed clear and unburdened—for the first time since his bitter experience at the river.

Gradually the landscape changes, becoming more rugged, with low, rocky outcrops.

In the late afternoon he reaches the vicinity of the camp. It took him longer today than it had taken the three of them that day. As he approaches the camp, he turns his thoughts to the people there. Will they know of Gert Smal's death? Will they have gone in search of them? Will they have concluded that the three of them are all dead? Will a few of the general's men by any chance have come to them with a message? What message?

The first thing he notices is that the horses are missing from their usual spot. He whistles the way they would do when approaching the camp from this direction—from the opposite side of the river—but he hears no answering whistle. He leads his horse up the steep incline. They move slowly, for the ground is uneven and his injured leg is painful after the long ride.

When at last he arrives at the camp, it is deserted.

It is as quiet as if no one ever put up camp here. A bitter, biting little wind is blowing. The shelters have been torn down. The stones of the fireplace have been scattered.

Reitz goes from one ruined shelter to another. They have all been torn apart, it appears. Of his own and Ben's shelters only a few solitary broken branches remain. No sign of the trunks or the journals.

They have gone, he decides. They left in a hurry. The English passed close by. That is why the general moved them to a safer place. They are gone and they are sure to have left him a message somewhere. He is bound to find them. They have taken the trunks and the journals along for safety.

In the entrance of the cave lie a few broken saddles. Cautiously he ventures deeper into the cave, where he has never been before, where the provisions were stored. There is nothing there, no mealie flour or biltong, or saddles or blankets, or whatever might have been kept there. Only the vague smell of meat and flour, half hidden by the cool, subterranean smell of soil, and the smell of bat droppings. He thinks he hears a squeaking noise and deeper, in the darkest part of the cave, the scurrying sounds of mouselike creatures.

When the sun goes down, it is suddenly piercingly cold.

Reitz builds a small fire in the mouth of the cave, under the overhanging rock, where they sat in the rain for two days. Long ago, it seems. Immeasurably long ago.

He sits with his back pressed against the rock wall behind him so that he can keep his eyes on the area in front, and at the same time hear what is happening in the cave behind him.

He eats some of the food Anna packed, and drinks some water. He wraps himself in the blanket she gave him. It is a clear night, and bitterly cold.

Despite the cold his face and head feel warm. This must be due to his distress. The horse is tethered to a small tree nearby. He feels grateful for its presence. He remains attuned to the smallest, slightest sound. Tomorrow he will search for a message. He tries to remember what Jan Buys said about the movements of the Khakis, but his mind has stopped dead, he cannot calculate, nor judge, nor predict their possible routes. His throat aches. He dozes off for short spells, keeps waking, tries to keep the fire going.

He dreams. He wakes a few times, for he imagines he heard a sound deep inside the cave. His body is freezing and his forehead burning. He dozes again and in his dream he hears voices in the cave behind him. As he moves deeper into the night and in and out of dreams, he thinks: They've left. He will never see them again.

The moon is full. The entire landscape awash in her remorseless light.

•

When he gets up the next morning he feels light-headed. His head is warm; there is pressure in his forehead; his eyes feel dry, as if there is sand in them.

His limbs are stiff; they lack all strength. Now and then a cold shiver racks his entire body.

The fire went out in the early hours and with difficulty he manages to get it going again. He drinks some water, but has no appetite.

He is scarcely able to rouse himself. Uncertain of what to do. Search for a message, go down to the river, wait?

In the brilliant morning light the camp appears deserted in a different way than the night before. The terrain appears unspoilt, innocent of all history. No one has ever been here. Nothing has ever happened here. The rocks that used to be smooth are overgrown with moss. A light breeze stirs the leaves of the low shrubs ever so slightly, hardly perceptibly.

Again he goes from one broken-down shelter to the next. For a long time he squats at the remains of his own shelter. He raises his head and sniffs the air. No smell except the heavy aroma of the veld. No tracks. No sign. No message. Except for the slight movement of the leaves, everything is motionless.

He could go in search of Oompie, but he lacks the strength. He will go down to the river, he decides. If no one appears, he will return to the farm. May God give him strength for the return journey.

·

For a long time Reitz sits in the morning sun with his back against the rock wall—he has no idea how long—before he goes down to the river to fetch water for his return journey.

He moves slowly because of his injured leg and his want of vigour. He avoids the place where he smoked Oompie's ungodly mixture, and goes instead to where Ben and he used to work every morning. On the cliff face and lower down the river the birds are chattering as they always did. The swallows have left. Some of the willow branches are entirely stripped of leaves. The wet river sand smells more strongly of mud, the air is more biting than before. It is unrecognisably desolate—they might as well never have been there, Ben and he.

The sharpness of the morning light hurts his eyes. The water is ice-cold when he washes his burning face. He fills his tin canteen with water and sets off on his way back.

Halfway up the winding path he catches a glimpse of Seun's skittering form behind one of the large, scattered boulders.

He calls out to him, but there is nothing but silence. He calls again. Some distance away Seun appears hesitantly from behind a rock.

He calls for the boy to approach, but the child is even more jittery than before. He keeps a safe distance.

"Please," he says to the child, "come closer—I won't do you any harm. Where are the others?"

Uncertainly the boy approaches. He is emaciated, so filthy and mangy that it looks as if he has been living under the ground.

"In God's name," Reitz asks, "where are the others?"

Painstakingly Seun pushes the word through his cleft lip: *Gone.*

"Did they leave with the general?" Reitz asks.

The boy shakes his head in denial.

"With the Khakis?" Reitz asks.

The boy nods. He sniffs. Wipes his arm across his face.

"Everyone?" Reitz asks.

The boy nods.

"Damnation," says Reitz softly.

"Ezekiel too?" he asks.

The boy shrugs, as if he does not know. He begins to whimper, his elbow in front of his face.

"Is he dead?" Reitz asks. "Did the Khakis kill him?"

The boy shrugs again. Snivels. His elbow still hiding his face.

"What did the Khakis do to him?" Reitz asks.

The boy shakes his head. He does not look at Reitz. His dirty face is streaked with tears.

"Don't you know?" Reitz inquires.

The boy keeps shaking his head. Looks away. Makes a motion as of a rifle being fired.

"Did they shoot him?" Reitz asks. His heart is hammering erratically.

The boy shrugs again, as if he does not know.

"Oh God," Reitz says.

He feels dizzy. His head feels fit to burst. His throat is thick.

"What did they do with everything in the camp—the food and things?" Reitz asks.

The boy struggles with the word. *Fire,* he says. The word issues tortuously from his disfigured mouth. He indicates with his arms to show how big.

Reitz's tongue feels numb.

He gets up. "You'd better come with me," he tells Seun, "you can't stay here."

But the boy shakes his head vehemently and begins to retreat.

"Come," he tells the child, "we have to go. There's nothing here for us any more."

But the boy shakes his head. He starts to whimper, sinks down on his haunches.

"Seun," says Reitz, "we don't have much time. I'm taking you to a safe place."

Reitz moves towards the boy—who turns quickly and moves away, nimbly picking his way among the rocks.

Reitz tries to follow him, but Seun is too quick.

He will wait here for the child. He does not have the strength to chase after him. He crawls in under the overhang of a large rock. For a long time he lies on the cool earth, motionless. He slips into a half-sleep in which Seun keeps appearing and disappearing. He tries to call the child, but cannot utter a word.

After a while he gets up. It takes him a long time to get back to the camp.

He calls out to Seun but only an empty echo comes back to him.

Again he searches listlessly under rocks, behind loose boulders, under shrubs and in the mouth of the cave. He no longer knows what he is looking for.

He scratches among the ashes of the fire. It was indeed a big fire, as Seun indicated, he sees now. He finds nothing that resembles the pages of a book. Nothing that resembles remains of any sort, except a small tin spoon.

He wraps himself in the blanket again; sits in the cave entrance leaning with his back against the rock face. He waits for Seun. The child will return. He knows he cannot stay here alone.

At times he is gripped by fever. He dreams that Seun has saddled his mare and left with her. He dreams Seun has a tame meerkat on his arm. Seun smiles coyly.

Reitz hovers between sleeping and waking. He is waiting for Seun to return. Someone is there, bending over him, he thinks it is Ezekiel. It is Ezekiel offering him water. He is glad. Where is the child? he asks. Ezekiel makes no reply.

In the late afternoon he wakes with a start. It is as if he heard a voice say clearly: Seun won't be back. He is gone.

The fever seems to have abated somewhat. He tries to get a fire going. He is not hungry, but has an unquenchable thirst. He drinks some of the water he fetched at the river that morning.

When he rises, his body is stiff. He calls for Seun again, though he knows he is not coming back. Half-heartedly he searches the area one last time.

During the night bouts of fever come and go. He sleeps for short snatches, dreams, awakes. He watches the passage of the moon in the sky. Listens to the small sounds of nocturnal animals; the dark, warm squeaking of batlike things in the cave behind him. The sky is wide and open, and night is more comforting than day. An owl calls. Somewhere close a nightbird takes fright and flies up. A jackal barks on the distant plain.

In the early hours of the morning, at first light, he leads his mount slowly down the winding path, and embarks on the return journey to the farm.

•

He does not know how long the journey lasts.

He prayed during the outward journey, but he no longer thinks of appealing to God. The fever has banished all thoughts of God.

He thinks he recognises landmarks, but he cannot be sure.

He alternates between burning heat and icy cold. Sometimes it takes a great effort to stay in the saddle. He slides off his horse and lies shivering under the nearest bush or shelter; under a small thorn tree or a sparse shrub or behind a shallow rock.

The fever burns his eyes, his nose, his mouth, his throat, his lungs and the palms of his hands with a dry, burning heat. He is stiff from his shoulders to the base of his spine. There is a burning pain between his shoulder blades that prevents him from breathing deeply. His thirst is almost unquenchable.

Once he clearly hears Ben say: Where shall we sleep tonight in this drought?

He sees someone kneeling in the shadows. No, he realises, it is an ant hill.

He sees water on the horizon.

He sees herds of buck. He sees a lionlike creature. He hears horses' hooves and voices. Let them shoot if they want to, he thinks.

In the heat of the day the crows croak hoarsely in a tree: caw, caw. Overhead the sky is spread like a sheet. A single bird of prey circles even higher.

In the late afternoon he sees in the distance the koppie where they were heading that day. That calamitous day when Ben was wounded.

A while later he passes through the drift on his way to the farm. The high, dry banks of the great river are first ahead and then behind him.

When he comes down the road leading to the house, Niggie runs to meet him with flapping skirts. Behind her is the youngest child with blood-red cheeks.

Niggie helps him from his horse.

Her body feels cool and firm, and he wants to throw his arms around her neck like someone adrift.

"Did you find the journals?" she asks close to his ear.

"No," he says.

"God help you," says Niggie, as she supports him to the house.

Ben, Tante, Anna and the older child are waiting on the stoep.

When he greets Ben, he looks briefly into his eyes and merely shakes his head.

Both Tante and Anna greet him with a handshake, both with concerned expressions. Tante has tears in her eyes; Anna's cheeks have an unnaturally high colour.

As on the first day when Ben and he arrived there, he has to lie down immediately, for his legs cannot carry him any longer.

This time it is Ben's turn to sit with him. Niggie stands in the doorway holding a basin. Sometimes Anna places a cool hand upon his brow.

CHAPTER 17

At the height of the fever Reitz is delirious. He is only vaguely aware of who is with him. The same words string through his head in the same unbroken sequence, over and over: Ghams, ghaps, ghabba, gharra. Ghams, ghaps, ghabba, gharra—like horses' hooves. *Or:* Ghwar, ghwap, ghoop. Ghwar, ghwap, ghoop. *Or:* Kriss, krass. Kriss, krass—like footsteps in grass. He cries out because there is no escape from them. Niggie gives him water.

After a day or two the fever subsides.

Ben sits by Reitz's bed; he does not talk.

When Niggie sits at his bedside, she talks. She tells him that Jan Buys came by again while he was gone, and told them that peace negotiations have indeed started, and that just the previous day Oom Sybrand van der Westhuizen of the neighbouring farm confirmed it. The situation is precarious. A number of commandos have already disbanded. The Boers have been forced to their knees. It is over, Niggie says, and plumps up his pillows. Anna was right, she says, it can't last any longer than the end of the month. Then we can pick up the pieces, Niggie says, and go on with our lives. God help you and Ben, who have lost your precious books. And deftly she straightens the sheets underneath him.

When he is feeling better, Reitz sits on the stoep with Ben. The younger child sits on the low wall. She plays with her dolls. Whenever possible, Niggie joins them too. In her presence Reitz speaks less; Ben and he feel less at ease with each other. Besides, she does most of the talking. As soon as she rises to perform some task inside, Reitz speaks to Ben. Ben listens attentively, making the odd noises in his throat to indicate assent or denial. At first Reitz was unable to listen to these sounds, but he has gradually become used to them.

Reitz describes to Ben what he found at the camp. He says: It was as if there had been no camp for all those months. It was as if no one had ever been there. As if it had all been imagined. If it wasn't for a few scattered branches where the shelters had been and the broken saddles in the cave entrance, there would be no sign that people had ever lived there. Everything razed to the ground. And what hasn't been destroyed, has been burned. I saw with my own eyes what an enormous fire it must have been.

(He does not mention that the trunks and journals were probably burned with the rest. Not only is he reluctant to say it out loud—he refuses even to think about it. By speaking the words, he might make them true.)

He says: The silence in the camp was frightening. There was moss growing on the rocks that I had never noticed before. Nature has begun to take over; all signs of human occupation have virtually been obliterated.

They sit in silence. The child speaks to her dolls in a whisper.

He says: Ben, it was no pleasant experience. And what happened to everyone there—that's even worse. (Reitz runs his hand over his face.) Why the English had to do *that*, on the eve of the peace treaty, is beyond me. Ben nods in agreement.

"Surely it was obvious to the Khakis that the group was by no means an active commando," he says. "And surely it was obvious that they weren't providing any other commandos with food—in fact, General Bergh's men had been providing *us* with food! Why should they be punished for mending saddles and darning blankets? Did you ever notice— were there any weapons in the cave? Even if there *were*. Even if they kept weapons there. It should have been obvious to the English. Young Abraham wasn't in his right mind. Seun even less so. Reuben missed a leg. Japie Stilgemoed was as good as stone-deaf. And the last thing Kosie Rijpma would do would be to even pick up a gun. And Ezekiel.

For God's sake—Ezekiel is black. What did they do to *him*? I couldn't get the truth out of the child. I wouldn't be surprised if they shot him. Neither the Boers nor the Khakis have any mercy for black helpers. Perhaps Seun got the story wrong. Perhaps he didn't quite understand what had happened. But if they had left with the general or gone off on their own, they would have taken Seun along. I don't know how he can survive there on his own. He looked like someone who . . . lives in aardvark holes, which he's probably doing. Living on insects and small animals. Scaly and scabby and even more bewildered than usual. It's my fault. If he trusted me, he might have come with me. I should have gone back sooner. Things might have been different. I wouldn't know in what way, though. I don't know what I could have done. Brought back the journals safely," he says with a laugh. "Brought back the journals and left the others to their own devices," he adds wryly.

"It's a terrible thing to have happened. I can't get it out of my mind. Especially young Abraham. He'll never survive as a prisoner of war. That all this should have happened so close to the end. For you it's much worse than for me, Ben. And for them perhaps a lot worse than for us. At times I think I should have done one thing, at other times another." He runs his hand across his face wearily.

Ben shakes his head vehemently, as if he wants to say: Don't torment yourself like this.

"I feel responsible for the loss of the journals—*and* for the fate of the others," Reitz says.

Niggie comes out on the stoep again. "Don't talk so much," she says. "You're wearing yourself out. Sometimes things happen in life that even God Himself would not have wanted. But what's happened has happened."

•

Because sleep eludes Reitz, and because Anna's forthright gaze speaks to him, he goes to her room again as soon as he has recovered from the fever.

As on the first time, she receives him without false modesty or pretensions of chasteness, but she refuses to allow any display of tenderness.

He finds her body lovely and abundant, unexpectedly paradisical—filled with promise of refuge and fulfilment.

As if she senses it, she says: I don't want to be a solace to you, and he says: You are more than that.

He wants to speak to her. What he has had to endure over the past weeks wells up unstoppably inside him. He does not want to have to hold anything back.

He wants to speak about the encounters with his wife at the river, five times in a row, when he had longed to meet her, but lost her for ever through Oompie's devilish sorcery.

He wants to say—he feels an urgent need to tell Anna—that he loved his wife, but that he cut himself off from her death and suppressed all thought of her. Until she *herself*—from the realm of the dead—made a claim on him.

He wants to tell her of the needless waste of Abraham's young life. He wants to speak of the extent to which Japie Stilgemoed's narration irked him. How Kosie Rijpma was unable to let go of the image of the dying Bettie Loots.

He wants to tell her of the immense loss of the journals. That he feels guilty, and responsible for their loss because he kept deferring his return to the camp.

He wants to tell her how hard it is for him that Ben has changed, and that they can no longer talk to each other the way they did before.

He also wants her to talk to *him*. But Anna is more reticent than he. Apparently she does not have much need of talk. Or she does not often allow herself to express her feelings.

She mostly listens to him in silence. He feels her reaction to his words in her body.

Sometimes he can feel her resistance. Her body that was pliant and receptive a moment ago, grows rigid in his arms. She no longer allows him to hold her or caress her. She turns from him. She does not want to hear.

You are *forcing* me, she says softly.

He does not understand what she means. Why is she willing to embrace him and receive him, but averse to what he wants to tell her? It wounds him. It makes him feel insecure. He feels disparaged.

More than refuge, more than solace, he wants something to be released in her as it is being released in him—something warm and life-giving. He does not want to staunch the flow.

But she is different. She has different needs. There are certain things she does not wish to talk about. She has no wish to speak of her sister. Niggie told him how hard it is for Anna that she and her sister were unreconciled before her death. She has no wish to speak of her husband. It must weigh on her mind—her husband's safety, her own premonitions. She has no wish to speak of her anxieties and fears. At night—when she lies beside him—she prefers to tell him in even tones about the flowers that once grew in her garden.

He lies in the dark and listens to her speak of dahlias and roses, phlox and chrysanthemums, daisies and gladioli, sweetpeas and velvety roses. Of the wealth of her summer garden, before it was ruined and withered.

•

Reitz sits with Ben, his face buried in his hands. He does not know how to broach the subject of Anna and himself. He groans softly. He runs his hands wearily over his face. He gazes at the low hills in the distance. Ben, he says, do you know me as someone who acts rashly? Indiscreetly?

Ben gives him a puzzled look.

Goodness, Ben, he says, how do you know me?

Ben looks at him; he smiles—though slightly bemused. On the slate he writes: *unwavering*. And: *stout-bodied grasshopper*.

Ben, don't tease me, says Reitz.

Yet, when he meets Anna's steady gaze at the table in the evenings, excitement and anticipation cause an uncontrollable fluttering in the pit of his stomach.

•

Reitz says to Ben: The more I think of it, Ben, the more convinced I am that it wasn't the Khakis who fired at us. My conversation with Jan

Buys confirmed my suspicion—Colonel Davenport came this way only later. I have a good idea which of the general's men were involved, and I'm convinced it happened without his knowledge. Why they killed Gert Smal, no one will ever know. Neither will we ever know whether they shot us because of those damned lectures, or whether they really believed we were deserters and traitors.

Perhaps they simply didn't like our faces—he imagines Ben might have remarked, drily. But Ben says nothing. Ben just looks at him. He looks at Reitz for a long time. His face is soft and open, the expression in his eyes amiable and compliant—the ironic look is no longer there. It is not clear *what* he is thinking. It is still not clear to Reitz whether Ben remembers at all what happened that day. Perhaps he will never again know with any certainty what Ben is thinking, he realises. Tears gather in his eyes, and he has to avert his face.

His heart is still heavy when he takes Anna in his arms that evening. Her fingers touch the hair on his chest. She says: If I do this, it feels as if I'm touching a dream I had last night.

What was your dream? he asks reluctantly, heavy of heart. But she makes no reply.

•

On the stoep Niggie says: Anna worries day and night. (At this she gives Reitz a meaningful glance; he blushes heavily and deeply.) She doesn't know what's to become of the farm. She and Johannes were prosperous people. But what wasn't taken by the Boers, was looted and ruined by the Khakis. There's no more livestock or grain. There's no pasture. The dams have fallen in disrepair. Everything is dried up and ruined. All the farm hands have left, except Betta and Jeremiah. The well is still fed by seepage, and there are the two springs and the two cows. But how will *that* help them on their feet again? God help Anna, if Johannes doesn't return—how will she, a woman on her own, rebuild this place?

Reitz asks Niggie—bashfully—when Anna last saw her husband. At the beginning, Niggie replies, during the first months of the war, Johannes used to stop by regularly, but in the past seven or eight months Anna has had no news of him.

He longs for Anna to tell him that she has dreamed, that she fears the worst, that she has had a premonition that she will never see her husband again. But she says nothing; she keeps silent about her husband.

She tells him that they used to have everything in the orchard—plums, peaches, apples, quinces, mulberries, figs. Sweet melons, grapes and loquats. And the veld was inordinately green in summer, she says.

CHAPTER 18

It is mid-May. Oom Sybrand comes round again to tell them it won't be long. The delegates elected by their commandos should have arrived at Vereeniging by now. May God grant that the peace negotiations are fair, he says.

Reitz does not know how to broach the subject of Ben's family. Once peace is declared, Ben will *have* to return to them. Before they came under fire that day, it was his resolve and his main purpose to find out what has become of his family. But since the shooting Ben has given no indication that he still wishes to do so—despite the fact that he is sufficiently recovered to undertake the return journey to his home town. Reitz does not wish to upset Ben. He lets the matter rest, uncertain of what to do.

Is Ben, like him, reluctant to leave the farm? Is he afraid of what he may find if he goes in search of his family? Has he accepted that he has lost *them* too, as he has lost his voice and his journal? Is it easier for him to remain here—in the close circle of Niggie's care? Is it possible—God help Ben if it is true—that he has feelings for her?

Before, he would have been able to talk to Ben about all of this. Before, when nothing escaped Ben's sharp, observant gaze.

But Ben has changed, he is passive and subdued. With great effort he is beginning to make himself understood again. What comes out is hardly more than a hoarse, throaty sound, virtually unintelligible, and Niggie is quick to warn that he should not exert his voice unduly.

There seems to be an understanding between Niggie and Ben. She is still attending to his needs, as she has done ever since their arrival.

Reitz has convinced Anna to take a renewed interest in her garden. He helps her; he hoes and weeds. She plants bulbs and attends to her roses again. It gives him great pleasure to work side by side with her like that.

He is alarmed at how much he is reaching out to Anna, how willing he is to love her. At first glance she seems reticent; she does not betray her emotions in their day-to-day contact. Her gaze remains forthright, poised.

But when they lie together, she meets him with growing eagerness. He thinks that she is less defensive. He thinks that she, too, is finding it important to open up herself to him.

He does not think he is imagining it—that she embraces him more fervently, regards him with greater tenderness. That her gaze in un-guarded moments is less unmoved.

This is how things have gone between the two of them, he thinks. At first he could penetrate her body but he scarcely dared say her name, and she kept her face averted. When he wanted to say how much pleas-ure he took in her body, she did not want to hear it; she stiffened in his arms. Gradually she permitted him more. Now she looks him in the eye during the act of love. There are no reservations between them any more, and she allows him to call out ardently to her in the throes of passion.

Anna, he says. Anna, my love. She listens. She never contradicts him any more. He feels his heart might break with gratitude and dread. But what dare he hope for the two of them together?

•

In the late afternoon Reitz and Anna often walk in the veld. She is knowledgeable—familiar with the names of flowers, shrubs and trees. He watches her kneel at a plant and carefully touch it with her awkward, tapered fingers. His heart overflows at the sight.

221

When they return, Niggie teases him. She sits with Ben, looks at Reitz archly, makes a comment. Ben smiles, slightly bewildered.

Sometimes Reitz questions Niggie about Anna. She is only too willing to talk, he to listen. He blushes sometimes: ashamed because he is discussing Anna with Niggie, but burning to learn everything about her, because she herself refuses to speak.

"Johannes is nothing but a bloody dry old man," Niggie says. "There's no fire between them." Niggie gives Reitz a knowing look; he reddens fiercely. "He's grumpy and morose, a real hypochondriac. I wouldn't be at all surprised if he didn't survive the war. Trouble with his lungs—always this little asthmatic cough. Considerably older than her as well. No, really," Niggie says, "Anna deserves better." Reitz feels his heart jump strangely. "In all these years I've never known what she sees in him. But Anna isn't one to show her feelings," she says.

Once when they are alone in the kitchen, Tante says: "My child, these must be difficult times for you. We can't know where our lives are going—or what our final destination will be."

At night Anna describes her dreams to him. He waits for her to say that she dreamed she and her husband would never see each other again—as she did once before in the kitchen, when it had not mattered to him yet.

But it seems her dreams no longer have any bearing on anything. Dreams where she goes on a journey, in a wagon or a horse-drawn cart, arriving at strange destinations, embracing children. And when the dead do come to her, it is her mother and father, or her sister, but never again her husband. Sometimes she dreams of landscapes, of plants and flowers—so different from his own dreams.

Tell me about your sister, he says.

You're forcing me, Anna says again. Her eyes are clear. They are greenish grey, like serpentine. The lines around her mouth are clearly visible. She looks directly at him. You *force* me to lay myself completely bare to you, she says.

But she does yield, and says: We were unreconciled at her death, but I love her children as if they were my own.

Some days he sees her watching the children—the orphaned girls, her sister's daughters. She touches the little one's cheek with a brief, tender gesture, or rests her hand for a moment on the older one's head.

When they lie together, he wants to repeat over and over again: Anna. Anna, my love. Anna, my dearest love.

•

Reitz tells Anna about his dream. I dreamed we were all taken away to a concentration camp. Even my elderly parents, who died long ago. In the dream there was no colour; everything was white. We had to leave everything behind, he says, *everything*.

When you die, she says, you have to leave everything behind.

Yes, he says, that is true.

Anna dreams. She dreams she is carrying a woman's head in her hands. The head has already begun to decompose. There is blood on her hands. The smell of putrefaction is so strong that her stomach contracts as if she is about to throw up.

She wakes, agitated and drenched with perspiration.

My poor love, Reitz says.

The woman had my name, she says softly.

My love, he says, don't let that upset you.

She turns in her heavy half-slumber, sighs and sleeps on.

In his narrow bed back in his own room early in the morning, Reitz dreams of his wife. Suddenly, out of the blue. She is sitting on a chair, a little distance removed from him. She is surrounded by light—as if she is bathed in the cool blue light of morning. She radiates a pristine gentleness, an unearthly beauty. He longs to go to her, deeply grateful that they can embrace once more. But in the dream he cannot bridge the gap between them.

The minute he wakes, even before he is properly awake, he tries but fails to recall her features.

If Ben could speak, he could ask him what the dream means. But Ben has changed and Reitz no longer has the courage to talk to him about this, or about his feelings for Anna.

•

During their rambles in the veld Anna asks Reitz about the rock formations in the area.

He explains that sedimentary rocks are most important to the geologist. He explains how they are formed by various deposits. For instance, fragments of existing rocks, or precipitations from mineral sources, or the remains of organisms like coal or marsh peat. He makes her hold a round piece of dolerite, as an example of igneous rock. She holds it in her hands and inspects it carefully. He watches her hands. He covers her hands with his own. She looks at the sky overhead as if she wants to read something in it. Then she looks him squarely in the eye.

Anna, he says, Anna, my love.

She makes no reply, but her cheeks are flushed.

In summer, she says, it used to be so beautiful here, when the red-necked falcons returned from their winter migration.

In the late afternoon a cold westerly wind comes up.

She longs for the gentle summer breeze, she says. So different from this harsh, bitter wind.

Do you remember its sound, do you remember the difference? he asks.

"Yes," she says. "Those times, those things, everything we've lost. The sound of the wind. The *exact* sound. When it comes over the hills at the back and passes around the corner of the house. The sound that surrounds you day and night, like a blessing. *That* I miss, and *that* we've lost."

"But, Anna," he says gently. He wants to ask her: Have we not gained something too? But her gaze discourages him.

That night he dreams that a dead man lies in a circle drawn on the ground and that he begs for water—a strange, inhuman sound. The others turn away, shocked. He is the only one who offers the man some limy water. Water white with lime deposits.

He wakes up, for it is he himself who has been moaning.

CHAPTER 19

Early one morning Oom Sybrand van der Westhuizen comes riding up to the house.

The peace treaty has been signed, he says. There is peace. To England goes the victory. So be it.

They all sit in the voorhuis and receive the news in silence.

Oom Sybrand is a hefty man with clear blue eyes and a short white beard. He has the defiant energy found in some old men—belligerent old men like Oom Mannes and Oom Honne, Reitz thinks. They are the kind who would never consider giving up.

Oom Sybrand says: After almost three years, *this*. Our land has been ravaged. Our people crushed. We shall never forgive England for this. *Never.*

Ben sits very straight, leaning forward slightly from the waist, his hands on his knees. At first he stares straight ahead, but then he raises his head a little and looks through the window.

Tante sits motionless, her hands folded in her lap. She looks at the floor in front of her and not once does she look up. Anna gazes over Oom Sybrand's shoulder into the distance, at a spot somewhere outside, it seems, in the veld. She is staring so fixedly that she seems scarcely to blink her eyes. Niggie's cheeks are flushed with dismay, and even she is speechless this morning.

The gaze of the oldest child travels from one grown-up to another to determine their reaction. The little one stands close to Tante, her face red, as if she has run far.

They have been expecting it for some time, but still it comes as a shock—like the death of a loved one after a long illness.

This is it then, Reitz thinks. This is as far as it goes.

•

That afternoon Reitz says to Ben: I'll go home with you Ben, to see how your wife and children are. What he neglects to say is: If they are still *there*. Ben nods, but makes a small, hopeless gesture.

Reitz imagines that Ben is anxious, now that the time has come to return. After he has delayed so long to discover the fate of his family. They will both find it hard to leave their safe haven of the past weeks. It is hard for Reitz to leave Anna. But he promised Ben, and who knows, who knows what the future has in store.

Now that their departure is imminent, Reitz comes to her bed with greater urgency. Anna, he says. Anna, my dearest love. For he is beginning to harbour the idea, the hope—faint, foolish perhaps—that he may well be able to return. That Anna and he will embark upon a new life together.

•

Anna insists that they take the horse, and they borrow another from Oom Sybrand. The plan is that one of them will return the animals later. Reitz takes it for granted that he will be the one.

Two days before their intended departure two young men ride into the yard early in the morning.

Like the day the burghers arrived there with the body on the wagon, they all stand waiting for the men in the kitchen doorway.

The riders dismount, tether the horses to the gatepost, and come walking towards the waiting group.

They exchange greetings. They are from Commandant Nel's commando. They are on their way home. They have a message for his wife from Johannes Baines. He was badly wounded at Bosbult, but is recovering well, and she can expect him shortly.

There is complete silence. In a tree nearby Reitz hears the soft cooing of a dove.

My child, Tante says, and takes a step towards Anna, but stops in her tracks when Anna turns away, her fingers covering her mouth in alarm.

God help her, Niggie says softly, she wasn't expecting *this*.

Soon afterwards the two young men depart amid thunderous hoofbeats.

•

That night Reitz lacks the courage to go to Anna. Did she not repeatedly remind him that she is a married woman? Did they not ignore it against their better judgment? But did she not say as well—with great certainty—that she is convinced she will never see her husband again?

He is unable to sleep. He is cold; he finds his small room oppressive. He steps out onto the cold, deserted yard. The moon is in her first quarter. The landscape bleak in the meagre light.

Early the next morning Reitz finds Anna in the kitchen.

She does not speak. She does not look at him—Anna, with her unyielding gaze. He sits at the table. She busies herself at the stove. Her movements, always so light and graceful, are stiff and awkward this morning.

"Anna," he says softly.

She turns her steadfast gaze on him. There are deep lines on either side of her mouth and her eyes are tired, but clear.

"He's still my husband," she says.

•

The night before their departure he goes to her for the last time.

They do not speak much. She allows him to hold her until they hear the first birds outside.

The two of us, she says, are twined together like a wreath made of thorn bush.

·

Early in the morning they take their leave, Ben and he.

Reitz says farewell to Jeremiah, he says farewell to Betta. He takes leave of the children. The little one throws her arms around him and holds him tightly. The face of the bigger one is flushed with emotion. He greets Tante. She looks him in the eye for a long time. God be with you, she says, takes his hand, and puts a small pouch in it. Take it, she says softly, you're going to need it. When he wants to protest, she says: I'm an old woman and I have a home. With that she folds his hand over the money and turns away.

He takes leave of Niggie. She embraces him and says softly: God grant that we see each other again.

He turns to Anna. He has put off this moment to the very last. She is pale, but she looks at him calmly and evenly. He has no words. He wants to say: I'll be back. But what would be the use? He holds her in his arms. They hold each other for a long time. She permits him to kiss her on the lips briefly—in the presence of all the others.

Then he turns away. Niggie helps Ben onto his horse.

He hears the little one cry as they ride away. He dare not turn round. Only once, as they are passing through the gate, does he turn to look at the small group standing there.

He dare not look at Ben.

When they are out of sight, in the open veld, Reitz asks Ben to halt for a moment. He gets off the horse, leans against her thin flank, and weeps as he has never wept before.

He weeps for his dead wife, banished to the realm of shadows for ever because of his folly. He weeps for the children—his own child who died so young and whom he never really mourned; the older child, who became a woman overnight, and the little one. He weeps about the fate of his camp-fellows. He weeps—bitterly—about Anna, because it has not been granted for them to love each other. He weeps because after this their lives will never be the same.

He stands like that for a long time, leaning against the horse's patient flank, before he raises his head, wipes his face on his sleeve, and motions to Ben that they may continue.

CHAPTER 20

They make slow progress through a devastated landscape. Farmhouses have been burned to the ground. In the fields nothing has remained of the crops. The grass and the pasture are yellowed through drought and frost. Towns are in ruins, the houses abandoned and looted. What has not been burned or ruined by human hand, has been withered by winter.

They move slowly. Reitz seldom speaks.

It strikes him how little interest the two of them show in their surroundings. Everything that would have claimed their attention before—the changing geological features of hills and plains, the rocks and dry riverbeds, the plants, insects and small creatures—they hardly react to any of these.

Along the way they encounter various groups of people. Burghers on horseback or on foot, returning to their home towns. Women and children on wagons or horse-drawn carts with their meagre possessions—most of them on their way back from the camps.

Reitz notices the anxiety and distaste on Ben's face as he looks at the women and children. He sees how torn he is between hope and aversion.

It seems that Ben wants to look, but at the same time is reluctant to do so, for surely he is afraid that somewhere among the disconsolate, pitiful bands he may recognise his own family.

Along the way they rest, eat some of the food Anna packed for them and drink some of the water.

Reitz eats slowly. He remembers her hands. Sometimes he finds it hard to swallow. The food was the last gift he would receive from her.

They sleep in the veld (wrapped in blankets Anna gave them), rather than attempt to find lodgings in the towns.

They move through Fauresmith and Reddersburg, heading for Wepener. After three days they reach Ben's home town.

The house stands empty, plundered. The windows are broken; mice and small mammals nest inside. Curtains, mattresses, linen, all have been destroyed or removed. Crockery lies shattered. Family portraits have been torn from the passage walls. In the pantry they find a few bottles of preserves, miraculously intact, and in a container a little flour with mites. At least they can cook some porridge. With the money Tante gave Reitz they buy provisions from the store.

From someone in town Ben hears that his wife and children were taken to the camp at Aliwal North almost a year ago.

They do their best to clean up the house. Sweep the rooms. Nail boards across the windows. They sleep on torn mattresses in front of the kitchen fire—the warmest place in the house—for at night it is freezing.

Ben moves like a sleepwalker. He is thin and pale. Sometimes Reitz finds the silence in the house unbearable. Ben's rasping noises do not make it easier.

By day Reitz inquires about Ben's family in town.

One day Ben's sister-in-law arrives. She has recently returned from camp. She brings bad news: His wife and two of his children died in camp; only his eldest daughter has survived. He can fetch the child from her.

Ben clasps his daugther to his chest for a long time when at last they are reunited. Wordlessly he holds her in his arms. The child stands passively in his embrace, her arms limp at her sides. Between them the silence is palpable.

She is a pretty girl of fourteen, with her father's broad face and gentle brown eyes. But her complexion is pallid and her expression that of an old person. She speaks so little that her muteness is like a reproach.

CHAPTER 21

Shortly after Ben's daughter has returned home, Reitz goes back to the Transvaal. There he continues to work at the topographical documentation and geological description of the area northwest of Pretoria with which he was occupied before the war.

He corresponds with Ben. Ben writes that he has made contact with Niggie, and that he is planning to pay a visit to the farm.

Two or three months later Ben writes that he is going to marry Niggie. His child has endured so much in her young life—Niggie will be a good mother to her. He has much to be thankful for today, Ben writes, though he remembers his late wife and children with great sorrow. Their suffering will be a blight on his memory for the rest of his days. But his daughter is a consolation and a support, and he thanks God that *she* at least has been saved for him.

He has discovered a new insect species, a beetle of the order *Coleoptera*. He named it after Niggie. One of the two species that he discovered and recorded in his journal during the war has in the meantime been registered by someone else. He has no regrets, however, for he is confident that he will come across the other species yet again. In the meantime he can make himself understood well enough, but he will never be able to speak normally again. They plan to settle in Colesberg, in the Cape Colony.

Anna and the girls are well, Ben writes. Niggie and he sometimes call on them. The girls have grown. Though their father and brothers have returned safely from commando, the girls are going to stay with Anna. She and Johannes are doing their best to rebuild the farm.

Reitz finds the mention of Anna's name difficult. Even after half a year he finds it hard to think of her at her husband's side.

Sometimes his longing for her is so fierce that it causes him pain.

Many questions remain unanswered for him. Why was Gert Smal so protective of Seun? Who was Oompie and where did he come from? What exactly happened on the day of the shooting? He would have liked to talk to Ben about these matters.

He intends visiting Ben and Niggie, and yet he keeps postponing it—without knowing the reason.

He studies every document, every official list of the names of prisoners of war that has been released, but he never finds the names of young Abraham Fouché or Willem Boshoff, Kosie Rijpma or Japie Stilgemoed. Neither does he ever hear word of the general and his company again.

Early the following year he receives a letter from Ben to say that Niggie is pregnant and Anna is making a slow recovery from a short but serious illness.

He sits at the window with the letter in his hand until night falls.

He has lost not one woman, but two. His wife is dead and has slipped back into the realm of shadows whence he called her forth.

But with Anna it is different. Anna is alive. Anna is there. But it is not destined for them to love each other.

He never imagined his life would seem so hopeless and devoid of prospect.

That day he knows—the day he receives Ben's letter—as surely as he has ever known anything, that he will never again know hope as he knew it during the brief period when he held Anna in his arms.

A few months later Reitz settles in Cape Town. He has no desire to spend any more time in the Transvaal. Not in the Transvaal nor in the Free State. Not in any place with familiar memories.

One day he comes across the farmer on whose farm they spent the night when they were on their way to find General Bergh.

After a brief exchange Reitz asks the man if he remembers his dream of the woman in the feathered hat.

The man gives him a surprised look and says: Yes, yes, he remembers the dream.

He gazes into the distance for a long time before he turns to Reitz and says: "That little hat was truly a remarkable thing."

GLOSSARY OF AFRIKAANS
AND SOUTH AFRICAN ENGLISH WORDS

AARDVARK: South African anteater with long ears and snout

AGTERRYER: mounted servant or helper who accompanies his employer on commando

BAAS: a master, boss, or employer; a title or form of address, e.g. *Baas Gertjie*

BILTONG: boneless meat which is salted and dried in strips

BOER: a Dutch or Afrikaans-speaking soldier fighting against British forces, especially during the Anglo-Boer Wars

DAGGA: marijuana

DASSIE: a rock rabbit or hyrax

DONGA: a dry gully or watercourse that has been eroded by running water

DRIFT: a shallow place where a river may be crossed

HANDSUPPER: member of the Boer forces who surrendered to the British

KAFFIR: black inhabitant of South Africa (now offensive)

KAROSS: a blanket of softened skins used as a bed or floor covering or cloak

KHAKI: Boer name for British soldier

KLIPSPRINGER: a small mountain antelope (literally rock-leaper)

KLOOF: a steep-sided valley, gorge, or ravine

KOPPIE: a small hill or hillock

KREUPELHOUT (also KREUPELBOOM): a dwarfish tree with twisted lower branches

KRIEDORING (also KAREEDORING): Karee thorn, shrub of the *Lycium* genus

LAAGER: any fortified place, permanent or temporary

LEGUAAN: a large amphibious monitor lizard

MEERKAT: a small southern African mammal similar to a mongoose

NEEF: a male cousin, or a form of address used by an older person when addressing a younger man, used often with a first name, e.g. *Neef Willem*

NIGGIE: a female cousin, or a form of address used by an older person when addressing a younger woman, used often with a first name, e.g. *Nig Anna*

OOM: uncle, a term or form of address for an older man, used alone or with a name, e.g. *Oom Mannes*

OOMPIE: diminutive of 'Oom'

OOM PAUL: Paul Kruger, president of the Transvaal Republic at the time of the Anglo-Boer War

POORT: a narrow pass or defile through mountains or hills

PREDIKANT: a minister of the Dutch Reformed Church; a preacher

RIEMPIE: a thin strip of softened leather, used for the backs and seats of chairs, for shoelaces, and as string

SEUN: boy, son; form of address for a young boy

sjambok: a heavy whip made of hide

SPOOR: the track or scent of an animal or person

STOEP: a porch or veranda

SUSSIE: little sister, form of address for a young girl

TAAIBOS: any of several shrubs or trees with tough, pliant branches or tough bark

TANTE: aunt, a polite form of address for an older woman

TREK (verb): go on a long, difficult journey

UITLANDER: white immigrant to the former Transvaal Republic, especially after the discovery of gold

VELD: open, uncultivated country or grassland in southern Africa

VELSKOEN: a rough shoe of untanned hide

VOORHUIS: the front room of a house

XHOSA: a member of a South African people traditionally from the Eastern Cape; language spoken by Xhosa people, currently referred to as isiXhosa (isi: a language)

Ingrid Winterbach is an artist and novelist whose work has won South Africa's M-Net Prize, Old Mutual Literary Prize, the University of Johannesburg Prize for Creative Writing, and the W. A. Hofmeyr Prize. *To Hell with Cronjé* won the 2004 Hertzog Prize, an honor she shares with the novelists Breyten Breytenbach and Etienne Leroux.

Elsa Silke translates from Afrikaans and was the winner of the 2006 South African Translator's Institute/Via Afrika Prize for her translation of Karel Schoeman's *This Life*.

Open Letter—the University of Rochester's nonprofit, literary translation press—is one of only a handful of publishing houses dedicated to increasing access to world literature for English readers. Publishing ten titles in translation each year, Open Letter searches for works that are extraordinary and influential, works that we hope will become the classics of tomorrow.

Making world literature available in English is crucial to opening our cultural borders, and its availability plays a vital role in maintaining a healthy and vibrant book culture. Open Letter strives to cultivate an audience for these works by helping readers discover imaginative, stunning works of fiction and by creating a constellation of international writing that is engaging, stimulating, and enduring.

Current and forthcoming titles from Open Letter include works from Argentina, Catalonia, France, Iceland, Russia, and numerous other countries.

www.openletterbooks.org